The Cauldron of Change

The Cauldron

MYTHS, MYSTERIES AND MAGICK OF THE GODDESS

# of Change

De-Anna Alba

delphi press Delphi Press, Inc. *Oak Park, Illinois*

Published 1993 by Delphi Press, Inc., Oak Park, Illinois, 60304. All
rights reserved. No part of this book may be reproduced in any form,
in print or electronically, except for brief excerpts used in newspaper
or magazine reviews, without the written consent of the publisher.

98 97 96 95 94 93 5 6 4 3 2 1

ISBN 0-878980-08-4

Library of Congress Catalogue Card Number 92-70478

The paper used in this publication meets the minimum requirements
of American National Standard for Information Services—Perma-
nence of Paper for Printed Library Materials, ANSIZ39 48-1984.

The text of this book is printed on recycled paper.

CONTENTS

To the Keeper of the Cauldron:
Threefold source of my inspiration.

ACKNOWLEDGEMENTS

I have met and worked with a large number of Wiccans and Pagans over the last 21 years and each has contributed to this book in one way or another. Many of them have confirmed my beliefs and practices. Others have given me lots of food for thought that has challenged my perceptions and stimulated thealogical growth and change within me. A few have encouraged me to write this book, and I would like to thank them in particular. I would like to thank Jade for helping my come up with the seed ideas for the Aradian Sabbat cycle. Math's technical support was considerable. Without his help I never would have gotten this book onto a computer disk in an acceptable form. Most especially, I would like to thank Rae. Her constant spiritual and emotional support encouraged me to see this book through to completion. I count her friendship among my most prized possessions. Finally, my thanks goes to Karen, my publisher, without whose help this book would not be in your hands right now.

INTRODUCTION

Dianic Wicca is a mystery religion based in nature and women's experience. It posits one or more feminine deities who are seen as dwelling within the being of every woman. It is an animistic religion in that it sees Goddess as the sentient core of everything in the world. As such, Dianic Wicca is a religion of immanence. It is also a religion of transcendence in that we realize She is "out there," too. The whole of Goddess is greater than the sum of Her parts (us, the world, the universe). She is the creative matrix from which everything arose.

In some minds this presents a paradox. The logical mind believes She has to be one or the other — either immanent or transcendent. The inner Self — the core of our being — *knows* She is both. This ability to hold a paradox — to say yes and yes to a seemingly either/ or situation — is another hallmark of Dianic Wicca and of Witchcraft in general.

The religious observances and the rituals involved in Dianic Wicca speak directly to this inner Goddess/Self in the language of symbol and metaphor, of gesture and imagery. Within the overall mystery of Dianic Witchcraft there are a number of lesser but significant mysteries which devolve from it. The symbolic words and actions contained in the ritual cycle of this book are a useful means by which to approach the greater/overall mystery. These symbols can act as short cuts, or secret ways, to the understanding of the overall mystery by bypassing the corrupted and authoritarian views of the dominant religions found in the Western world. This catalyzing effect is not triggered by verbal or literary analysis (ie: through the intellect). It comes as a surprising and inward certainty through participation in symbolic language, images and actions. It activates and brings to consciousness that part of us which is directly connected to Goddess. This allows us to purposefully direct the actions and events in our lives. The ability to consciously effect change for the better in ourselves and in our sphere of action (the world around us) is called Magick (here spelled with a "k" to distinguish it from the magic tricks of the stage magician).

The rituals of Dianic Wicca are Magickal rituals. They work because we learn to tap the energy matrix of the universe which seeks to dynamically maintain the cyclical nature of life and death and move it along the evolutionary spiral toward wholeness, integration and internal consistency. When that is achieved in one area of existence, it pushes us, as individuals and as a world community, to do it in other areas. So the cycle begins again. These cycles, reflected in ourselves and in the world in which we live, are most especially reflected in the bodies of women. Women all over the world are beginning to suspect and to come to know that there is a sacred connection between the cycles of their own bodies, the cycles of their lives, and the greater seasonal and evolutionary cycles of the Earth. They are looking for and exploring their own connection to the divine feminine, to each other, and to the experiences of their foremothers, from the first births to the present. They are learning that women's intuition, often dismissed as silly, can be a major part of their decisionmaking process. It can prepare them for future events and can enable them to read between the lines when dealing with others. It is a psychic skill given to all women, to be developed for their personal and mutual benefit.

Women are coming to Dianic Wicca in a variety of ways and for a number of reasons. Some come from the feminist movement, seeking the women's strength and power they sense in the religion. The ecology movement brings in those looking for a connection between the Earth and the sacred: Mother Nature as Goddess and the sacredness of all beings. Dianic Wicca is rooted in the Earth but reaches for the stars. Women on the cutting edge of science and technology often find their work dovetails with Dianic belief and practice. Others leave the Judeo-Christian models because they perceive prejudices against women in those systems. Older women facing their own mortality find comfort and self-affirmation in our respect for the aging process and our mysteries regarding life and death and life again. The mysteries of the Mother Goddess attract women who want to, or do, find power and self-esteem in their own mothering abilities.

Lesbian women are among Dianic Wicca's strongest and most active supporters. It validates their lives in ways our society and its religions do not even begin to approach. Heterosexual women who

2

live and work in male dominated environments find Dianic Wicca brings a much needed balance into their lives. Bisexual women find honor and acceptance here as well.

Today thousands of women the world over identify themselves as practicing Dianic Witches. They work alone or gather in small groups on the Full Moons (Esbats) and the Solar festivals (Sabbats). Occasionally, large groups will come together to share knowledge, women's wisdom and ritual in workshops, conferences, gatherings and festivals. But the basic working unit of Dianic Wicca is the small group, or coven. This book addresses coven practice.

However, as you will see, much of the information and many of the rituals can be used by the solo practitioner with little or no modification. If you find a given ritual totally unworkable in individual practice, develop your own. Simply take the basic theme(s) from what is given here and come up with something along similar lines which is suitable for one.

Dianic Wicca presents a lovely tapestry of form and color to those women who seek it out. It is not a codified religion with commandments etched in stone. Many threads, in a variety of textures and hues, make up the beliefs and practices of the Dianic Witch. I've tried to present some of them here. I have by no means covered the variety of permutations founds within every aspect of Dianic Wicca. There is no one, true, and only way to practice Dianic Wicca or to worship the Goddess. Each woman must find her own way to the Goddess. This book is meant only to shine a little Moonlight on the subject and perhaps to guide you a little way along Her path. May it help you find what you seek.

De-Anna Alba
Beltane 1992

CHAPTER ONE

Dianic Thealogy

As stated in the introduction Dianic Wicca is a mystery religion rooted in nature. The endless cycle of life and death is celebrated in the Solar, Lunar, and personal cycles of women, and through this celebration the Lesser Mysteries are revealed and the Greater Mystery is approached. Dianic Wicca can only be truly understood through experiencing its wisdom and rituals. This means that each woman will define it differently in some ways. It is a religion which, like nature, celebrates and encourages diversity. However, there are a few core beliefs that most Dianic Witches hold in common.

First and foremost, the divine is viewed and experienced as feminine. This is perhaps its most radical departure from the majority of world religions. God is Goddess. Dianic Wicca focuses entirely on deity as female.

To those who question the wisdom of this I can offer the following: Is it wise to conceive of deity only as masculine, as do the revealed traditions of Christianity, Judaism and Islam? Is it wise to see the creator of the universe as male when it is the female that manifests creation? Is it wise to think any single understanding of the divine is right for everyone?

There are several Dianic creation myths. Some believe She danced everything into existence, that the energy thrown off by Her dancing and spinning body coalesced into the myriad different forms found in the universe. Others believe She sang all into being. This is the origin of the creative and Magickal power of words. Still others believe She birthed all from the waters of Her womb.

A few Dianics who feel a need to explain the presence and the role of the male in the scheme of things believe that the divinity of the male came from the Great Goddess. She wanted to create something very other from Herself. She wanted a companion, a son and, sometimes, a lover. He is differentiated from Her own divinity. He then spends the rest of His life cycle trying to become one with Her again, in a repetitive cycle of life, death and rebirth. His life is finite, but repetitive. Hers is eternal. As Her child, He is divine but He does not approximate Her on the scale of divinity. His purposes are limited while Hers are all-encompassing.

The Goddess of Dianic Wicca, and of western European Witch-craft in general, is conceived primarily as a Moon Goddess having three aspects that correspond to the phases of the Moon. They are the Maiden (waxing crescent), the Mother (full Moon) and the Crone (waning crescent). Each contains aspects of the other. Whether they are experienced as three separate Goddesses or as facets of one Goddess depends on to whom you talk or the aim of the ritual being experienced. However, it is not uncommon to feel it in both ways. Each is equally valid.

The Maiden is the divine girl child who constantly grows and acquires knowledge and experience. Hers is an instinctual nature and Her behavior is determined by Her wants and needs at the moment. Her experience is felt mostly in Her body and in Her emotions. She can be given to excesses for good or ill. Reason and control of self for the benefit of the self are developing within Her, but are far from down pat. On this instinctual level She is the soul of nature — the wild and the free. She loves totally and is filled with joyous sexual passion. She hates vehemently and does away with that which She dislikes, just as all children wish to do. A part of Her dwells in all women.

The Mother is the Great, Cosmic, Mother of Us All. It is She who birthed the world and lovingly tends its (and our) growth. Hers is the ability to create, whether it be children, great works of art and science or universes unending. Her hand guides the mysteries of the life cycle. Her heart beats at the center of all that is, was and will be. From Her comes our freedom to act as we will. She is expansive and fertile, moist, expectant and full. She is enthroned in heaven as Mary, the Mother of God. By the light of Her full face do we work our Magick and in Her honor do we gather. A part of Her dwells in all women.

The Crone is the Wise One, the Dark Shining One, the Ancient of Days. As guide of the inner Self and director of the soul She forces us to face ourselves, our fears and our secret yearnings. She measures the thread of our lives and cuts it off only to begin spinning it again. Hers is the wisdom of experience, the insight of age — the lesson and its learning. She is wizened and dry, sterile and contracting. Her all-seeing eye peers at us in partiality from behind Her veil of mystery. A part of Her dwells in all women.

But the Goddess of Dianic Witches is also much more than a Moon Goddess. She is also Mother Nature, Mother Earth, Gaia of the green and growing, Mountain Mother of craggy peaks. Running water is Her life's blood and the oceans are the waters of Her womb. Her spark of life and fiery passions burn within Her living core. The air is Her breath of inspiration, and storms its blowing out.

Dianics worship Her as Creatrix of the Universe as well. It is She who sets the stars in their courses and spins the galaxies in space. As Queen of Heaven She sits at the hub of the universe, whirling around without motion. In Her hands are the rising and setting of Sun and Moon, the birth and death of planets.

Women's Witchcraft sees Her as the Goddess of the Sun too, — the face of morning and of noon, the sleepy eye of setting, the life-giving light and heat. It is the Solar life cycle of the Sun Goddess that is celebrated at the eight Sabbats of the Witch's year, as presented in the ritual section of this book.

The Ritual Cycle

The mythic cycle and the rituals found in this book are of my own creation. I make no claim as to their historicity, except to say that they are based on the legend of the descent of the Goddess Aradia as found in Geoffrey Leland's book, *Aradia: Gospel of the Witches*. The legend, briefly stated, says that the Goddess Diana sent Her daughter, Aradia, to Earth to help the poor and oppressed by teaching them the Magick and thealogy of Witchcraft. Any similarity with Leland's book ends there.

Dianic Wicca has not really employed a central mythic cycle that is woman-identified and yet encompasses the life cycle of all beings on Earth as well as the seasonal cycle of the Earth Herself. Dianic Wicca celebrates these mysteries, but not in any internally consistent and cohesive manner. Since I prefer weavings to webs, I needed my practice of Dianic Wicca to become a woven fabric of lovely close-fitted threads that combined to make a luminous garment cloaked with mystery and Magick, instead of a colourful variety of tenuously interconnected threads with gaping holes between them which left me dangling by a silver thread in mid-air. Although I appreciate Arachne and Her lessons, they alone are not enough to support the totality of me. In speaking with other women I often heard similar sentiments given voice, hence the ritual cycle found here.

Having had twenty years of experience with Wiccan and western European Pagan rituals, I knew that the mysteries we all observe, reverence and celebrate are essentially the same. How they are portrayed varies slightly and significantly from tradition to tradition and from group to group, but the central ideas remain the same. In short, a deity incarnates on Earth and through the example of His, now Her, life cycle and actions teaches us about ourselves and each other; a variety of cycles and how to use them for our benefit; and the nature of divinity. This deity usually is thought of as male. Here, She is female and She is the Solar Daughter of a Lunar Mother. Her mysteries are observed on the eight solar festivals, or Sabbats. Those of Her Mother are incorporated into the Full Moon observances, although you will find the presence of each in the other.

Aradia has never struck me as being a lunar deity. Just because She is born of a Moon Goddess does not mean She has to be a Moon child. Diana Herself is far more than a Moon Goddess, and to limit either to a singular, lunar, manifestation seems extremely myopic.

I have always connected the name "Aradia" with the word "radiant," which leads me to thoughts of radiant heat, fire and the Sun. In addition, Aradia came to Earth. As such, She would experience the same life cycle as the rest of us. In essence She takes on the role of the Sun-king, whose life cycle is celebrated in the eight major festivals of western European Paganism and other traditions of Witchcraft.

Although there are similarities between the cycle of the Sun-king/Hero and the Aradian cycle, there are major differences as well. Here is the eight-spoked Wheel of Life as ritually presented in this book:

1) Aradia is born at the Spring Equinox (March 21), the primary birthing time within the animal kingdom;
2) at Beltaine (May 1) Her rite of passage into womanhood (menarche) is celebrated;

3) the Summer Solstice (June 21) finds Her enjoying Her sexuality to its fullest extent;

4) at Lammas (August 1) She chooses a permanent partner;

5) she becomes Crone at the Fall Equinox (September 21);

6) at Samhain (All Hallows Eve/Halloween) (October 31) She passes from the Earth and returns to Her Mother in the Summerland;

7) the Great Mother announces She is with child at the Winter Solstice (December 21) and the light begins to grow within Her and within Her womb of the heavens;

8) at Imbolc (February 2) the Daughter quickens within the womb of the Mother and Aradia is born again at the Spring Equinox, thus completing the cycle.

After all this talk about *the* Goddess I should make it clear that Dianic Wicca is, in the main, polytheistic. It posits many Moon Goddesses, Sun Goddesses, Earth Goddesses, etc. Women draw on Goddesses from a variety of cultures, mythologies and traditions in creating their rituals. Some believe that all Goddesses are simply facets of one Great Goddess. Others believe each Goddess is a separate entity. A few, myself included, feel such an affinity with and closeness to one particular Goddess that She becomes the Great Goddess for us. That is not to say that we don't acknowledge others from time to time or as the situation merits. It's just that this one deity, our Matron deity, is our personal favorite and/or the one we feel has helped us the most.

Although Dianic Wicca is primarily concerned with cycles and patterns, some of us do acknowledge the element of chaos (or chance) as operative in the world. We even have Goddesses to cover this aspect of existence. Hail Eris!

Women Witches do not believe in sin, original sin and evil, as do other religions. We certainly don't believe a woman's body is evil because it is the gateway through which sinners are born into the world, as does Christian orthodoxy! We have no personification/ deification of evil like the devil, or the seven deadly sins. We do believe in and understand the law of cause and effect operative within the universe. We call it karma. From this simple law come a couple of our own maxims and our particular belief in, and understanding of, karma.

I will discuss one maxim, "An it harm none, do what ye will," in chapter 2. The other maxim, which is more directly related to karma, states that whatever good we do will be returned to us threefold, and likewise any bad. This is commonly called "The Threefold Law of Return." In modern day street parlance it might be stated as, "what goes around comes around" — and around and around! It may come around immediately or quite soon. It may come around in this lifetime or in any of our others. But, it *will* come around.

Here we see that the ultimate responsibility for our actions rests with the individual. I reap a bountiful harvest from what I sow and I decide what to sow. There is no judgmental deity imposing this from outside, no grand accountant keeping a tally. It is a simple law of motion. What I set in motion has an immediate, an intermediate and a long-term effect. It is similar to the ripple effect.

My karma centers on my soul or spirit, though. My karma is not visited on my offspring, now or "until the seventh generation." There is no "the sins of the mothers . . ." within Witchcraft. My child does not pay my karmic debts, I do.

There is also such a thing a group karma. In a functional coven the energies contributed to the coven by each individual help to create a group energy. This group energy is that which is used to take Magickal action and, as such, is capable of creating karma for the group. In other words, each individual in the group takes on a portion of the responsibility for the actions of the group. In this way she adds a portion of the group karma to her own individual karma. When it comes time for the group to reap its karmic threefold return, each woman in the group will share in that return in equal measure.

Women's Craft has no universal, sacred or actual scapegoat who takes on our sins, suffers for them and dies that we might be absolved. Dianic Witchcraft has no suffering saviour. Nor do we sacrifice goats or any other animal to atone for our sins. (This is the origin of the word "scapegoat" — a goat that allows us to escape our punishment for transgressions against God. In ancient Israel the priests would ritually transfer the sins of the people to a goat and either set it loose to wander in the desert until it died, or would sacrifice it within the confines of the Temple, depending on which historical era you are looking at.) We do not expect an animal or another person (not unheard of within Catholicism) to suffer for us. Nor does the Goddess demand/require anything in sacrifice from us. Ritual murder of any kind or for any reason is not the way of a Witch!

A belief in karma and a belief in reincarnation often go hand-in-hand, and so they do in Dianic Craft. For most of us, our belief in reincarnation differs from the Eastern or New Age philosophy. We do not believe the world is a grand illusion. Nor is it a place of trial and tribulation we must endure before going on to better things. For us, the Earth is sacred and we look forward to returning to it again and again. We do not want to "get off the wheel," "go to heaven" or "pass over permanently." We like it here. We enjoy incarnation on Earth and consider it sacred. It is our hope that when we do reincarnate it will be with many of the friends and loved ones we have now, and probably have had in the past. As in Eastern traditions, many of us believe that we need to experience all there is to experience here on Earth and for that reason we will incarnate in many guises and in a variety of life situations. We feel the spirit needs to know and experience as much as it can in order to understand, not to escape.

A lot of us also believe, as did the Celts, in the transmigration of souls. Simply put, we believe we can come back as anything — animal, vegetable or mineral. The choice is ours. We are not assigned lives, we choose them.

Some of us also believe that, "once a Witch, always a Witch." We feel that the special psychic skills we have and our understanding of cycles, seasons and divinity, is not only passed down to our offspring, but remains constant within us throughout our reincarnations. It is in the blood, or the DNA — our genetic programming — or within the latent capacities of our minds.

Another major thealogical question addressed by Dianics is, "Where does Goddess dwell?" Goddess is everywhere, within and without. She is in our innermost thoughts and in our wildest imaginings. She sits at the center of the universe and enfolds it to Her breast. She is in the Earth under our feet, in the air we breathe and in the water we drink. The spark of Her essence ignites our passions, whether they be sexual, social, political or spiritual in nature. She animates mammals, reptiles and amphibians. She enlivens the plant world and imparts Her substance to minerals.

She is as close as our heartbeat and is rooted in our wombs. She is as distant as the farthest star. She is all.

Dianic Wicca, and Pagan religions in general, are nature religions and are animistic. The belief is that Goddess is present in all of Nature and that a spark of Her divinity abides in all living things. As a result, Dianics do not view the world as stratified/structured hierarchically. All is sacred and equally worthy because of that indwelling sacredness. No form of being is superior to any other, and we are all connected to each other in the web of life.

Dianics place particular emphasis on the indwelling of Goddess within each woman. I think it is fairly safe to say that all of us were brought up in religious systems that separated the female from the divine. The Bible, and the ecclesiastical and civil history of the Christian church, are littered with examples of the vilification of woman as the tool of the devil and the gate through which sin entered the world. Hebrew tradition and the Islamic faith are not exempt from similar charges.

When women discover Dianic Wicca and its belief in a Goddess who inspirits them and the universe, they are thrilled and empowered in many ways. Most feel like they have finally come home or can at last put a label on feelings related to the divinity of the feminine and the sanctity of Nature and women's bodies.

Viewing the female body and its processes as sacred is a central feature of Dianic Wicca. The life process itself, from birth to death, is honored. Our connection with the Moon Goddess is emphasized through our monthly menstrual cycle and there are rituals, ranging from the elaborate to the simple, centered around women's blood. (See the Beltaine Ritual in chapter 7). Women are connected to each other and to the Goddess through the shared experience of the monthly shedding of blood. This shared fertility cycle was the first Magick and is the foundation of Witchcraft. Robert Briffault in *The Mothers* states that, in essence, women were the original priestesses, magicians, prophets and shamans by virtue of this first Magick. He goes on to say that the monthly cycles of women and the Moon are so similar as to make the analogy between them universal in religious imagery. In his view, all Moon cults are menstrual cults and he presents an astounding array of information and evidence to corroborate his view.

The first Magick was (and is) fertility Magick. "All communities [then and now] do in actuality depend on the blood sacrifice of the menstruating woman, for without menstruation there is no ovulation, and therefore no people."[1] This monthly cycle is mirrored in the phases of the Moon. This fertility cycle of the female later was assimilated into the yearly fertility cycle of the land, as depicted by the Sabbats. The bloody sacrifice of the Divine King/Solar Hero embraced by many ancient cultures and most Pagans and Wiccans of mixed traditions can be interpreted in this light.

The menstrual cycle "also has to do with the alteration of feelings during the cycle — and it would be natural to personify these alterations in dream images and stories — which, as depictions of processes essential to life, might well take their place in community rites. If the particular rise of instinct at menstruation is powerful, then it would be natural to depict it in terms of power politics: since it would be an opposite experience to the maternal feelings of ovulation, an overmastering Divine King might be a natural image, who is sacrificed in blood for fertility's sake, but who returns constantly. This blood king, whose image might be given horns, since the appearance of the animal and human womb is horned with its beautiful swept-back Fallopian tubes, would be a mediator between life and death."[2] Joseph Campbell's *Masks of God* lends a lot of support to these views, especially when discussing Cretan and Sumerian religion, the slain bull motif and its relation to the Great Goddess.[3]

There are other connections between the monthly blood of women, the Moon, the womb itself and the Goddess. The name of the Great Goddess in most cultures means womb or vulva. Hera means womb. She is called "panton genthia" — origin of all things — which is, of course, the womb. The "widowhood" of Hera refers to Her Crone phase and was associated with Her menses at the New Moon.[4]

Astarte means womb, or "that which issues from the womb." Pallas Athena means "vulva-vulva." Eileithyia — Greek Goddess of childbirth — means "fluid of generation" (i.e., menses). In the Native American Dakotan language Wakan means "spiritual," "sacred" and "menstrual".[5] Our word, menstruation, means "moon-change."

The Witch word, "Sabbat" has two possible meanings not given in standard texts on Witchcraft, and both are connected to the Great Goddess. It may derive from "Sabbatu," a Babylonian word referring to the menstruation of the Goddess Ishtar at the Full Moon. It was a holiday—or a time when no work was done—which echoes Hebrew customs regarding their Sabbat(h). Sabbath was another name for Shekinah, the female spirit of God in Hebrew tradition (the Hebrew Goddess). The Sabbath is the Goddess' day of celebration. It is also connected to the Akkadian "Shabbattu" or "Shapattu," which was their name for the feast of the Full Moon, celebrating the menses of the Goddess. Working, cooking and travel were/are not allowed. The same taboos are put on menstruating women in a variety of indigenous cultures.[6]

To return to the discussion of where the Goddess dwells, all this talk of the immanence of the Goddess — Her presence within us and Her nearness to us on Earth, in the Earth and within the matrix of Nature — does not negate Her transcendence. You don't hear many Dianics talking about this, but our actions within a ritual setting indicate that we hold this belief as well. Not only is the Goddess within us, She is "out there" too — amongst the stars in deep space. Many invocations I've heard (and written) speak of this. When we invoke the Goddess we look up at the sky or ceiling, or at least tilt the head up slightly. If we truly felt She existed only within us, we would be looking at our wombs when we invoke Her. If She is only a Goddess of the Earth (i. e., nature) we should be looking at the ground or the floor. But we don't. Most often we open our arms and raise them slightly and tilt our heads up as if expecting to receive something from "on high." Transcendence in this case does not means separated or withdrawn from us, it means differently located; the Sacred Other who is yet at one with us and connected to us, whose totality of being extends beyond our Earth-related and individual perceptions of Her.

Opinions on the extent of the Goddess' power vary within Dianic thought. Some say She can only act in the world through us. For them, miracles and divine intervention is the stuff of legend, not reality. When they say, "It's in the hands of the Goddess" they mean, "It is right here in my own two hands. The Goddess in me will work through me to create change." Others say She needs our help through prayers and invocations to Her. This worship gives

Her additional power that She can use to work in the world through us and possibly on Her own. Still others believe Her to be omnipotent. Though She can and does work through the individual and her "own two hands, " she can operate as She will in the world. Miracles do happen and divine intervention is possible. Prayer and invocation is done because it fills a need in the ritualist, not in the Goddess.

Lest you think the Dianic notion of the existence of one or more female deities was created by feminists within the last 20 years or so, it should be pointed out that there is a plethora of historical and prehistorical evidence for the existence of Goddess worship within a variety of world cultures. Pick up any book about mythology and you will find Her in many forms. In recent years a number of books have been written which deal specifically with Goddesses and Goddess worship. For those interested in pursuing Goddess history and prehistory, Goddess lore and the history of Goddess worship, I highly recommend the works of Marija Gimbutas, Merlin Stone, Pat Monaghan and Barbara Walker. I would also recommend you glean what you can from the works of Joseph Campbell, Robert Graves, Robert Briffault and others.

Beginning with the ascendancy and finally the domination of the male and religions centered around Gods, it becomes more and more difficult to trace the thread of the Goddess running throughout the web of the world and Western culture in particular. Although the thread has become twisted, knotted and obscured at times, in my opinion it has never broken. The Goddess lives on, even within the Judeo-Christian traditions.

The nature of the divine feminine within Christianity has been split in two camps: the pliant, acceptable image of sanctity (virgin/ maiden) and the threatening image of dark power (whether that be the dark moisture of fecundity that is the Earth and the Mother, or the awe-inspiring power of the Crone — who is usually reduced to demon status).

The presence of Goddess within the Judaic tradition can be seen in Proverbs 8:22-30, where we read that the Shekinah (the Hebrew Goddess) and God are partners. At the time of the fall from paradise the Shekinah decided to descend with Adam and Eve. She went into voluntary exile with humanity. She inhabited the Ark of the Covenant, going before it in the desert as a cloud and a pillar of flame: a visible presence of God's dwelling among the Israelites. (For the Jews, the Ark takes on the significance of the Grail found within esoteric Christianity: the subject of an interior quest.) She is the female counterpart of God. The Qabalistic texts call her God's wife. Her imagery stems from that of the Canaanite and Mesopotamian Astarte, or Ishtar, who reigned supreme in heaven with Her consort. In biblical books of wisdom the Shekinah is also called Chokmah, or wisdom. She is the hope of restoration with God.[7] It is She who is celebrated at the Hebrew Sabbath beginning on Friday night.

Although Mary is often restricted to the image of good virgin and blessed Mother of God (a passive vehicle for male power), She is the one to whom Catholics turn in prayer in order to get things done. It is She who most often appears to the faithful in visions. She is, in fact, the Great Goddess Herself. She is identified with the Moon and is often seen depicted in Renaissance painting with the Moon beneath Her feet. And it is She, according to Briffault, who created the world.[8] According to Briffaut, St. Alphonse stated that "At the command of Mary all obey, even God."[9] Though the Protestant Reformation removed all trace of the Goddess from Christianity, the Holy Spirit of the Christian trinity is theologically understood by some today as stemming from its origin as part of the Divine Feminine — the holy motherhood of God.

Most everyone would agree that prayer and invocation are a method of strengthening our connection to the Goddess. They are a means of opening up a channel of communication. The development of a broad range of psychic skills, from meditation and visualization to channeling, or aspecting, as well as various forms of divination, are important ways of establishing communication with the Goddess. These skills are usually considered part and parcel of each Dianic Witch and are, or can be, taught and developed within each woman. This makes "women's intuition" a sacred skill instead of the butt of jokes, something dismissed in an off-handed way, or purposely down-played. These skills will be discussed further in chapters 3, 5, and 7.

Magick as Thealogy

Dianic Wicca is, at its core a Magickal religion. The use of spells and rituals to create change for the better in the life of the individual, the coven, the community and the world is central to its thealogy. Working in concert with the Goddess and the creative energy available in the universe, we can improve our spiritual lives and our daily lives as well.

When most Witches end a spell they say, "So mote it be!" This means, "so *must* it be," not "so *might* it maybe be." "So mote it be!" leaves no room for doubt. It is an emphatic statement of what will occur as a result of the knowledgeable use of Goddess/creative energy in accordance with the Wiccan Rede (see chapter 2). Magick has been performed and a change in reality *will* take place.

This belief in our ability to do Magick — to change our lives — carries with it a concomitant belief that we can (and do) create our own reality. If we do not believe that, what is the basis for believing the Magick we do will work at all?

Many women in Dianic Craft have a great deal of trouble with the concept of taking responsibility for one's life circumstances. They feel it is akin to blaming the victim for the crime and is quite possibly classist and racist. They feel women do not choose to oppress themselves, but are instead oppressed by a more powerful other. After all, why would a woman choose a life of poverty, abuse, racial discrimination, sexual abuse or harassment? I do not have definitive answers to these questions, but I would like to take a stab at them by offering the following opinions. First of all, most people are not aware that they can create their own reality. On the whole, our society does not teach or encourage this idea. We are taught to look to recognized authorities for answers instead of to ourselves. We are taught to respect authority in others and to assume that someone else knows better than we do.

Our schools do not teach us how to think for ourselves. They teach us how to accumulate and to regurgitate known information. They teach us the tyrannies of time — on time, in time, last time and next time; and sameness — fit in, like and be liked. The bell rings and we all change classes; it rings again, and it's time for lunch. This makes us good automatons for the work force. We learn regimentation and to "go with the flow." All of these things numb the brain and stifle creative and critical thinking.

The religious traditions within which most of us have been brought up teach us that, even though we have free will, we are doomed to making mostly poor choices because we are sinners, deceived by the devil, or are simply unworthy of a happy, healthy

17

life for one reason or another. After all, life on earth is a trial according to them. It only gets good when we get to heaven. Thus, we learn not to expect good things to happen to us — especially if we are women. Eve and evil are synonymous. All evil entered the world through woman. All this not only numbs the brain, it deadens the spirit. Then there is an economy fraught with difficulties for just about everyone, but especially for women.

This morass of inculcated beliefs and lessons leads us to be inattentive to what goes on around us and within our sphere of action. This inattentiveness is what creates the reality we make for ourselves. It is the unconscious Magick we do. It is when we realize that it is possible to create change in our lives and to begin to make conscious choices about how that life will be that we realize we do create our own reality, and that it is just a matter of paying full attention all the time and acting (or not acting) on the information received through that attentiveness. It is easier said than done. Lapses in attention and in confidence in our own inner knowing lead to the problems in our lives. These same principles work on the group or societal level as well as the individual level.

Lack of group attention to the environment, unthinking acceptance of the idea that "it is our right and responsibility to dominate and subdue nature" has led to ecological disasters. Our complacency and lack of critical and compassionate thinking on such issues as slavery, colonialism and manifest destiny has led to racism, classism and the creation of the "third world."

This idea of lapses in attention also goes a long way in explaining why a person's Magick may not always work. In a very real sense the hands of the Goddess are at the ends of the wrists of every person through whose life She becomes manifest. Too often people think that if they do a ritual (that is, if they work Magick) to effect a change of some kind, all they have to do is to "give it to the Goddess;" "release the cone to manifest it;" "send it into the world to do its work;" or whatever the phrase flavor of the month is, and they're done. Now the change will happen. Or, if they are careful to do the ritual at the correct phase of the Moon, when the Moon is in the right sign, at the correct planetary hour, if they repeat the ritual nightly from New Moon to Full Moon, or repeat it often enough, that the change will automatically occur. I call this the "Bewitched Syndrome" (BS). You know what I mean — with the wave of a wand (or with the twitch of a nose), POOF!, you get what you want. It is not likely. Magick needs a vehicle through which to become manifest and that vehicle is most often the ritualist herself. She still has to get out there and work for it.

For example, if you do a ritual to get the job that is best for you and all concerned, at the perfect rate of pay, and then don't go out and fill out a few job applications or send out resumes, you are not likely to get that perfect job. The Magick will create the opportunities. You have to recognize them and act on them. If you do ritual(s) to clean up the environment and save the Earth Mother, and then do not make every attempt to clean up the environment within your own home, your ritual is not likely to have the effect you desired.

Internal disbelief will also contribute to the ineffectiveness of a ritual. If you do not believe in Magick and therefore do not believe it can work, or if you do not believe you are capable/powerful enough to make it work, it won't and you aren't. Or, if you are doing a Magickal working for something you feel in your heart-of-hearts is hopeless, hopeless it shall remain. You must be open to the possibility of change in order to create change.

The other possibility (to my mind at least) is divine intervention. Although I know the Goddess dwells in me and works through me, I do not and cannot contain the totality of what She is and what She knows. I trust Her judgement just as I trust my own. However, I also know that I do not always see all sides of every issue, that I am sometimes subjective when objectivity is called for and that, though I am psychic, I am not all-seeing. I trust Her to know and do what is best, even if I cannot see it at the time. I am Her child and like any mother She has my best interests at heart. I get upset like anyone else when I don't get my Magickal way. But it has been my experience that there is always a good reason for it and that reason will become clear to me in time. Sometimes it takes a very long time. And I am still waiting, watching and listening attentively on several things. But, She hasn't let me down yet, so I am still hopeful. If you do not believe in the possibility of divine intervention, this last bit of information will not apply to you. However, the other suggestions given here probably will.

CHAPTER TWO

Ethics

Morals, as I understand them, are a code of conduct imposed on the individual from the outside. Ethics are standards of behavior imposed from within by the individual's own good judgement. Developing a personal code of ethics requires knowledge of your inner Self far beyond that of the person following the dictates of an externally applied law or commandment.

The Craft does not have a stern and judgmental deity who metes out punishment for perceived offenses. It does not have a set of commandments detailing contractual obligations to be met by a body of believers choosing to worship the deity. Nor does it have a system of jurisprudence dictating individual or coven standards of behavior or practice, as given by some overall governing body. It does, however, have a fairly strong system of ethics based around the Wiccan Rede, which states, "An it harm none, do what you will." This is the only law within the Craft.

In its exoteric expression, Christianity fails to give any sense of personal responsibility for ones actions and redemption. All comes from an outside agency. "The devil made me do it." "By the grace of God, through faith, are you saved." "May God have mercy on your soul." Free will, while granted by God to humanity alone, led to the fall and generally is not seen as something to be exercised positively in an attempt to end their separation from God. Sin, and original sin, seems to keep Christians from exercising their free will in ways that will help themselves. They seem to see themselves as destined to sin and to make wrong choices.

On the surface, the Wiccan Rede appears to grant one complete freedom to do whatever one wants so long as no harm is caused. Complete freedom implies complete responsibility as well, and "harm" is never defined. It is left up to the individual or to the coven to decide on a case-by-case basis. Important things to consider in deciding what causes harm are personal and group karma and the threefold law of return. It requires a great deal of thought, foresight, and insight into the Self and the situation in order to make a proper determination. And, because each situation is different, one set of decisions around a particular issue may not be applicable the next time the issue arises. Or, different individuals and different covens may arrive at different conclusions when presented with the same ethical dilemma. For example, more than a few mainstream Craft and Pagan practitioners believe it is not a good idea to invoke or work with the energies of the Crone. They consider Her too powerful, too dangerous, too unpredictable or just plain nasty. Others, including most Dianics, can't imagine not calling on Her and working with Her energies because She is a part of ourselves and the cycle.

It is also possible to become so concerned with causing harm that one is unable to act at all. In order to prevent this most people put a qualifier on any Magickal work they are doing. That condition is that the result or aim of the spell be "in accordance with free will and for the good of all." Another way to look at this is to realize there is a difference between harm and hurt. Harm is intentional. Hurt is accidental. These definitions can go a long way in eliminating the "what if" game many of us play in deciding a course of action.

The biggest ethical questions in the Craft center around the Magickal use of power. The power/energy present in the universe and within the Self is neutral. It has neither a positive or a negative charge in and of itself. It is the intention of the practioner that determines whether the power will be used for positive or negative purposes.

You are causing harm any time you intend to manipulate someone against her/his will. Such harm usually comes under the heading of negative Magick. Obvious examples of this include Magickally attacking someone (called blasting) or preventing a person from succeeding in a chosen course of action (called binding). Praying for the death of Supreme Court justices — an action taken by several Evangelical and Fundamentalist Christian groups during the Reagan administration — is a glaring example of the use of negative Magick.

Another example that is not so obvious is Love Magick. Love Magick entails doing a Magickal ritual to gain or keep a lover. At first glance this type of work might seem to be harmless, but, upon closer scrutiny we find that a love spell is an attempt to make someone love us whether that person wants to or not. It takes away the loved one's free will and, thus, has caused harm.

Something else to consider here is the sending of healing energy to someone who has not requested it or who has not accepted your offer of Magickal help. Although you may feel that sending healing energy to the individual would be for her own good and could only help her, she may feel otherwise. Perhaps the person you wish to heal is of a religious faith that believes Witches are evil and any power they can muster comes from the devil. Maybe the person prefers to work on her own healing without aid from others. There is also the chance that she may be enjoying being sick for a while. Being the center of attention during an illness, or being unable to work for a while, can be powerful reasons to remain sick. To invade someone's body or mind with Magickal energy of any kind is an act of negative Magick, unless you have the person's permission to do so.

How you approach someone with the offer of a healing is an ethical issue. Do you tell everyone to whom you offer a healing that you are a Witch? That could be unwise. Or do you say, to a Catholic for example, "May I light a candle for you?" Of course, then you will need to make sure that the healing you send centers around a candle burning spell.

Many people believe in the healing power of prayer. An offer to pray for someone is often readily accepted. Praying to, or invoking the aid of a deity in many ways are barely indistinguishable. And calling on a Goddess of healing can help the sender of the prayer as well as the recipient.

There are those, particularly within Dianic Craft, who feel that it is acceptable to use power for anything, including binding and blasting. They cite the legend of Aradia from Leland's *Aradia: Gospel of the Witches* and parts of "The Charge of the Goddess," itself largely based on passages from *Aradia*, as their justification. The legend states that Aradia came to Earth at the behest of Her mother, Diana, to teach the poor and oppressed the ways of Witchcraft and Magick. They were then to use it to obtain a better life for themselves. The "Charge" itself speaks of freedom and a release from the slavery of oppression. Although *Aradia* states that She taught them to bind and to blast, the "Charge" goes on to say that the only law of the Goddess is love. It is hard to love someone or something and call for its destruction or cessation at the same time. The Crone destroys in order to create new life and growth, not to revel in the destruction. She does not end oppression in one area by causing it in another.

The Ethics of Paying

Many people in mainstream Craft and Paganism feel that it is wrong to charge money for teaching the Craft. Dianics, for the most part, do not believe this to be true. Both sides of this issue have a knee jerk reaction to the opposing belief.

People who follow a very traditional path believe that the teachings of the Craft — the religious philosophy and its practical application through the eight Sabbats and thirteen Moon observances (Esbats) — should be available to appropriate seekers regardless of the candidate's ability to pay. They also believe that taking money for teaching or performing the rituals of the Craft corrupts both the teacher and the rituals — a concept borrowed from the traditions of Ceremonial Magick.

Dianics, on the other hand, believe that lack of adequate compensation for work performed and complete access to right livlihood have been major sources of women's oppression for at least the last two thousand years. To them, serving as public educator regarding the Craft and serving as ritual Priestess in a public setting are both right livlihoods deserving of fair compensation.

Please keep in mind that no one is talking about being paid for regular coven work. This issue is whether or not Wanda the Witch, who is teaching an introductory course on Witchcraft at the local occult, new age, or feminist bookstore is ethically correct in charging a fee for those classes. Likewise, is it acceptable for Patty Priestess to charge money for a ticket to attend the Spring Equinox ritual she will be leading at the women's center or in the Unitarian Church's basement? Basically, the Dianics would say yes on both counts, and the traditionalist would say no. Most everyone agrees that it is fair to ask the students in the first case to provide or to pay for their own class supplies, and most also feel it is alright for Patty Priestess to ask for a minimal donation to cover any rental fees involved in using the site.

24

So the questions really are: 1) is the time, knowledge and skill of the public leader worth anything and does that deserve compensation; 2) is it fair to exclude people from access to Wiccan spirituality based solely on ability to pay; 3) do you or do you not accept the old occult maxim that, when it comes to Magick and/or spirituality, money taints everything it touches; 4) if you do not feel it is fair to limit access based on ability to pay, what can be done to meet your monetary needs while attempting to meet the spiritual needs of seekers as well?

Although this is an issue for each potential teacher or Priestess to decide for herself, I can offer some food for thought. There is a difference between need and want. Do you need to charge for teaching the Craft, or do you want to? (Basically, do you or do you not need the money to support yourself and any children you have?) If you choose to charge a fee, consider using a sliding scale. That scale needs to be a realistic one, it should incorporate the ability to pay of a single mother with children, the working poor, the middle class housewife, the single working woman and the corporate executive. Child care options also need to be considered.

Perhaps you could teach a class on a Craft-related topic like divination, astrology, or ritual construction, and charge for that. Or, you could solicit donations by putting a labelled basket at the door. In this case, you have to be prepared to be happy with what you get. If you have skills or training in psychic or psychological counselling from a religious perspective, you might make yourself available for paid consultations before or after the Craft class or ritual.

Another way to look at this is to realize that, even though you may wish to keep your Craft classes and rituals free of charge, it is just as important that you not be laying out any personal expense to provide them. It is perfectly fine to expect the sponsor or sponsoring organization to provide you with transportation (or money for same) and any meals or housing that may be necessary. If you have handout sheets, send the sponsor(s) a copy of each and ask that one copy of each be made available to each attendee. Or, ask for the funds necessary to photocopy them yourself. There are creative solutions to the ethics of paying, all you have to do is put your mind to it to find them.

The Ethics of Touch

From the very beginning of participation within a Magickal group, each person needs to determine what levels of physical closeness are appropriate for her within the Circle. Each individual within a group must clearly state her expectations and limitations regarding levels of intimacy between coven members. The group as a whole needs to reach some kind of consensus concerning this issue. And anyone seeking entrance into a group or seeking training from an individual needs to know exactly what the group or individual stance on this issue is. Coercion of any kind is unacceptable. Casual touching, such as holding hands in a Circle as a method of linking energies in order to raise power, can be disconcerting to someone who does not know why it is being done. A friendly group hug can be downright frightening to a woman with a history of sexual abuse. Cruising the Circle for potential lovers is inappropriate and invasive. Offering training in exchange for sexual favors is inexcusable and is the worst kind of oppression/manipulation. Dianic covens are no more exempt from these potential problems then are mainstream covens.

If you are inviting a new woman to share a Circle with you, be sure to discuss these issues with her before the ritual. She probably won't bring it up herself. Then do what it takes to make her feel comfortable. If holding hands to raise power makes her uneasy, use another method. If you share a group hug at the end of the ritual, be sure she is comfortable with that. Do not just sweep her into the hug and assume she will like it. The anointing procedure(s) suggested in chapter 7 may be something to discuss prior to the ritual, as well. If she would rather not be touched in this way, perhaps you could all "smudge" with incense smoke by directing it toward each person with a feather. That does not involve touching, yet it fulfills the Magickal intention of the anointing procedure. If you will be using your red cords to link yourselves together, be sure you have an extra one for her and explain its use and purpose. Skip it and do something else if she is uncomfortable with the idea. (See chapter 4 for more information about the red cord.)

If you are doing a more public ritual, one in which the sacred space will be shared by a large number of women who are unused to working together and who come from a variety of coven backgrounds, it is probably best to skip all forms of touch. Here again, it is important to explain the ritual before it begins so that everyone can feel comfortable about participating.

We often assume that because we are all women, and because all of us are Dianic Witches, that we will all automatically be comfortable with a certain degree of familiarity while working together. This is most definitely not the case. So, ask before you act. Explain, do not expect everyone to understand what you are doing and why.

The Ethics of Learning

The diversity of belief and practice within Dianic Wicca and Paganism, and our preference for autonomous small groups, can be seen as both a great strength and a great weakness. One of the areas where it can function as a weakness is in the training of newcomers to the Craft. There is no codified set of beliefs and practices to be passed on and no agreed upon method of communicating the content of religious and Magickal material to the seeker. As a result, it is up to each coven to find a method of instructing newcomers in the ways and means of becoming a functional member of their religious body.

Standards will differ from group to group. However, each potential member has a right to expect that some concerted effort will be made to instruct her in some way. If no such information regarding training is forthcoming from those she seeks to join, she should ask for a general outline of the coven's teaching style and the content of their lessons before joining the group.

Teaching styles may vary widely, but generally fall into two catagories: the teacher-student model and the guide-seeker model. Each is worthy, and each may be used within the same coven under different circumstances. The power dynamics of each are quite different, however, and should be addressed before training begins and throughout the process if things are to remain on an ethical and equitable footing. In either case, a course outline of material to be absorbed should be presented and then followed, and the responsibilities of each party should be clearly understood — in writing if necessary.

The teacher-student model implies a one-up, one-down relationship. The teacher knows all and will impart it to the student who knows little or nothing. The guide-seeker model posits a more

27

equal relationship. Both have "the answers" within. The guide's job is to help the seeker find her own answers, not to provide them for her. In the teacher-student model, it is the teacher's responsibility to provide answers. In the guide-seeker model, it is the responsibility of the seeker to provide her own answers. The guide merely points the way or facilitates the discovery. Each relationship has a potential for manipulation. Here are some things to look out for: if the teacher or guide expects sexual favors in exchange for instruction/guidance, find another group or another teacher/guide. If it seems to you that she is not sticking to the course outline but is instead preaching her own agenda, bring it out into the open and discuss it with the individual teacher/guide or with the entire coven, if you feel that is necessary. If you feel information is being withheld from you, say so and ask why, there may or may not be good reasons. If your feelings or concerns are being given short shrift or are being dismissed entirely, reconsider your decision to study with that person/group. If you are expected to do a certain amount of work for the person or group in exchange for training, is that exchange a fair one?

Once the basic training is over, whether that happens before you are actually accepted into the group or whether it happens after membership has been established, you have a right to expect continued training if you wish it. For example, you should expect to be able to gradually assume a bigger and bigger role in conducting ritual. Your particular areas of talent or expertise should be tapped, used and developed. Your growth and training should not stop with the basics unless you want it to. If your growth needs are not being met, say so. It is up to you to see to it that your needs are taken care of. If nothing more is forthcoming from the group, it may be time to find another group or to start one of your own.

If the group you are joining is a brand new group and has not yet developed a system of mutual study and training, be sure to develop one that fits the needs of all concerned. It often works best if those with a specific area of Wiccan/Magickal interest take on the responsibility for learning as much as they can about it and then share it with the rest of the group through lectures, discussions, workshops or whatever. In this way each woman is allowed to pursue her special interest(s) and each has a chance to take a leadership role in passing on to others what she has learned.

The Ethics of Politics

Dianic Witches, perhaps more than any other branch of Paganism and Witchcraft, believe that the spiritual is political. What is meant by this is that one's personal political views are a reflection of her spiritual beliefs. Furthermore, it is felt that those beliefs should prompt appropriate action within the political, socio-economic and cultural arenas of day-to-day life. I think the key to being able to deal with this issue ethically is to remember that we all can agree to disagree. How each individual woman Witch interprets commonly held and privately held Dianic Wiccan beliefs will determine what actions (or inactions) she will decide to take in the realm of the political.

There is a tendency within both the Dianic and the feminist communities to judge the political action and beliefs of others against a more or less commonly held majority opinion as to what constitutes proper belief and its application to real world issues. Individuals are judged as either politically correct or politically incorrect — right or wrong.

Although Dianic Wicca does not presume to tell any individual woman what she should or should not believe spiritually, this same courtesy is not always extended to that woman in the realm of the political. This inconsistency deserves some attention and examination. Why do we find it threatening when someone does not apply her beliefs in the manner we have chosen? Why do we find it necessary to judge her wrong, unethical or unenlightened when she has chosen a different expression of her beliefs? Is it ethical on our part to make such judgments?

My answer to the last question is, no. I don't have answers for anyone but myself. Everyone certainly has the right to strongly held opinions and, to a certain extent, it is probably natural to feel absolutely right in holding those opinions and to wonder why some women do not. I do question the vociferous protest that comes from many women when confronted with a sister who believes and acts differently. Such condemnations seem to run contrary to the spirit of Dianic Wicca, and Paganism in general.

Another area that comes under the umbrella of the spiritual is political centers around how we act in response to the laws of the land. Although we live in a pluralistic society that usually allows for the free expression of any religion, in the eyes of the government that freedom of religious expression does not exempt us from complying with the law of the land. The right of religious expression does not always hold up in court in cases where the two conflict. How are we to act ethically when this issue arises?

Although state and local laws may differ from state to state, there are some pretty commonly occurring laws that can be addressed in this context. My aim here is not to tell you what to do or not do, but to make you aware of some things worthy of consideration. Young women who have not yet reached the age of majority often seek us out. They feel the Goddess has touched their lives, or that our beliefs and practices are right for them. They want to join our circles. If we agree to this without first receiving written permission from parents or legal guardians, we are leaving ourselves open to a variety of charges in every state in the union. These charges can range from kidnapping and child abuse to contributing to the delinquency of a minor. Freedom of religious expression will not hold water in these cases.

Witches have always been known as healers and the midwives of rites of passage. Ever since the dawn of state-sponsored Christianity and "modern" (read: male) medical practice, Witches have been persecuted, imprisoned and killed for their beliefs, particularly in regard to their medical practices. It remains so today. Midwifery — the right of one knowledgeable and skilled woman to attend the birth of another knowledgeable woman — is illegal in most states unless the midwife is a board-certified doctor or a certified nurse practioner. Although this is slowly beginning to change in some states, it is illegal for a lay midwife to attend a birth. Some states do, however, allow a lay midwife to attend a birth if it takes place within the context of a religious ceremony.

The dissemination of information regarding the use of herbs and other alternative methods of healing by those without medical degrees is called practicing medicine without a license. Although Witchcraft has a long association with the knowledge and use of alternative methods of healing, it would be hard to prove it is a necessary tenet of the Craft in a court of law.

In keeping with their beliefs, Witches support the right of individuals to decide how their lives will be led. Part of deciding how a life will be led can include the right of the individual to decide how and when it will end. Not only have Wise Women/ Witches historically been the midwives of birth, they also have been the midwives of death. Euthanasia — active or passive — does not present a moral or ethical dilemma to most Witches. Yet, to willingly assist someone who wishes to die would land us in court charged with murder.

Though I have cited just a few of the types of cases where Wiccan belief and practice could conflict with the laws of the land, what do we do in these types of cases? Do we comply with the law? Do we covertly or surreptitiously circumvent the law? Do we challenge it in court? Do we seek to change it in the legislature? Or, do we do nothing?

The Ethics of Drugs and Alcohol

Dianic Wicca takes no stand in particular in regard to the use of drugs and alcohol. As with everything else, the individual is free to make her own decisions regarding their use. However, women Witches do understand the potential for abuse inherent in the use of these substances and, therefore, do not generally include their use in a ritual. Women have found that, like any other cross-section of society, there are those within the Dianic community who have problems with substance abuse. Not wanting to contribute to the problems of these women, and not wanting to exclude those in recovery from full participation in the ritual experience, the once fairly traditional use of wine has been dropped from the ritual format and replaced with spring water, herbal teas, cider, red Kool-Aid or any other non-alcoholic beverage. Some women do bring wine to share during the feasting portion of a ritual, or perhaps to drink with a shared meal prior to the ritual. No one is expected to partake, though you may be offered the option.

With this issue, like any other in Dianic Craft, please feel free to do what is best for you. If you are new to a group or are attending a large function wherein those facilitating the ritual are unknown to you, it might be a good idea to ask whether a drink will be shared in the context of the ritual. If so, and if you are concerned about what it might be, ask what will be in the cup. If it is an herbal blend, ask what it consists of. If the ritual leaders are unwilling to tell you, reconsider your participation in the ritual. That information should

31

be made available to anyone. Witches, remembering the Rede, do not want to cause harm — either intentionally or unintentionally.

Another ethical consideration comes into play when deciding whether to use drugs within a ritual setting. Drug use is illegal. The judicial system, for the most part, has not upheld the rights of claimants who use drugs within a religious context. As with the use of alcohol, dependency and recovery are also worthy of consideration. The use of drugs as aids to attaining altered states of consciousness is questionable. There are other, and better, ways to attain that type of experience. (See chapter 3 for a discussion of the alternatives.)

The Ethics of Ecology

Since Witches believe that the Earth and everything on it is sacred, it follows that we would be concerned with ecology and environmentalism. In fact, many women have come to Dianic Craft out of a deep concern for the plight of the Earth and the beings that dwell upon Her. Many have been environmental activists for quite some time. Wiccan beliefs and concerns regarding ecology and environmentalism are somewhat different than either the traditional model of environmentalism or the philosophy of deep ecology. Witches bring a sense of the sacred to the environmental movement.

Women Witches are environmentally active because we belief the Earth is alive and the diversity of that alive-ness found on Earth is to be honored, celebrated and named holy. Natural diversity is not just valuable as a resource for human exploitation. Not only does natural diversity have its own intrinsic value (deep ecology view), that diversity is sacred. And we do not rank species according to their value for humanity or according to the amount of brain power they have (how close they come to approximating humans). For women Witches all species are equals and are part of the whole to which we all belong.

Because we feel we are all a part of a singular whole, we understand that in degrading the environment, or in degrading other people or other species within the environment, we degrade ourselves. When a species becomes extinct a part of us dies as well, and a manifestation of divinity is forever gone from the world and from ourselves. So you will often find Dianics involved in campaigns to save endangered species.

Dianics also believe that the way in which we live our lives and the ways we treat other beings and our environment, whether it be our immediate environment or the global environment, are outward reflections of our inner spirituality. If we believe the Earth is the body of the Goddess and that body is sacred, then we do not wish to see it littered with trash and pockmarked with landfills full to overflowing. Recycling then becomes more than a fashionable way to be politically correct, it becomes an ethical obligation.

Pollution is not just seen as a threat to economic growth, it is seen as a symptom of an unhealthy alienation from Nature/Goddess. Its control is seen as a way of reconnecting with, or strengthening, the spirit of Nature/Goddess.

How we make choices regarding population control, land use, land management and distribution/ownership all become ethical considerations in addition to the political and/or socio-economic conundrums they already are. Quality of living, or quality of life, becomes a matter of our participation in and acceptance of our connection with the divine in Nature and in each other.

The Ethics of Sexism, Racism and Ableism

Dianic care and concern for these issues arises out of both feminist philosophy and Dianic thealogy. Feminists have long fought sexism and gender politics. Dianics know and understand that many of the women who seek out Goddess centered religions do so in order to heal the wounds inflicted on them by a patriarchal society. Whether those wounds have been physical or mental, Goddess religion and Dianic Craft actively seek to heal them and to empower its women with a knowledge of the divine feminine within themselves and within the world. This knowledge often gives women the inner strength to get out of bad situations and to improve their lives, loves, and their view of themselves.

Dianic thealogy encourages women to see that we are all interconnected. We are each a part of an ecological, systemic and living whole, incorporating the totality of existence on Earth. This view precludes racism and ableism in a couple of ways. First, we see everything and everyone as a unique, sacred and necessary part of the whole. Removal or suppression/oppression of any part diminishes the sacred within the world and depletes the ecosystem. Viewed in this way, racism and ableism become blasphemy. Second, because we are all interconnected, to harm, oppress or ignore the special needs of any part of the whole, hurts the whole. Stated more personally and more simply: What hurts another hurts me.

For these reasons Dianic women have been in the forefront of the Pagan movement in inviting women of different racial and ethnic backgrounds to participate in their rituals, and have been the strongest voices in insisting that Pagan gathering places and ritual formats become accessible to the physically challenged and differently abled. For these same reasons they were also among the first to insist on alternatives to alcohol in the ritual cup.

Because Dianics do not discriminate against anyone on the basis of race or ethnic background, you'll often find quite an eclectic flavor to many Dianic Circles. When women of color join a Dianic Circle they often bring with them a variety of Pagan beliefs and practices from their native cultures. Others in the group are usually eager to learn about these alternatives in religious belief and Magickal practice and are quick to incorporate them into their existing Circle format and ritual practice. In this way the racial and ethnic diversity of the group is honored and celebrated and everyone is made to feel at home and an integral part of the group.

Dianics respect cultural diversity and ethnic integrity. This is in keeping with our honoring and naming sacred the diversity found in Nature. While we respect the rights of others to determine their spirituality for themselves, and make no attempt to convert others to our beliefs, we similarly make no attempt to incorporate the beliefs of others into our own unless invited to do so by those participating in ritual with us.

CHAPTER THREE

MAGICK

Magick is the ability to effect change for the better in ourselves and in our sphere of action, it is the art and science of achieving our goals. Its only admonishment is that we cause no harm. It works through the imagination, in concert with the vast pool of creative energy available in the universe. It is this pool from which we draw when painting a picture, raising a child or developing a computer program. This pool of creative energy is variously called etheric substance, Goddess, Magickal energy, Goddess energy, power of the Goddess, Magickal power or, most commonly, power.

Witches believe this power comes from the Goddess, that it is a part of Her essence. Since we are also a part of Her essence and partake in small measure of Her divinity, this creative or Magickal energy/power is inherent within us as well. This is referred to as personal power. We make Magick by accessing this power within and combining it with the power available in the universe. With it, we can transform our lives and the world.

The skills necessary to access this power and to direct it to our intended goal are derived primarily from our psychic and emotional makeup. We become more powerful, and more successful in our Magickal workings and in our lives, as we gain mastery over these skills.

In order to do Magick (to use power to achieve our goals) we must first believe it is possible to do so. Or, at least we must be open to the possibility. At its root, the ability to do Magick (to create our own reality) exists because we believe it does. It begins as a matter of faith and later becomes a matter of knowing. There is some evidence to support our belief in our ability to create our own reality, and thus, to do Magick.

Perhaps the most convincing evidence comes from the scientific realm of particle physics, and is called the Heisenberg Principle of Uncertainty. Due to recent technological advancements we are now able to see sub-atomic particles. We can either see the speed at which they travel or we can see their location. We cannot see both at once. Which phenomena gets seen depends entirely on which the observer chooses to see. It is not determined by the particles themselves. It is determined by the observer. The root of this particle activity is chaos. The reality of its manifestation is only determined subjectively — by what the observer *wants* to see. If, when viewing sub-atomic particles the observer thinks, "I want to measure velocity," speed is what is observed. If the same observer then changes her mind and thinks, "I want to see positioning," location is seen. If the observer tries to blank her mind and just look, she sees nothing until the idea of speed or location flickers briefly in her mind. Then she sees that flicker of thought manifest itself before her eyes, according to the choice she made. If we can make these choices at the sub-atomic level, at the level of the building blocks of nature, surely we can use those building blocks to create whatever reality we wish. Magick becomes a matter of knowing, not just believing.

The building blocks a Witch uses in doing Magick are called the Four Cornerstones of Magick, or the Witch's Pyramid. They are: to know, to will, to dare, and to keep silent.

To know means you have developed the skills necessary to do Magick. To will means you know how to raise power and send it. To dare means you will actually do it and you know it will work. You have faith in your own abilities and in your connection to the Goddess. It means you are willing to do Magick and to approach alternate states of reality — something thought of as dangerous, tricky, even evil by most people. It means you have the courage to face the totality of your Self and your deepest feelings. To keep silent means exactly that. It means you do not tell everyone you meet about what you are involved in and what Magick you have done.

To Know

The skills and knowledge necessary for a successful Magickal operation include the ability to meditate and visualize; knowing various techniques for raising and directing power; basic knowledge of the system of correspondences; knowing the Magickal times and seasons; and knowing Magickal principles/laws.

Meditation and visualization are the foundation skills of a Witch. Meditation allows access to the Goddess within and to the different levels of your Self that lie beyond or behind your personality. Through its daily use psychic skills begin to develop or are enhanced, and the deep mind is opened to receiving information from other planes of reality as well as from the Goddess, your true Self, and a variety of Otherworld beings whose realms you may choose to visit. Visualization allows you to create before your mind's eye the Magickal realities you intend to make manifest on the Earth plane. This same mental imaging will become a focal point for concentrating on an intended goal during the portion of a ritual in which you raise and send forth power.

The ability to meditate and visualize successfully takes more training than you might guess. I have often heard it said that all you need to be able to meditate and visualize is a good imagination and the ability to daydream. While these skills are important, it doesn't end there. The daydream must be a controlled one, and you must be able to narrow your field of attention when meditating and visualizing. You must be able to block out extraneous mental chatter or images, and then you must learn to follow the meditation or maintain the visualization for an extended period of time without becoming distracted.

Here are some tips and exercises that may help: Begin by doing this work at the same time every day. Your mind and body will come to expect it at that time, and will become more receptive to it through repetition. Try to do it at a relaxed time of the day — before work if you are an early riser, or in the evening after work and household chores are completed. I do not recommend doing it in bed right before falling asleep at night. It is too easy for you to simply fall asleep. Falling asleep during a meditation/visualization is an ego defense against letting go. Meditate earlier in the day and sit up to do so.

It will help if you can go to a quiet part of the house to do this work. Dim light or candlelight is more relaxing and conducive than is harsh or glaring light. If blocking out sound is a problem, try covering it with "white noise." White noise is a constant, non-musical sound. I have found that turning on a fan works well. It hides other noise, its sound is not obnoxious, and it keeps me cool in the Summer. In fact, the constant whirring of the fan actually helps induce my meditative state.

Light incense if you would like, just be sure to use the same scent each time. The left brain will do anything to avoid giving up control to the right brain. Scent is one of the greatest memory stimulators known. The left brain will latch on to that and flood your mind with memories associated with each new scent you use, instead of allowing the meditative state to take hold. Also, using the same scent each time will come to act as another trigger to your body and deep mind, indicating it is time to relax and meditate. Sandalwood is particularly suited to inducing psychic/meditative states. It calms the mind and allows the spiritual aspects of Self to come to the fore and do their work, whether it be meditation/visualization, divination or Magickal workings.

First, you must learn to relax. Make a note of the time when you start. Close your eyes. Get comfortable in your chair or on the floor. Breathe slowly, deeply and rhythmically. Feel the tension drain from your body. Tense and release your various muscles, beginning with the toes and moving on up to the head and neck. Shake or rotate your joints to help loosen them if you need to — shake your hands and wrists, rotate your ankles, wiggle your hips, and shake your shoulders.

Now you need to calm and open your mind. You must first get rid of the mental chatter and extraneous images running through it. To do this, imagine yourself sitting at the base of a tree by the bank of a stream. All of the daily hassles and agendas you need to dismiss from your mind are written on the leaves of the tree. Slowly, one-by-one, they drop from the tree into the water, and the stream carries them away. As they drop you see what is written on each leaf. You watch it fall into the water and move away. As you see it go you know that particular item has been removed from your mind. When all the leaves have fallen and have been carried away, you are ready to begin a visualization exercise.

Unless you are an experienced meditator it is highly unlikely you will be able to accomplish this stilling of the mind in one sitting. Generally, you will find yourself thinking about the content of a leaf that has already washed away. When that happens, see the leaf fall and be gone again. Should it happen again, with the same leaf or any other, stop the exercise and note the time. Jot down your beginning and ending times in what will become your Magickal Journal.

When learning a new skill like this it is important to measure your success in small increments, instead of in terms of the overall picture. By keeping track of your daily starting and ending times you will be able to measure your success against the lengthening seconds and minutes, instead of against accomplishing the entire exercise. You will find this will help you avoid frustration and self-chastisement. When the day comes when you are able to have all leaves fall from the tree and keep your mind in a still and open state for a couple of minutes, you will be ready to begin visualization exercises.

In learning to visualize, it is best to start with the concrete and move by stages to the abstract. When you are ready to begin visualization exercises, place a lit candle in front of your place of meditation. If it is at or near eye level, so much the better. Use a single taper of a color of your own choosing. Use the same candle in the same holder each time. In the beginning, bright colors are easier to visualize than pastels.

Light your candle, close your eyes, relax, and do your leaf meditation as described above. When your mind is stilled, open your eyes and gaze at your candle for about a minute or so. Make a mental note of the time and look at your candle again. Now close your eyes and see it in your mind's eye. See the flame, the color and shape of the candle and its holder. When the image shifts or mental chatter creeps in, stop the exercise and note the time. Jot starting and ending times in your journal after writing a description of the exercise. Repeat this daily, noting times, until you can maintain the visualization in your stilled mind for five minutes.

Next time, repeat the exercise, but this time blow out the candle in your mind's eye while retaining the image of the candle itself. You will probably find that, when you mentally blow out the visualized candle, the entire image will disappear. Try to bring it back. If you can't bring it back, stop the exercise and note what happened and the times in your journal.

When you can hold the image of the snuffed candle in your mind for a couple of minutes, mentally make the flame reappear and hold that image for two minutes. Note your progress in your journal daily.

Next, remove the candle entirely before beginning the exercise. Now relax, still and open your mind, open your eyes and gaze briefly at the spot where the candle was. Close your eyes, see the spot and produce the lit candle before your mind's eye. Now open your eyes and gaze at the blank spot where the actual candle used to be, but retain the image of the burning candle in your mind. When you can do all of this, you are ready for the next visualization exercise.

Pick a more complicated object with a different shape and color. Choose something with two colors or something that has a single colored background with a single shape of a different color superimposed on it. For example, use a piece of cardboard painted red with a gold star on it, or a ball that is half green and half blue. Now repeat the above process in gradual increments: 1) hold the visualization of the object for five minutes; 2) turn it over, upside down or sideways in actuality, then in your mind; 3) right it again, see it in your mind and turn it in your mind; 4) remove the object and create it in your mind only; 5) create it in your mind, open your eyes and still see it in your mind. Now add another step: create it in your mind, open your eyes and see the image. Now project the visualization to the actual location the object once held. See it in your mind's eye, out there in front of you. Keep daily notes in your journal.

Repeat this entire process using more and more difficult objects until you can see an entire painting in your mind and projected before you. Then do a closeup of the painting. Make the image of the painting fill the entire visual field of your mind. Now you can move on to creating visualizations in your mind without the aid of an object in front of you. Start with the plain and simple and gradually work up to the more elaborate and complicated. Finally, create moving objects in your mind's eye and visualize their motion. Gradually add stationary and other moving objects to the scene until it were as though you were watching a movie in your mind.

Now that you can meditate and visualize fully you can move on to other forms of meditation/visualization. You can relax, still your mind and ask your Goddess Self to help you solve a particular problem or make decisions. You will be able to see, hear or feel possible and likely solutions/decisions in your mind's eye (or ear), or feel what is right at a gut level. Be sure you remain focused. If your left brain tries to interfere with extraneous thoughts, pull yourself back on course. If you see things unrelated to the problem, fade them out. If these types of things keep re-occurring, end the meditation for the day and jot down notes in your journal. Act on any related information you received. The more you practice, the better you will get at it.

You can use these same meditative and visualization techniques to give yourself a boost in energy, to heal yourself on all levels, to commune with the Goddess and to open your psychic centers for divination. You will also use these techniques in Magickal workings, alone or with others.

One of the more common group uses of meditation/visualization is the guided meditation/visualization. In this case a facilitator or guide will talk you through a particular mental imaging. She may or may not preface the working with an exercise to relax and/or still the mind. You may be expected to do this quickly for yourself.

During the guided portion of the exercise (usually a journey of some sort) the facilitator will tell you what to see and/or feel in general terms. Once the mental destination is reached, she will give you time to explore and to find answers on your own. She will then guide you back to your point of origin within the visualization and guide your return to normal awareness.

Do not allow your left brain to distract you during the guided portions of the exercise. See what you are told to see and mentally do what you are told to do. If you go off on your own tangent you will have failed the exercise and will have detracted from the group's goal. It is important to complete the exercise as it is and not let your left brain run away with you.

The System of Correspondences

There is a basic system of correspondences used by most Witches. It is based in Ceremonial Magick and has been in use by Witches and Magicians for at least several hundred years. You can make up your own system or you can use systems from other traditions like Native American, Celtic, Norse, Voudoun, or Santeria. Those systems are not specifically Wiccan and are in some cases, like the Celtic and the Norse, incomplete or possibly inaccurate because of the lack of surviving documentation from those cultures.

There is also a great deal to be said for a great number of people using the same correspondences over an extended period of time. This process builds up a Magickal charge behind each symbol, which accumulates additional power with each use over the passage of time. Through this process each symbol becomes so inspirited and enlivened with power that it reflects that power back to us when we call upon it or use it in a ritual/Magickal context. The same can be said for the repetitive use of a ritual or cycle of rituals over an extended period of time. The more often you repeat them, the stronger the psychic charge they build up and the better they are able to point one to the Mysteries. The more often the deep mind is exposed to the Mysteries the greater the opportunity for experiencing and understanding them and the lessons they have to teach.

Here then is the basic system of correspondences. It comes to us from Ceremonial Magick and Alchemy and has been in use for at least three hundred years. It is based on the four directions and the four elements of Earth, Air, Fire and Water. I am sure you will be able to add items to each category as familiarity and experience grows. This is not meant to be an exhaustive listing. (The format for the listing is borrowed, with thanks, from Starhawk's book, *The Spiral Dance*.)

East

Element: Air

Color: Yellow

Season: Spring

Season of Life: Youth

Time of Day: Dawn/morning

Magickal Tool: Athame, censer

Associations: Of the mind — intellect, clarity, discernment, wisdom, knowledge, abstract thinking, logic, the spoken word, the wind and breath.

Animal: Eagle, hawk, birds in general

Elemental Spirits: Sylphs/Fairies

Signs of the Zodiac: Aquarius, Gemini, Libra (the Air signs)

Gem: Topaz, amber, citron

Sense: Smell

Goddesses: Arianrhod, Nuit, Iris, Ostara; Goddesses of dawn and Spring

South

Element: Fire

Color: Red, red-orange; fiery colors

Season: Summer

Season of Life: Maturity

Time of Day: Noon, mid-day

Magickal Tool: Wand, censer (the fiery coal within it)

Associations: The will, the Sun, passion, transformation, energy, heat, flame, embers, life blood, purification by fire, fires of all kinds, volcanoes, eruptions, explosions, violent change, the solar plexus, the heart.

Animal: Lion, horse

Elemental Spirits: Salamanders

Signs of the Zodiac: Aries, Leo, Sagittarius (the Fire signs)

Gem: Fire opal, ruby, carnelian, garnet

Sense: Sight

Goddesses: Sekhmet, Bridgit, Hestia, Pele, Vesta, Aradia, Ameratsu, Lucina

West

Element: Water

Color: Blue, blue-green

Season: Fall

Season of Life: Old Age

Time of Day: Evening, twilight

Magickal Tool: Cup or chalice

Associations: Intuition, psychic abilities, love, emotions, deep feelings, the unconscious, the womb, generation, fertility, water of all kinds, wells, tides, the Moon, menstrual blood, amniotic fluid, saliva, the third eye, wisdom

Animal: Sea serpents, leviathan of the deep, dragons, fish, sea lions, creatures of water

Elemental Spirits: Undines, mermaids

Signs of the Zodiac: Pisces, Cancer, Scorpio (the Water signs)

Gems: Aquamarine, beryl, opal, ambergris

Sense: Taste

Goddesses: Aphrodite, Tiamat, Mari, Yemaya

North

Element: Earth

Color: Green, brown

Season: Winter

Season of Life: Death/rebirth

Time of Day: Midnight, darkest night

Magickal Tool: Pentacle, salt, wheat, corn

Associations: Manifestation, the body, physicality, fertility, vegetation, mystery, silence, growth, money/material gain, common sense, caves, mountains, fields, standing stones, metals, manifested creativity.

Animal: Bull, cow, stag, deer, snakes, bear

Elemental Spirits: Gnomes, dwarves

Signs of the Zodiac: Taurus, Virgo, Capricorn (the Earth signs)

Gems: Rock crystal, emerald, jet, quartz, granite, bedrock, salt

Sense: Touch

Goddesses: Hathor, Ceres, Demeter, Gaia, Bo-Ann, Persephone, Kore

Some Witches include a fifth element in some or all of their workings. Here are its correspondences:

Spirit

Location/Direction: Center; up, down and all around

Color: Purple or white, rainbow, clear, black

Season: The cycle itself

Season of Life: All life, life beyond death, rebirth

Time: Beyond time, all time, the eternal now, the Lunar and Solar cycles

Magickal Tool: Cauldron

Associations: The presence of the Goddess, immanence, transcendence, omnipresence, the void, all and nothing, within and without, the center of the universe and the Self.

Animal: Sphinx, owl

Gems: Diamond, amethyst

Sense: Hearing

Goddesses: Isis, Cerridwen, Shekinah, your personal matron deity

Magickal Times and Seasons

Pray to the Moon when She is round

Luck with you shall then abound

What you seek for shall be found

In sea or sky or solid ground.

—Old Witch Verse[1]

The Magick of Witchcraft is closely tied to the phases of the Moon. Rituals of increase — of bringing things to yourself and into the world — are started on the night of the New Moon crescent and are completed on the night of the Full Moon. Rituals of decrease — of removing or stopping things — take place during the Waning Moon. Generally speaking, Magick is not attempted during the Dark of the Moon. However, some women find this a good time to do rituals of an inner, personal nature, particularly if the Dark of the Moon coincides with their Moon Time.

The bleeding time, no matter when it occurs in the Lunar cycle, is a particularly powerful time for women. Psychic abilities are usually strongest during the menstrual cycle, and many women feel a need to turn inward, to be alone, to seek personal visions, to contact the inner plane (Otherworld), to draw on ancestral connections or to spend time in other Magickal and creative pursuits.

The Full Moon is considered the time of greatest power in the lunation. For this reason the night of the Full Moon is the traditional meeting time for Witches. The Goddess is honored and invoked, and Magickal operations are undertaken and/or completed. Since many covens do not meet at the New Moon as well as the Full Moon, they do all their Magick on the night of the Full Moon. Individuals, of course, may choose to begin their own Magickal operations beginning at the New Moon crescent and continuing nightly until the Full Moon is reached. It may be helpful as well to consider the sign of the zodiac the Moon is in when beginning and/or completing a Magickal operation, although it is not absolutely necessary.

Witches also take the Solar cycle into consideration when doing Magick. Each of the eight Sabbats (major festivals of the Witch's liturgical year) are associated with particular things in the life cycle of the Goddess, Her Daughter, Her women and the Earth. The four seasons act as indicators as well. Spells associated with new beginnings are best done in the Spring. Magick associated with maturation, abundance and variety are associated with Summer. The Fall brings spells related to harvest and endings. The Winter is a good time for things associated with hibernation or turning inward, and the creativity of planning, ingesting and gestating new ideas in preparation for their birth in Spring.

Another option for deciding the timing of a spell would be to use astrological/planetary correspondences as well as the Moon's location within a sign on any given day. Most Witches purchase an astrological calendar each year to help them keep track of the Moon's movement through the signs of the zodiac. Planetary correspondences are as follows:

☽ Moon: Cycles; birth, generation, fertility; intuition, psychic abilities; emotions; inspiration, poetry; water, travel by water; women; Monday

☉ Sun: Success; happiness, joy; light; leadership; advancement; growth; healing; innate power; friendship; Sunday

☿ Mercury: Communication; creativity; cleverness; intelligence; science; memory; thievery; business transaction; travel by car/vehicle; writing; Wednesday

♀ Venus: Love, sexuality, sensuality, pleasure, attraction, friendship; harmony, beauty, art; the aesthetically pleasing; Friday

♂ Mars: Strength, aggression, conflict, war, anger, struggle; surgery; Tuesday

♃ Jupiter: Royalty, leadership, politics, power, success, responsibility, public acclaim; business, wealth; Thursday

♄ Saturn: Knowledge; death; history, time; limitations, restriction, obstacles; Saturday

Here is an example of how to use this information: Suppose that I want to do a ritual to aid me in writing this book. I would probably do it on a Wednesday because Wednesday is the day of Mercury, and Mercury rules creativity, communication and the written word. If I was just starting the book, or starting a new chapter, I'd want to begin the ritual at the New Moon. If I had hit a rough spot and was looking for additional inspiration, I would do the ritual at or near the Full Moon. If I wanted to critique what I had done and/ or rewrite something, I would probably do it during a Waning Moon. It would also help mental work, especially that involving the use of words, if the Moon was in an Air sign.

The three outer planets (Uranus, Neptune and Pluto) are often not used in traditional Magickal workings because they had not as yet been discovered when this system of correspondences was codified. You are welcome to seek out a good book on astrology and add their correspondences to your own set of tables, and use their energies to your best advantage.

To Will

Magick is often referred to as an art. Like the development of skill in any other art form, the development of Magickal skill requires time, attention, effort and discipline. Its ultimate goal is to cause changes for the better within ourselves and our environment. In so doing we not only effect change in accordance with our will, we come to know ourselves and, finally, to know more about the nature of the Divine.

Although Wiccan Magick is thought of as simple (or low) Magick within many occult circles, it still requires the self-discipline of practice and repetition to master its techniques. Wiccan Magick is most often sympathetic (or imitative) Magick. In other words, its Magickal actions are done in imitation of natural processes. The action itself may seem simplistic to an outside observer. However, those simple actions are backed up with the full force of a Magickally trained and fully operational mind, and an open and properly focused and channelled emotional, psychic and physical self. It also takes an iron-clad will, one that will brook no opposition. The Magick *will* work. The ritual *will* be effective. The power raised and sent forth *will* become manifest in the world (or within the Self).

Meditation, visualization, focused attention and the development of the psychic senses (see "To Dare" below) are the fundamentals of Magick. Concentrated work on developing these disciplines can go a long way in strengthening the Magickal will as well. The daily practice of these skills, the keeping of a Magickal journal of your progress and the focused attention each of these things entails, requires an act of will in itself.

Another oft cited and effective method of developing Magickal will and self-discipline is the breaking of a habit. If you choose to do this, start with something small. Save the truly Herculean efforts for later. For example, don't start out by trying to quit smoking. Instead, begin by deciding not to cross your legs at the ankles for a month. It may sound silly, but it will develop your self-discipline, focused attention and degree of persistence all at the same time.

Another good exercise is to try to make it through a day without speaking a negative. This one is of particular value to one who works Magick. The deeper levels of your mind and your Self, upon which and through which Magick works, do not respond to, or understand, negatives. For example, if you have decided to use an affirmation to effect a change in yourself, it must be stated in positive terms in order for it to work. If you say, "I am not sick today," your deep mind takes out/does not register the negative world. So in effect your affirmation becomes, "I am sick today." The same thought, stated in positive terms would be, "I am well today" or, "I am feeling fine today."

You will be surprised at how difficult it will be to speak without negatives. When you realize you have made a mistake, "discipline" yourself in some way so that your body comes to know/becomes aware of the Magickal process. Since you will be channelling your Magick through your body, it will help if it, too, has its own more or less automatic awareness of how Magick works through it. This is often referred to as "body knowing." So, stomp your foot or snap your fingers each time a negative comes out of your mouth.

Magickal will is much more than the self-discipline it takes to learn the basic skills, however. It also entails knowing what you really want and then taking action to see to it that you get it — ethically, and in accordance with the free will of others. Knowing what you want requires a deep communication with your deep Self as well as a trust in your own volition. This inner knowing of what you want/need is often called "true will" and contains within it the ability to risk the consequences of your actions. In other words, to take responsibility for your actions. The true will has no need to dominate others, merely to direct the Self in accordance with the common good.

The will directs the power when working Magick. The power is drawn from the matrix of creative power in the universe; is collected and amplified within the body and within the Circle itself; is shaped to its intended purpose through visualization; is expelled from the body and the Circle through the cone of power, and is sent to do its intended task by the force of the will. Without this willed sending of the power, the Magick is not released into manifestation.

This Magickal will is used and developed in day-to-day living by following through on what you say you are going to do. You make a choice, or come to a decision about something, and then act on it. Lack of follow-through weakens will. This is the basis of the Witch's maxim: "A Witch's word is her bond." If you promise to do (or not do) something and then do not comply, you have weakened your will and its use in a Magickal context is weakened as well. A Witch's day-to-day life is a reflection of her Magickal/spiritual life. There is no separation between the two.

Methods of Magick and the Raising of Power

Although the development of meditation and visualization skills have been discussed at some length already, I have not yet presented information as to their applications within a Magickal context. Perhaps the most frequent Magickal use of meditation and/or visualization is as a method of focus when in the process of raising energy.

For example, when doing a healing it is helpful to have a picture of the sick one to pass around the Circle. Everyone then has a chance to see what the person looks like. They then retain that picture within their mind as they raise the power necessary to effect the healing. Then, when the power is released, everyone visualizes it being sent to that person, who is now visualized at her present location. In other words, the visualized image has been projected outward along with the power. The visualized image becomes one with the person — is the person — and she absorbs the power via the projected image. If it is known to the group, her actual surroundings at the time the power is released can be visualized, and the group actually can "see" the power reach her there. This gives an added sense of completion to the work.

Often no picture is available and the one who knows the ill person will give a verbal description of her appearance, the ailment and the power to be sent. Based on this information the visualization must be entirely created within the mind's eye. In either case, the facilitator will ask that the participants visualize the healing taking place and/or to visualize the result of the healing as they send the power out.

There is another method of sending the healing when only one woman knows what the sick person actually looks like. In this case the Witch who knows the ill person will act as a channel for the healing power raised by the other participants. At a previously agreed upon signal the participants will direct the power they have raised to the channel. She will add her own power to that of the others as it comes to her. She then visualizes her sick friend as she sends the accumulated healing power to her. She sees her receive the power, sees the healing power start to work its Magick and finally, sees her friend as completely healed. The other Witches in the Circle Magickally support the channel by sending her thoughts of support and healing while the channel directs the power. Or, they may all chant, "Be healed" over and over again for the duration of the sending.

Other uses of meditation/visualization include opening the Self to receive information from other planes of reality (see "Trance" and "To Dare" below); to go within the Self to explore/discover personal and/or group symbols and totems and their relationship to other Magickal/spiritual symbols, stories or myths from the Western European tradition, or any other tradition with which the individual or group feels an affinity; to relax and reduce stress levels at the end of a hard day or prior to Magickal work; to establish a personal and/or group astral temple; or to re-energize yourself when you find yourself tired, droopy or uninspired.

Chanting, Singing and Rhythm

Much of the raising of power consists of bringing power down, or to the Circle, and then bringing it through and out of your body by effecting changes in your body/metabolism to encourage this. Chanting is one method of fulfilling both of these functions.

Beethoven was once asked how he could continue to compose such magnificent music even though he had lost his hearing. He answered, "I hear the music of the spheres." I think that is a very telling statement about the relationship to sources of power and information (and hence world view) that a singer/musician has. Music is the universal language. It breaks down barriers between people and reaches out to touch the stars. It can be used to overcome fears and to instill self-confidence.

Sing a happy song in English to a group of children in a foreign land who do not understand a word you are saying, and soon they will be smiling, laughing, perhaps dancing and vocalizing along with you. Ask a child who stutters to sing with you and she will no longer stutter. This is power. This is connecting with each other and with the Goddess on a deep level that surpasses our usual view of ourselves, each other and the world.

In ritual, once one gets over any initial stage fright, lets go of the ego and concentrates on the music she is producing, she has access to inspiration and hence, information. Free-form chanting has become quite common in Wiccan rituals. This is chanting whatever notes come to mind in whatever way works best. Each person is totally free to do it however she likes, with no expectations or standards of performance involved. Because no one cares what she sounds like, she relaxes and sings the Goddess within her. She opens up to the Goddess and lets the Goddess direct her voice — the Goddess sings her.

Everyone usually starts with an "aum" (pronounced ohm), but it changes in various ways from there, depending on what each person is prompted to do by the Goddess. The aum chant itself — the repetition of aum on a single note — comes to us from the Eastern tradition of Buddhism. It is thought, among other things, to balance the four elements in the body and to invoke an Indian trinity of deities. A stands for Vishnu, U stands for Shiva and M stands for Brahma. By the elements, A stands for Agni, or Fire; U stands for Varuna, or Water; and M stands for Marut, or Air. Earth is represented by the body itself, which is producing the sounds. This oft repeated word, or any oft repeated word or brief phrase, is called a mantra. Often I will hear phrases of praise or invocation/ prayer coming from various participants. I often get "told" by the Goddess voice within me what to sing and then sing it.

Clairaudience (psychic hearing) is connected to the throat chakra. By singing, you are using the throat chakra and thus opening yourself up to information from the universe via clairaudience. The more frequently you do this, the better a clairaudient channel you become. I have seen it happen time and time again. When someone starts chanting repetitively, she gets the information that she needs. Perhaps she was thinking about a specific problem she has and was wondering what to do about it when she began chanting. Suddenly she will get an insight into what she needs to do and will often start singing about what it is she needs to do and will start asking the universe/Goddess to help her do it. Singing becomes a way of channeling the power of the universe and bringing it to focus within.

Singing and music, particularly drumming or the use of rhythm instruments, can be used to raise power as well. For this purpose it is best to use a chant with as few words as possible so no one has to concentrate on remembering the words and can, instead, concentrate on using the music as a way to channel power through themselves and apply it to the task at hand. For example, in doing a healing we often have chanted "Heal her" while sending energy to the sick person. This chant will start very softly and slowly and gain in speed and volume as the power is raised. Soon it becomes a very staccato shout, and the power is finally released into the person.

We do the same type of thing when working on issues that involve our own growth and development, or when we send energy to the Earth to heal Her. The point is that the music is used to effect a change of some sort. In the process it changes our view of ourselves and the world around us.

Since the beginning of time people from every culture around the world have believed that they could communicate best with their Gods through music, and that music could heal their bodies and bring peace and enlightenment to their minds. Pythagoras (perhaps the most famous student of the Oracle at Delphi) is the person who investigated and developed these theories to the highest degree. He said, "Perfect music comprehends all things." He was particularly concerned with mathematical proportion in music, and with its vibratory harmonies within the universe. He believed, as do modern day occultists, Witches and Magicians, that everything within the universe has a specific vibratory rate. Simply put, the denser the object, the slower the vibratory rate and the lower the pitch. As you ascend the universe to the more etheric substances (including the Gods) the vibratory rate becomes faster, hence higher in pitch.

Pythagoras found that certain vibrations resonated in harmony with each other (or were of the same nature), and that when one note resonated it set off sympathetic (harmonious) vibrations with other notes (things) higher up the vibratory scale. In this way, contact could be established with the Gods, creating a musical channel between Them and us. This is evident in something called the overtone series. When you sound a note, other pitches called overtones, which are usually inaudible to the human ear, sound simultaneously with the given pitch. These are higher than the original pitch, and are in the same intervallic relationships as found in the successive divisions of a string. Each note has an overtone series that follows the same pattern. Thus contact is established with various entities within the universe and a channel is opened between them and us.

Occasionally, under certain acoustic or meditative conditions, some of these overtones can be heard floating above the notes you are singing (particularly if you are singing in a group and each person is singing *exactly* the same note). Hearing them is quite a Magickal/powerful experience and I have heard people refer to it as hearing choirs of angels. This is a very apt description of what has taken place on a Magickal, vibratory level.

If you want to strengthen this connection to other planes and other realities, you add rhythm. Rhythm is the pulse-rate of the universe and another way to contact its various forms of "aliveness," either by itself or in concert with melody (and harmony). The process is similar. Everything has a pulse rate as well as a vibratory rate with which we can connect.

Plato said, "Rhythm and harmony find their way into the inward places of the soul, on which they mightily fasten." This, in a nutshell, explains how much music effects healing, the emotions and the mind. It was said of the bards of Great Britain and Ireland that they could bring on fits of laughter or tears, cause a room full of people to fall asleep or incite a war simply by playing their harps in different ways. And it is well known that the piping of Scots war pipes caused the Roman Legion to run from the battlefield screaming in terror. Bagpipers always led the Scots into battle and the Romans never did conquer Scotland. Instead, they built Hadrian's Wall to keep the Scots out of the territory they had conquered and left them entirely alone!

Besides the use of chant (and/or dance) in group ritual to effect change, it is also used frequently in individual ritual/Magickal work. It is used to effect a change of personal consciousness — to give one a new way to look at the Self or a particular situation in which one is involved. It can be used to overcome fears, to calm the nerves, to incite to action, to change anger, grief, or remorse, into positive expressions or to reinforce the positive within one and within life in general. This all implies that the individual ritualist is performing the music or dance herself. This does not mean that a person cannot effect change within herself by listening to the music/words of another, just that it will be far more effective sooner if the individual ritualist does the work herself.

Ritual is occasionally performed in order to effect a non-participant, but not nearly as often as active, personal participation. An example of this would be the playing of a single instrument to facilitate a group meditation/visualization. Or, the performance of a mystery play which incorporates music and dance or gesture as a way of communicating a message of religious importance to an audience. The effect here is much more subtle than in direct participation, and may take longer to effect the consciousness of the observer/hearer than does the direct participation of the ritualist working to effect a more immediate change in herself or her environment.

The role of music in ceremony varies from group to group. Some groups use little or no music in their rituals. Others incorporate music in just about every facet of the ritual, using it to cast the Circle, call the Quarters, invoke the Goddess, attune themselves to meditation, raise power, ground the energy and close the Circle.

You will find strong modal elements harking back to ancient times in the melodic content of the spontaneous or free-form chants, and even in some of the more "standard" chants. Many of us create harmonies for the "standard" chants as well, and often these harmonies take the form of singing parallel fourths, fifths, and octaves. This is a complete no-no in any composition or theory class in the modern world. The open sound produced by these parallel intervals produce a very haunting and Magickal quality that you don't find in most "properly" composed music. In fact, I remember hearing that the pope, sometime back in the Dark Ages, actually outlawed the use of certain modes and these open intervals in harmonization precisely because of the Magickal qualities they produced.

As previously mentioned, music is a good way of getting into a meditative state and remaining open to input from the Goddess/universe. Certain types of music are very relaxing and very pleasant to listen to. Focusing on them can put you in a relaxed and open state. The somewhat passive act focuses your attention on the music. In other words, the mental chatter that goes on in your head almost constantly is turned off.

Not all music will do this, however. It must not be antidystalic, as is much of rock music and just about all New Wave music. It must flow naturally with the rhythms of the body. The strongest rhythm of the body is the heartbeat or the pulse rate. Music to induce meditation must compliment this or augment it, not go against it. Therefore, it must be fairly slow and steady, or may slow down slightly as the meditation progresses, because the heart rate will usually slow down during meditation. It should be instrumental music, because most of us tend to get caught up in listening to the words when we hear vocal music. Acoustical instruments are better than electric or amplified instruments. The instruments must be soft enough that the attention is not dominated by the sound, merely enhanced by it. It often helps if the music imitates the sounds of nature, such as the songs of birds, the babbling of a brook or the wind in the trees.

I would also like to add that a person playing music can enter into a meditative state if she has a facility with her instrument and is comfortable with what she is playing. I have often sat down to play the piano when I was angry and needed to calm down, or when I had a problem and I needed to still my mind in order to relax and get some new insight. Sometimes I have to start with a real pounder when working off anger, but I gradually mellow it out until I reach a state of total relaxation and openness induced by the pieces I am playing. I also use wordless songs or chants on open vowel sounds as a way of relaxing and opening myself. For me, it is a form of worship that has had a profound impact on my life. I let go and let the Goddess sing me, and I feel a connection with Her that I am unable to duplicate in other ways.

Dance and Movement

Dance and movement are often connected with the use of chanting, singing and music in a ritual setting. It is another way to raise power. Here again, the dance begins slowly and gains in speed as the power is raised, and stops abruptly when the energy is released.

It is another way of raising power through the body by effecting a change in the metabolic/pulse rate. As the blood pumps faster and faster and the rate of breathing increases, the pulse and vibratory rates of the body increase. As they increase, the power, or flow of energy through the body, increases. When the power is at its peak, the dance abruptly stops and the power is released to its intended goal.

These dances usually take the form of circle dances. Occasionally a ritual will also incorporate a meeting dance, which is one of the purposes of the spiral dance. Spiral dances may also enhance the group worship experience, if each person concentrates on the symbolism of the spiral as the dance is being performed. Other Magickal dances would include dances done as sympathetic Magick. In this case the dance imitates something that we would like to have take place. It's a way to show the Goddess/the spirit world something that we would like to have take place. Or it can be used to connect with our inner selves in a special, wordless way. For example, some belly dancing movements — particularly the belly rolls — were developed and originally done in imitation of what happens to a woman's body during labor and delivery. A woman in labor, seeing this done in her presence during her labor and delivery, was helped to relax and "go with the flow" of the labor in this way. There is even some evidence that women actually danced the babies from their bodies in this way, finally squatting down over a shallow pit dug in the ground to push the baby out into the waiting arms of another woman.

In some ancient cultures (and in some modern subcultures like the Pagans who have decided to use the technique), dances in the Spring fertility festivals involved a lot of leaping and jumping in the air. This was their way of showing the newly planted crops how high they wanted them to grow. The dancers believed that the higher they jumped, the higher the crops would grow. Many times this dance would take place as a sort of procession around the newly planted fields, to insure optimum growth of all the plants within the field. In fact, many folk dances are remnants of Pagan Magickal dances. Some reels, round dances and square dances actually trace the pattern of the casting of a Circle and the invocation of the Quarters on the dance floor.

Breath of Fire

The Breath of Fire is another way of changing the metabolism to bring power in and push it through and out of the body. It also activates or encourages the solar plexus — the seat of will in the chakra system. (The solar plexus area runs from just below the breastbone to the base of the navel.) The Breath of Fire clears the lungs, oxygenates the blood and raises the metabolic rate which, again, increases the body's vibratory rate, thereby making it a stronger and more apt channel for the creative/Magickal energy that is drawn into the body, amplified within its confines and then released to do its work.

In occult parlance the creative energy/power available in the universe is often seen as being present in the air. Through Magickal intent it can be drawn to us and brought within us through the breathing process. In practice the Breath of Fire is usually preceded by several "cleansing breaths." The idea here is to take several deep but leisurely breaths to clear the lungs and to clean out any accumulated "gunk" — psychic or otherwise. It is an "out with the bad air, in with the good" type of exercise. Visualize the air passages as being cleaned out and fully opened in this process. Since the breaths being taken are deep, belly-breaths, in which the stomach area expands on the inhalation and contracts/sinks in on the exhalations, visualize the solar plexus as cleansed and opened as well.

Following immediately upon the heels of the cleansing breaths is the Breath of Fire itself. The goal of the ritual is planted firmly in the mind and held there by visualization. All those in the Circle hold hands. Deep breaths are taken and released in unison. The breaths slowly, rhythmically and steadily increase in speed until everyone is literally panting. When the woman chosen to facilitate this ritual (Facilitating Priestess) feels this energy has reached its peak, she shouts a single word — usually, "Now!" — and everyone releases the power and sends it on its way to its intended goal. All visualize the power going to its mark and hitting it/being absorbed by it.

At the "Now!", everyone forces an exhalation from her body. The exhalation is sustained for several seconds. The power is visualized as going out on the breath. Participants usually make some kind of gesture with the arms and hands as well. If all are holding hands, participants often raise their arms to release the cone of power. Or, if participants are not holding hands, they may stretch their arms forward, fingers extended, in which case the power is visualized as being released and directed through the arms, hands and fingers. Some are wont to stomp a foot and/or lunge forward on one leg in addition to the individual arm/hand movements to release the power. Do whatever works best for you or the group.

Now let's back up a minute and I will try to describe the metaphysical visualization process during the Breath of Fire. In addition to holding the Magickal aim in mind, the spell worker is also aware of and focused on the following: On the inhalation the power is visualized/felt as coming into the body through the nose and mouth, and proceeding down into the lungs and solar plexus as well as throughout the bloodstream. The exhalation is lesser or incomplete (not all air is expelled), and is seen as settling the power within the body in order to make room for the accumulation of more power on the next inhalation. As more and more power is accumulated within the body, the solar plexus chakra begins to spin faster and faster as the breathing gradually speeds up. The blood flows more freely and pumps more quickly, carrying the power throughout the body and raising its vibrational rate. The body may actually begin to shake or vibrate as the power reaches its peak. At this point the power is highly charged and ready for release. Hold on to it until told to release it. The facilitating priestess will sense when all are at this point, and will shout "Now!"

If you are all holding hands, you can visualize/feel the power whirling around the Circle through your linked arms/hands. The left hand absorbs the power and pushes it through your body to the right arm. The right arm/hand pushes it out and into the left hand of the woman to the right, and thus it continues around the Circle. Its speed increases with the rate of breathing. You may even visualize this power as radiating outward from your bodies and coalescing with the power available within the space of the Circle. As it whirls faster and faster, it creates an upward spiraling vortex. This is the cone of power. At the sending it shoots upward and onward toward its goal. Your forced and maintained final exhalation and any movements or gestures you make at the same time contribute to the cone of power and help send it on its way.

Now, here is my own personal Dianic twist on this process. I only use/visualize this process in Dianic Circles. You are welcome to use it if it works for you and/or your group. Some women may find, as I have, that the seat of the will to create — the ability to manifest change in the world or within the Self — does not lay in their solar plexus, but in the womb. On a very basic level, the womb is the source of female creativity. It is where babies take root and grow. It is the seat of one of the greatest creative processes in the natural world.

As power is raised during the Breath of Fire, the rate of breathing accelerates until the individual is panting. This reminds me of the transitional phase of the birthing process. Not only is a woman panting at this stage of labor, she is also filled with Goddess power. Doctors, birthing attendants and others present often remark as to how the woman is "not herself" during transition. She is in an altered state of consciousness and in possession of physical strength she does not ordinarily have. Anyone who has had a baby or has seen a baby being born can attest to the incredible power the womb can exert in pushing the baby out. This is analogous to the sending of the power in the Breath of Fire.

I often use this imagery when doing a Breath of Fire in a women's Circle: Not only do I visualize my womb as the seat of power and creativity that will change the reality I am trying to shape, I see it as the accumulator/container of that power as I raise the energy within myself. After all, the womb has to hold more and more energy and power as a baby develops and grows. In the panting/ transition phase I visualize and feel that power growing and coalescing in my womb as it moves toward manifestation/birth. My connection to the Goddess is strongest at this point. When told to release the power, I stand astride to allow free passage of the power out of my womb through the birth canal, and I push it out as though birthing a baby.

In keeping with the symbolism of the cauldron that runs throughout the rituals in this book, you may wish the group to visualize themselves as standing on the rim of a cauldron (the Circle itself) or as being the sides of the cauldron. In either case, the power would be seen as the swirling, seething contents of the cauldron stirred by the hand of the Goddess. The fires beneath the cauldron are stoked by each breath of every woman present.

One of several things can be visualized when sending the power. In my opinion, the least desirable option would be to see the cauldron as boiling over as the power is released. This lacks an image of focused and directed power. But, it may be useful if the idea of the Magick spilling over the Earth is appropo to the spell being worked. Another option would be to see the steam arising from the boiling cauldron as the cone of power that is being released. This has the upward image many people prefer in visualizing the sending of the cone. Finally, stirring a cauldron at a faster and faster pace (as the breathing speeds up) would tend to create a downward spiraling vortex within the cauldron. This vortex could be seen as spiraling farther and farther down into the Underworld (the Otherworldly realm seen as within the Earth Herself) until it reaches the Fairy Mound at its center. It accumulates more and more Otherworld power as it descends, until it finally hits bottom and bounces upward again into the "real world" and on to its intended destination, carrying its extra Otherworld Magickal charge with it. If the group is not comfortable with this particular imagery, try visualizing the vortex as Diana's bow. It is drawn back until it can go no further, and the arrow of Magick must shoot forward and out to its intended target.

No matter how the imagery of the Breath of Fire is done, once the breath has been released and the power has been sent, it will be necessary to spend a few moments "grounding out." People often feel an odd combination of being out of breath/tired and yet retain a somewhat higher rate of bodily vibration/energy after the release of the cone of power. In order to calm down, and to release the excess energy and center the Self again, they will sink to the ground/floor and place their hands flat on the ground/floor. They then visualize/feel themselves giving the excess energy to the Earth to heal Her, to feed the spirit world and to re-center themselves. When they are done, they will thump the ground, clap once, snap their fingers, slap their thighs a couple of times, or do something that indicates to their mind and body that the spell has been completed and that the Magickal link/channel has been broken, shut off or closed down. At this point they are ready to proceed with the remainder of the ritual or with the next power raising.

Invocation

An invocation is a set of spoken, chanted or sung words intended to call the presence of divinity to the Magick Circle. Not only is it meant to attract the attention and presence of deity, it is also meant to arouse the inner fire within the individual speaker or hearer. It is meant to open the heart, mind, emotions and body of the speaker or listener to the mysteries of the deity being invoked. It is a way to enhance the comprehension and experience of divinity within the individual.

The language of invocation presents a paradox. The words chosen are extremely important on the one hand, yet they tend toward irrelevancy on the other. Magick and the Mysteries arise out of non-literate consciousness. That is, they can only be understood through experience. No amount of reading, study, ritual recitation or lecture attendance will give you Magick or elucidate the Mysteries. Intellectual understanding of its processes and outer forms do not substitute for the wisdom gained through the actual experience of them.

However, words do have power. Not in their literal definition, but in the set of symbolic images they trigger within consciousness. They can be conceptual models leading to a stream of awareness or inner cognition. This is what the wording of an invocation attempts to prompt within the individual. The "calling down" of the deity is an attempt to make Her real, apparent, active and understandable within the Circle and within each woman.

Some feel that it is best, or at least advantageous, to invoke deities in the mother tongue of the deity or in the Hebrew language of the Qabalists. I disagree. Since the purpose of invocation is to draw deity to us — for us to come to know the Goddess — it is more important to do so in a language understood by all participants. If these other "mother tongues" are the group's own mother tongue(s) as well, by all means have at it. But if they are not, skip it. It's hard to come to "know the Goddess" when one is tripping over words or wondering if the pronunciation is correct, not to mention having only a vague idea of what it all means!

Of course, in solitary work everyone is free to follow her heart's desire. Some may wish to contact deities from their own cultural/ethnic background and may wish to use the appropriate language to do so. This may be especially true if one is already fluent in the language of her ancestors. It may prompt others to learn their ancestral tongue — perhaps even in its old or archaic forms. Once facility is achieved, an invocation in the mother tongue can be a powerful Magickal experience.

Spells, Charms and Incantations

While we are on the subject of words and the power (or lack of it) behind words, let's take a look at spells, charms and incantations. First of all, these words can be used interchangeably. There is little or no difference in actual meaning between them. There may be a difference in common usage, however.

Spells are often thought to be sinister or more intense than charms, which are thought to be more beguiling or "cutesy" than spells. In popular usage, incantations are more closely aligned with spells than with charms, and are usually thought of as being chanted rather than spoken. I use them interchangeably in this book. They are all powerful uses of "the word." Whether they are sinister or not depends on their intent. Power is neither positive or negative — good or bad — it just is. It is the intent of the user that determines its effect. Witches are admonished to do no harm. So, spells are definitely *not* sinister. They can, however, be very powerful.

The purpose of a spell is to generate energy and emotion within the core being of the speaker/hearer. From this switched-on being comes the ability to raise and direct Magickal power. Magickal power, in the case of spells, is best generated by Magickal language. Magickal language is produced through the use of repeated rhythmic patterns of speech — often through rhyme as well — and always through the Magickal/religious content/symbolism of what is being said, intoned, whispered or shouted. Good content/symbolism invokes excitement, Mystery, power and awe within the individual. The deep Self is awakened, the pulse rate strengthens and quickens, breathing changes and often becomes rhythmic, the psychic centers open and the presence of the Goddess and power is felt. The body often begins to sway or move. Fingers or spine may tingle. Goose bumps may rise. The hair on the back of the neck may bristle. Effective Magickal language encourages visualization of the goal to be accomplished. It encourages the participant to believe the Magick can and will happen.

A good spell need not be long and involved. The best ones are often short and can be picked up and repeated easily by all participants. Longer spells often have a refrain or a chorus that is short and easily learned and repeated by all, either in a call and response fashion or at the culmination of the spell. On a practical level, poetry is often used because it is easier to learn and remember than is a long (or short) passage of prose. On a more Magickal level, poetry is often used because it comes the closest to conveying the feelings associated with the symbolic meanings of the words used. When poetry is used, it usually has a rhythmic element to it to encourage learning and repetition.

Spells are often used in combination with dance or other movements designed to imitate the intention of the spell. A spell to stomp out pollution might include rhythmic stomping on the ground; a spoken spell may precede a Breath of Fire; a spoken spell may be used in combination with a dance that gets faster and faster as the power is raised and the words are repeated until the Facilitating Priestess calls for the sending of the energy. Another option is to begin the spell in a whisper and to gradually increase the volume, and sometimes the speed, as the power is raised until finally the spell is released with a shout.

Incenses, Essences and Herbal Brews

Witches have long used herbs and aromatherapy for healing the body and the mind. But incense and herbs have a Magickal application apart from health and healing. They have Magickal associations that can be used in working spells and in making amulets. They also can aid one in achieving light trance states and other altered states of consciousness. The rituals in this book often call for their use in aiding relaxation, calming and quieting the mind, opening the psychic centers, arousing the passions and in the creation of amulets for use in individual spells. Their Magickal properties and uses, as well as the composition of various brews and amulets, are explained in the rituals in which they are used.

You will notice that I do not use, nor do I recommend the use of, addictive or psychoactive drugs, plants or even alcohol in the rituals. Not only are most of these items illegal and/or detrimental to health, they can become dangerous crutches too often relied upon when attempting to achieve altered states of consciousness. The herbs and essences used in this book are not addictive, not illegal, not detrimental to your health and will not force you into an altered state of consciousness you may not be prepared to handle. They will merely nudge you in that direction by making it easier for you to achieve those states on your own, through your own knowledge of the techniques and skills required.

I do acknowledge that there is at least some historical evidence that psychoactive plants have been used by Witches, seers and prophetesses. There are even a few recipes extant for the famous Witch's Flying Ointment. However, old names for the plants are often given and we cannot be sure of their modern/botanical equivalent, and the proportions used are not given. They are therefore best left alone.

The preparation and burning of incenses has been associated with Witchcraft, Magick and Pagan religions for thousands of years. Smoke and/or the breathing of fumes was, and still is, associated with the mystical or psychic experience. The Bible includes references to seeing God in a smoke-filled temple. The Delphic oracle is thought to have inhaled the "vapors" of specific plants and the Underworld itself before giving prophecy. Priestesses of a number of Goddesses throughout the ancient world tended sacred fires, seeing their Goddess and the future in both the smoke and the embers of those fires. Witches and Magicians are still believed to be able to see the spirits of the dead (as well as deity) in the smoke rising from a burning censer, a steaming cauldron or a Sabbat fire.

Moreover, certain incenses have religious and Magickal associations. For example, frankincense is both a cleansing and protecting incense. Its smoke is used in the consecration of sacred space, ritual tools and the practioner. It aids concentration and heightens awareness. It is used to invoke Moon Goddesses, Demeter and

Goddess in general. Sandalwood aids all forms of divination, meditation and trance work. It calms the mind and brings forth the spiritual essence of being. It brings success. It is a particular favorite of Venus. Other incenses and blends of incenses are specified in some of the rituals below.

Scent triggers the memory. It also can motivate or enhance actions and/or emotions. For example, most people find musk and/or patchouli sexually stimulating. Once you know that sandalwood aids meditation, just smelling it will help you enter a meditative state.

Finally, incense provides sensory stimulation, and sensory stimulation is important to good ritual. Ritual should be a feast for the eyes, the ears, the nose and the senses of taste and touch. All can serve to focus one's total attention and awareness, to encourage emotion and to trigger a stream of symbolic associations, understandings and cognitions. Each alone, or in combination with the others, can lead to an experience of the Mysteries.

Sex and the Sacred

Within Witchcraft, and Paganism in general, noncoercive sexual intimacy between two people is considered both sacred and a source of potential power. The Goddess has told us specifically that "all acts of love and pleasure are My rituals." In this one sentence same sex love is honored, approved and sanctified; bisexuality finds acceptance, veneration and respect; heterosexuality is lifted out of the morass of sin, guilt and degradation and named a blessing and a gift.

The Magickal aspects of sex involve more than ego. They are an attempt to light the inner fire which transforms the Self, strengthens the inner individual behind the personality, and allows one to come to know the divine within the Self and within the partner. Its power can initiate spiritual change/rebirth in the inner and outer worlds and can illuminate certain Mysteries. It can tie one to the Earth and release one from it. It can transcend time and space in the eternal here and now. It can make the cauldron churn and froth and can recreate the world.

Sex is the thing that has suffered the most since the advent of the Judeo-Christian and Islamic religions. In order to return to the

Goddess centered understandings of sexuality as sacred we have to wade through thousands of years of programming that tells us sex is bad/dirty/evil. Sexual expression, whether alone or with a totally trusted partner is, on a smaller/individual level, a reflection of the creative process that formed the Earth and set the planets in motion within the starry heavens. Its energy can be used/directed toward Magickal goals in an attempt to *create* change. Or, that energy can be directed toward the spirit of the Earth and all Her creations to enhance their luminosity, to add to the sacred strength of their spirits, to increase or strengthen their aliveness.

This use of sexuality/sensuality to create change or to enhance aliveness does not imply the victimization or martyrdom of the participants. Enjoyment of the experience is not offered up on the altar of Magickal aims. Sex Magick allows one to experience both the totality of the physical/sensual experience and the totality of the Magickal creative process, which is occurring simultaneously.

An image of what is to be created or changed is held in the mind. As pleasure in the physical sensations of the body and/or the body of the partner increases and the emotional sharing of love grows, the Magickal image is fed or enhanced. Sexual release is not postponed in order to gather more power for the spell. It is being constantly fed/strengthened as lovemaking progresses. When the sexual energy peaks and is released, the spell is released with it to do its work in the world. Images of the Magickal changes taking place are envisioned in the warm afterglow of love realized and inspirited.

To Dare

It takes a fair amount of daring to be a Witch, and even more to be a Dianic Witch. To name oneself a woman of spirit who worships one or more Goddesses; seeks and finds female sources of power within the Self and the universe; draws wisdom and strength from the cycles of the Earth and the female body; believes in and works Magick; and who envisions and attempts to model a society devoid of patriarchal pitfalls is to fly in the face of "conventional wisdom," religion and all inculcated beliefs about the "natural" order of things. The Dianic Witch is often judged harshly by other Witches, and by Pagans in general. This is particularly true of those who feel

, a polarity-based (male and female) Pagan or Wiccan practice is the one, true and only enlightened way to worship the divinities and to work Magick! If the Dianic Witch is also a lesbian or bisexual woman, still more fuel is added to the fires of persecution. The dominant culture cannot handle it, nor is homophobia unknown in the Pagan community. On the other hand, a lesbian prejudice against heterosexual women pursuing Dianic Witchcraft is far from unknown either.

Since Dianic Wicca posits a totally different view of religion, the world and reality, the Dianic Witch often feels isolated and alone until she is able to connect with other women like herself. Old friendships often fade away or lessen in intensity. Estrangement from the family often occurs, particularly if she attempts to express her beliefs and views, even in veiled or general terms. Coming out of the broom closet to family and friends can be risky. Self doubt comes easily when she meets with disapproval. To hold fast to her beliefs and practices in spite of all this can become a real act of courage and daring.

Like the Delphic Oracle, Witchcraft insists, "Know Thyself." Like the oracle, Witchcraft believes that the best route to knowing the Goddess is through the Self. In the final analysis the only thing standing between each of us and the Goddess is our own foibles and failings — our own inability to face and deal with what is lacking and what is excessive within ourselves. As those things begin to transform, so does our ability to know and to experience the totality of the Goddess. But this is often hard, and even frightening, personal spiritual work. To undertake it and to stick with it takes courage and taps sources of inner strength of which we are often unaware.

Witchcraft implies a belief in and the use of Magick. Some come to the Craft expecting to be given forbidden secrets that will enable them to instantly get or change whatever they want. This is the Bewitched Syndrome (BS) again. They are disappointed to learn it does not work like that. These people usually lose interest quickly and fall away.

Others, primarily interested in Goddess worship, are at first fearful of, or in doubt about, the Craft's use of Magick. They carry within them the Judeo-Christian program that teaches that Magickal skill comes from the devil. They feel it just might be inherently evil to work Magick.

Still others, particularly those who pride themselves on their abilities to reason and to be logical, feel that working Magick is silly, childish and illogical, and that its practitioners are quite benighted. Yet their curiosity is piqued, and they wonder if Witches might not be right after all.

For each of these types of women, participation in a Magickal working is an act of daring: daring to buck conventional wisdom; daring to try something that might be dangerous, yet exciting, and that will lead to instant gratification (BS); daring to find out for oneself whether Magick is evil or not; daring to try and work with and comprehend power that arises from, or is channeled through and used by, other parts of the Self besides the logical and rational self.

What it boils down to is this: Working Magick requires an act of faith. Magick uses energies of consciousness that the modern intellect denies has any existence at all. It can only be proven through experience. The initial opening to that experience requires faith. It is a faith in the Goddess not to lead you into something evil. You need faith in those with whom you are working. You must believe they will not lead you into something dangerous. You must have faith that your can connect with powers inside of you and within the universe other than the purely logical, rational and even-tempered. Finally, for the beginner and the old hand alike, you must believe that it will work. Faith is the vise of your Magickal will. If there is just the slightest doubt in your mind that a spell won't work, it won't.

Working Magick also requires a psychic and emotional investment in the spell being worked. Emotional investment in just about anything is something our current society finds quite dangerous and, therefore, something to be feared. For this reason, our society rejects emotionalism and psychic awareness utterly. It does this by belittling, humiliating, squelching, denying, shunning, imprisoning and institutionalizing those who act out of these modes of being. Society teaches us to find our own emotional and psychic makeup unacceptable and dangerous, and to find such things suspect in others. Here again the Witch is challenging the system. It takes a great deal of courage and daring to honor, celebrate, and encourage psychic development and emotional integrity. Magick works best when it is heartfelt!

States of Non-Ordinary Reality

One form of Magick, most often used by the individual for personal exploration but available for use by the group, involves altered states of consciousness. Here I am referring to trance states, astral projection, Otherworld journeying, shape shifting, channeling or aspecting the Goddess — which, by Wiccan definition, is more akin to seership or prophecy than to mediumship — and some divinatory practices. This area of Witchcraft is where Witchcraft and Shamanism cross paths. In fact, by loose definition, Witchcraft could be seen as Western Europe's form of Shamanism.

This form of Magick is based firmly on the fact that there are other realities and other modes of being besides the consciousness, consensus reality, and life forms we experience each day. There is more than one world, and the things and beings within those other worlds are not symbolic, but are very real within their own realms. And, it is possible to enter and leave these other realms at will once the requisite skills have been developed. One of the doorways to these other realities lies in the mind, with an imagination trained by meditation/visualization and trance work.

Trance is perhaps best described as a higher octave of meditation. By trance I do not mean the definition usually associated with trance mediumship (i.e., the abdication of the body by the spirit of the Self in order to allow something else to come through it). It is not necessary or even desirable to leave the body or set the Self aside in order to achieve a trance state. It is necessary to quell the personality, or ego, however. This is done through meditation and visualization.

It is important to note here that the ego/personality is not the same as the Self (also known as the inner Self or true Self). The Self remains in control and aware throughout the trance process. It is the true Self that can see and communicate with Otherworld entities in the trance state, and which can "channel the Goddess." (See chapters 5 and 6 for further information on channeling or aspecting the Goddess.)

In a trance state the attention is turned inward, and the world of ordinary sensory perception is blocked out or lessened in favor of a reality of a different type. The gateway to these Other worlds is through the focused and trained mind of the skilled meditator. In this deeply meditative or trance state we see with our inner eye.

Sounds are heard within the mind. We touch, smell and taste inwardly in this visionary state. This visionary state is both subjective and objective. The interpretation of forms and symbols seen are subjective, masking or revealing objective energies and entities. These energies and entities can appear in forms that will endure and be perceived in the same shape by more than one person. Some of these forms or energies can be attached to a place or objects. This is the original meaning of consecration.

Trance states stimulate creativity and personal growth. The psychic abilities are enhanced. Solutions to problems arise. We are better able to channel power into the outer world. We experience the Goddess on a more profound level. By the same token the trance state will lead us to our personal "dweller on the threshold" - the accumulation or representation of all within ourselves that we would rather forget, ignore or otherwise not deal with. This must be confronted, examined, taken apart and reassembled in another, healthier, pattern in order for Magickal growth to continue.

Entering a trance state requires safe space. Safe space means different things to different people. For some it may simply mean a place where they will be undisturbed — a place away from the phone, the TV and the kids. To others it may mean they need to be in the presence of an experienced teacher or guide. Still others prefer to be within a fully cast Wiccan Circle to which the Watchers have been summoned as guardians. (You will find more on this in chapter 6.) A few may want all three of these conditions to be met.

A trance experience usually consists of four phases aligned with the four quarters of the Magick Circle. Corresponding to the East is the trance induction itself, which consists of relaxation and the focusing of the Magickal attention on the knowledge of what is about to happen. This can come either through an oral explanation from a teacher or guide, or will be based on past experiences of the inward turning. The journey itself corresponds with the South. This involves traveling within to the heart of the matter. Again, this may be assisted by a teacher or guide. This will either be a physical teacher or guide present in the Circle/room with the traveller, or an Otherworld guide who has appeared to help the journeyer. The physical guide, if present, may suggest the appearance of the Otherworld guide. Or, if the journeyer is alone, a guide may appear on its own. If so, this being will arise out of the past trance

experiences of the traveller as well as her present understanding of
the Twilight Way.

The heart of the matter, or the mystical experience being sought,
corresponds to the West. At this point the physical guide, if present,
will fall silent and/or the Otherworld guide will disappear. The
traveller proceeds alone. What is experienced here will be both
subjective and objective, and will be different for each individual in
the group if the trance work is being undertaken in a group setting.
The return to the "real" world of day-to-day living is associated
with the North. It is deliberate and fairly quick. The traveller
returns to normal consciousness, is fully awake and fully energized.

It is important in trance work that there be clearly audible cues
to help induce the trance, to signal the arrival of the Otherworld
guide, to stimulate the guide's disappearance and the beginning of
the mystical experience, and to begin the return to "normal"
consciousness. These cues may be verbal and may come from a
teacher or guide who is physically present and facilitating the
experience. Or, they may be musical, rhythmic or a combination of
the two. If you are undertaking a trance experience unaided by a
physical guide or facilitator, it would be a good idea to tape record
the induction and various cues along the way and to play it for
yourself when you wish to journey inward.

Not all trance states need to be this deep or this intense, however.
There are many instances of light trances in which a state of non-
ordinary reality is reached and information previously unavailable
suddenly or subtly enters the opened mind. This may occur when
listening to music, when daydreaming or when watching the
passing scenery through a car window. The same four steps will
occur: A relaxed and open state will occur first; a journey or some
action will take place within the mind; a mystical experience/new
understanding will be reached, and a return to ordinary consciousness will end the sequence.

Astral Projection

While trance work involves Otherworld journeys within the mind,
astral projection involves an Otherworld journey with the astral
body. The astral body is that part of us which survives the death of
the physical body. It has also been called the spirit or the soul.

Astral projection, or soul flight as it is sometimes called, is not all that mysterious or unusual.

Astral projection is almost taken for granted in popular occult circles, and within some psychological models. The theory here is that dreams are actually astral projection. The action that we see ourselves taking in dreams is taken by our astral bodies/soul, or spirit selves. Evidence of this phenomena are the thudding heart, pounding pulse and the gasp for air that accompanies a sudden and unexpected arousal from sleep. It is believed that these physiological responses are caused by the rapid return of the astral body (literally, the "star" body) to the physical body - a sort of crash landing as it were. The mental disorientation that often accompanies such a rude awakening is taken as further evidence of the soul's nightly flight.

It is also possible to consciously project (send forth) the astral body through the active use of trance states. In this case, waking consciousness is willed into the astral body, and the traveller feels the astral body and consciousness separate from the physical body. When the astral body looks back at the physical body, it will appear motionless and inert. The astral seer will also notice a thin, luminous, silver cord running from the solar plexus of the body to the solar plexus of the astral body. This silver cord is an umbilical cord of sorts, sustaining the physical body and connecting the astral body to the world of form we all know and love.

For those of you who would like to try to develop the ability to travel in full awareness in the astral body, here are a few hints. Some people find it helps to fast on the day of the attempt. There is less to weigh you down so to speak. I personally do not find this to be true. Listening to my stomach growl is not at all conducive to my trance state or to my ability to detach mentally from my body. Eating lightly does it for me.

If you are worried about being interrupted, wait until you are alone in the house or until everyone is asleep. If you are worried about the safety of your body while you are gone, cast a Circle around it — either physically, by actually going through the motions, or mentally, by going through the motions in your mind's eye only. Lock the door(s) if that makes you feel better. Lay down if you feel your body may fall over while you are gone. Disconnecting the phone is a good idea, too.

Relax and put yourself in a trance state. It may help you to visualize and feel your astral body beginning to rise to the surface of your body, and from there to slowly and gradually begin to float out of your body. Do not presume that your astral body will float out of your physical body in a manner that is parallel to your posture. If you are lying down, it might sit up first and then float upward and become vertical. If you are like me, your astral body will fall out of your physical body. Mine falls downward and to the right if I am sitting up. This startles me so much that I snap right back into waking consciousness, certain that I have fallen over. Then I have to start the whole process over again. So, I lie down to begin with.

When I begin my astral projection lying down, it feels as though my astral body sinks into the mattress before taking flight. It's sort of like drawing a bow. You have got to pull back before you let the arrow fly. That feels alright to me because I know my body cannot fall, and I like the connection between Artemis and the bow. I feel as though I am going to Her realm, or as though I am being shot from Her bow, and can feel safe in my flight knowing whence I came. I know Her aim is true and that my experience will be a good one.

Mastering this skill requires a strange sense of emotional detachment and ego neutrality. Learning to project my astral body did not come easily. I remember that the first time I got out of my body successfully and turned around to look at my body lying there on the bed, I got really excited and shouted, "I did it!" Whereupon I immediately found myself back in my body and unable to get out of it again for several days.

Once you have learned to get out of your body, make haste slowly. Float around your room at first. Be very observant. How does your room look when viewed from the far left upper corner? Although you will be able to "walk" through doors and walls in your astral body, you may find this prospect disconcerting at first. Go through an already open door into the rest of the house. How does it look from this new perspective? From the house move out into your neighborhood. Expand your travels gradually.

You might find it fun to test your perceptions while in your astral body. Go see what someone is doing in another part of the house and verify it with her later. Tell a coven sister that you would like to come visit her. If you get her permission, drop in on her and make note of the time and what she is doing. Verify it with her the next day. Perhaps she sensed your presence while your astral body was there. This testing of your astral abilities will verify your perceptions for you, and will help you learn to trust your astral senses when you venture into unfamiliar territory.

Time, space and everyday reality are no longer barriers for you when traveling in your astral body. A "flight" to Europe can take place in an instant. Entrance into other states of reality can occur just as quickly. You can visit what seems like the past, even the mythic past, yet it is not really the past because other realities, like our own, exist in the eternal now or the constant present. Remember that linear time is an artificial construct. The eternal now will also enable you to visit "the future" as well.

This non-ordinary reality has a variety of names. One or more of them may be familiar to you. The most common name in occult parlance is the astral plane. Shamanistic traditions speak of travels in the Spirit World. The Australian aboriginals speak of the Dream Time or the Dream World. Celtic lore speaks of going in and out of Faery or journeying to the Underworld, the Otherworld, or the land beneath (or across) the sea. Other mythic references to non-ordinary realities include the Land Behind the North Wind, the Isle of Apples, Avalon, the dwelling place of the Gods, the Innerworld, the Elemental kingdoms, the Devic kingdom, the stairway to the stars, heaven, and others. Nearly every culture in every era and location has made reference to it/them. Witches most commonly call it the astral plane or Summerland.

So, why would you want to visit these places? Several reasons come to mind. Astral projection is an excellent method of delivering long distance healing. You can travel to the astral plane to seek advice and aid from spirit helpers in order to effect a physical, emotional or psychological healing for yourself or another whose permission you have secured. It can be a way of gaining access to information about past cultures and belief systems, and of experiencing those traditions. I am sure you can think of other ethical applications as well. Having the guidance of someone who has done this before, or who is journeying with you, can lend a much needed sense of objectivity to this particular, fairly subjective, type of experience.

In your astral travels you will likely meet other beings. Some may appear to be human, others will not. They are not apparitions, visual fantasies or psychological constructs. They are real beings existing in their own realm. Most Otherworld interactions, sights, and beings are reflections of patterns that did, do or will exist in the "real" world. It is important to remember that the astral plane can act as a womb in which creative energies can shape "real" world realities socially, politically, environmentally and personally. The astral substance is very responsive to thoughts and emotions and can be used Magickally to bring about change, as in healings.

Astral projection has long been thought one of the skills of a Witch. Hysterical and tortured exposes of flying Witches reported during the burning times refer not to actual physical flight, but to astral projection or soul flight. Though it is a skill associated with Witchcraft, you need not do it if it frightens you or feels wrong to you. You will not be less of a Witch because you choose not to pursue astral projection.

Shape Shifting

Another accusation once levelled at Witches was that they had the ability to shape shift, or turn into an animal. Here again, the actual skill was misunderstood, misapplied and blown way out of proportion. Shape shifting does not involve physically turning into an animal. It involves becoming one with an animal (or plant) in your mind while retaining your own, human, cognitive and observational abilities. It is another use of a trance state, here used to gain knowledge and information from a different perspective.

Witchcraft finds all beings of value and does not rank them according to the strength of their brain or body, or according to their usefulness in serving humanity. Wiccans believe all beings have a unique and necessary place in the overall scheme of things, partake of the same spirit as do we ourselves, and have valuable lessons to share with us should we care to look closely enough. The best way to look closely enough is to become one with them. By doing so we learn to look at the world through their eyes. We find out what they need to survive and how they go about the business of survival. We experience how they relate to each other, their young, and the land. We experience their strengths and weaknesses and come to understand their place in the web of life. Then, in our waking state, we can thank them for sharing themselves with us by working on the environmental and ecological issues necessary to assure their continued survival, and we can bring their wisdom into our own lives and interactions.

What might one learn from "becoming" an animal via a trance state? Animals have been symbolic of a variety of things for millennia. For example, depending on the culture, birds have represented contact with the spirit world because they fly up to heaven and back down to earth. They nest in trees for the most part, so are seen as living between heaven (the spirit world) and Earth. Some believed them to be the keepers of written language because certain letters of the alphabet can be seen in the flight of a flock of birds. To others, being birdlike is to gain objectivity and perspective because one can get a view from above — one can see the whole picture — and can gain insight not normally available to the earthbound.

Because of this ability to fly to the spirit world and/or get the best perspective/insight, shamans often wore cloaks of bird feathers. The cloak served as a reminder of their sacred task, both to themselves and to others, and was used to act as a trigger to the trance experience through which they gained spirit knowledge and healing for their community, tribe or clan.

Certain Goddesses and colleges of Priestesses were associated with or named for birds. These women gave prophecy through song and poetry, and were later vilified in patriarchal myth as the sirens and Dei Lorelei. These same Priestesses often schooled youngsters in reading, writing, mathematics and the divinatory arts — hence another association of birds (Priestesses) with letters, learning and prophetic wisdom.

Other examples might include "becoming" a cat to learn to take joy and pleasure in the physical body. "Becoming" a wolf can teach one a great many things about living and working communally. "Become" a mole to learn how to bring down a mountain. That mountain could be anything perceived as an immovable object: an addiction, a bad habit, an unjust law, institutional racism, patriarchy, your biggest problem. (For more information on shape shifting see chapter 7. The August Full Moon ritual uses shape shifting within its format.)

Divination

Divination in all its many forms falls on the "to dare" side of the Witch's Pyramid. Divination is the art of learning things through nonrational or nonordinary methods. Often it seeks to find out how things will be, although it can also identify how things truly are and how things once were.

It is not really known how divination works. There are a couple of possible explanations for it, however. The first of these is an examination of the true nature of time. Time as we know it is a man-made concept. But, time is not really linear, moving from past to present or to the future. Time is cyclical and, within broad parameters, repetitive. Anyone who has lived and worked for a period of time without a calendar and a watch knows this. Without calendars and clocks we soon lose track of time. We do not know what day of the week it is, what the date is, or even what time it is. All we know is that it's morning, mid-day, evening, twilight, or dark. And the next day and night will be just the same. The weather may differ, the seasons will change in their own cycle, what we do may change with the weather or the season, but there is no sense of linear movement through time. There is no sense of progress forward or backward. All that matters is the present and the pattern (the cycles) — the eternal now. All time is now. This means that on some level, information being sought about "the future" is available in the present.

Divination looks at the infinite variety in the overall pattern as well as the patterns within the questioner's life, and extrapolates (or "predicts") likely outcomes based on this information. It is important to remember that these "likely outcomes" are not etched in stone. There is nothing fatalistic about a divinatory reading. If you do not like what you see or hear, you can change it through your own effort.

Most forms of divination rely to some degree upon the psychic skills of the reader in providing helpful insight to the querent (questioner). Some do not. For example, the use of a pendulum does not require psychic ability or training. The pendulum will answer "yes" or "no" to a question. All that needs to be done is to hold the pendulum perpendicular to the ground, still it, and ask question that can be answered by a yes or a no. For some people the pendulum will rotate clockwise for yes or counterclockwise for no.

For others, it will swing back and forth for yes and from side to side for no. The answer is clear and does not require interpretation.

Astrology is often considered a divinatory art. However, the method of setting up a chart (determining how the signs and planets are arranged on the chart for each individual) involves no psychic skills whatsoever. Some basic math skills, the date, time and place of the person's birth, and a good ephemeris for the birth year are all that is needed. Even the interpretation of what the chart means can be drawn from more or less standardized material. However, the best astrologers are those who use their intuitive skills in conjunction with the standardized material in helping their clients understand themselves.

The tarot is perhaps the best known system of divination, and it is the one most often associated with Witches. There are a variety of tarot decks available and each usually comes with its own book explaining the interpretation of each card (which may be helpful in familiarizing you with the deck, but may not be of much help in an actual reading). These books will also detail a variety of different layouts, or patterns, in which the cards are placed on the table. The meaning of the symbols on each card are then interpreted in relation to the question, to the card's position in the layout, and to the other cards in the layout.

No one knows where the tarot came from. It suddenly appeared in France and Italy in the late fourteenth century. All kinds of extravagant claims have been made regarding the origin of the deck. Some see them as embodying the teachings of early mystery schools (matriarchal or otherwise), as having originated in Atlantis or Egypt, or as being the result of a meeting of Arab occult philosophers who decided to condense all their wisdom into a set of pictures placed on playing cards. These cards would be used for gaming by the ignorant masses, and thus would insure their survival until such time as worthy occult students of the future could absorb their true meaning.

The images on the cards and the interpretations of their meanings have changed almost since the day of their appearance on the European scene. And they continue to do so today. Women, who objected to the patriarchal overtone of some of the cards, have developed a variety of woman-centered or Goddess-guided tarot decks. There are now Native American tarots—decks that draw on

Native American beliefs and symbolism — Celtic tarots, Unicorn tarots, and others. (Personally, I think a Sesame Street Tarot has great potential. The Amazing Mumford as the Magician, Miss Piggy as the Empress, Bert and Ernie as the Lovers . . .)

No matter what its origin, the tarot is a divination system that seems to work. How well it works depends in large part on how well the user connects intuitively with the symbols on the cards. This is why it is so important that anyone wishing to read the tarot choose a deck that resonates well with her. Being politically correct and reading with a women's deck is not as important as reading with a deck that works well for you. The "patriarchal" decks need not be interpreted in a patriarchal manner. The rule of thumb here, as in so much of the Craft is: if it works, use it!

How do they work? Briefly, the querent and the reader agree upon the layout to be used. The querent shuffles and cuts the cards while concentrating on her question, thereby determining which cards will come up in the reading. In this way she determines what it is she needs to know or to learn from the reading. The reader lays out the requisite number of cards in the pattern selected. The cards are then interpreted on a card-by-card basis according to the appearance of the card (what picture is shown), its position in the layout, its relationship to the question at hand, and its relationship to the other cards in the layout. An answer or a set of probabilities is arrived at as a result of the interpretations.

These interpretations are based on psychic impression. How that impression comes to each individual will depend on the type of psychic skills she has. If she is a clairvoyant, the symbols on the card will trigger pictures in her mind related to the question and to the querent's life — spiritual, mental, emotional, financial and/or physical — which she will then put into words for the querent. If she is clairaudient, the symbols on the cards will trigger words in her mind that she will then share in some way with the querent. If she is hypersentient, the symbols on the cards will evoke certain feelings within her, which she must then interpret for the querent.

Who does the interpretation depends on the attitudes of the querent. Many are silent and wish to be enlightened by the reader. Others, and most Dianic Witches fall into this category, ask questions of the reader regarding her interpretations, or actually participate in the interpretation in a joint venture. This is the preferred method. In it the querent is taking responsibility for her own reading and, after all, it is her situation that the reader is addressing. In this case, the reader and the cards themselves become a catalyst or guide to the querent's discovery of her own answers, instead of being some sort of mystical adept who knows all, sees all and tells all, with knowledge inaccessible to most.

This is much healthier for the reader as well. Often readers are expected to make decisions for querents and to tell them how to run their lives in general. That way, when the querent blows it in some way, or things do not work out exactly as the reader implied, it becomes the reader's fault and the querent is allowed to escape personal responsibility for her life (again). On the other hand, if things do go according to the plan detailed in a reading, the reader is then deified and the querent loses an opportunity to validate herself as a successful and competent person in charge of a fulfilling life.

Although there are several other forms of divination which employ symbol systems like runic reading, stone casting and, to some extent, the I Ching, it is beyond the scope of this book to cover them all. I would like to move now to a discussion of divination via direct psychic cognition. This, for some, is where we get really daring. Witchcraft has always honored and encouraged the psychic skills of its practitioners. And Goddess worship has a long history of direct contact with the Goddess via the psychic abilities of Her Priestesses. The Delphic Oracle (always a woman) was the supreme spiritual authority of the known world for two thousand years. Rulers, politicians and warriors sought and heeded her Goddess-given advice. Scholars, philosophers, and some say even the Druids studied at her feet. The papacy pales by comparison. Even at the rise of the patriarchal Olympians, when Apollo supposedly "took over" the site and Zeus "married" Hera, still the people came to hear the Goddess-inspired words of a woman. Still they kept her counsel.

So why today is such direct speaking from the Goddess, called variously prophecy, channeling, seership or aspecting, considered suspect at best and dangerous, silly, or evil at worst? Because it is so powerful! Because it is dangerous — dangerous to those who support the status quo. It is dangerous because it proves we do not need some great man standing between us and God to interpret God's will for us. Because, through its use, we can hear Her for ourselves every time we cast a circle and call Her to us through our own voices or through the voice of the Facilitating Priestess. Such prophecy is an important part of women's spiritual heritage.

While some women do see its potential value, they also see its potential for abuse. Like any other use of Goddess energy, it can be applied for good or ill. However, in the small group structure in which it is most often used, the potential for abuse is minimal. And, like anything else, it is the responsibility of each woman in the group to see to it that its expressions are genuine and its uses responsibly and reasonably employed.

Others find it suspect because they mistakenly believe it to be a form of mediumship or possession, which it definitely is not. The ability to "channel the Goddess"/give prophecy does not involve displacement of the inner being of the speaker. The inner Self, or true Self, is present and in control of the ability at all times. Indeed, if we believe that a spark of Her divinity lies at the root of the inner self, if we believe Goddess dwells within us, why should displacement occur? There is nothing that needs removal to make way for the divine. She is already there. She merely needs to be revealed, and prophecy is by definition direct revelation from (of) God/dess. The experience is measured, controlled, calm and coherent. It is not frenzied, wild and out of control.

The process as it pertains to Witchcraft is called, "Drawing Down the Moon". Does that mean that the Goddess energy you are drawing down to yourself/your Circle is located outside of yourself after all? The answer is yes, and no. Here is another of the paradoxes of Witchcraft. Witches believe that everything partakes of the same spirit. This spirit, which enlivens all, is called the Goddess by Dianic Witches. Because everything that is contains this spirit, we are all interrelated. The Goddess in me is the same as the Goddess of the Moon. The spirit that animates people animates plants, other animals, and all forms of matter on Earth and throughout the universe. So, although "the other" seems outside of us, it is at one with us. It contains a spark of the same spirit. Therefore, the Goddess that is "drawn down" in prophecy is both within the speaker and outside of her as well. We tend to think of ourselves as separate, closed systems interacting with other separate, closed systems. In this way the Goddess can seem a divine other as well as the divine within.

The Moon is a symbol of the divine female. The Moon Goddess of Dianic Witches reminds us of all that is sacred about femaleness.

The Moon demonstrates the cyclical nature of things in Her waxing and waning. In Her ever-changing face we see life, growth, decay, death and life again, just as we see it within the cycles of our own bodies and within the world around us. So, to "draw down the Moon" is to remind ourselves of the sacred all-pervading nature of the divine woman. In fact the phrase — to draw down the Moon — can also refer to the menstrual cycle. The menstrual blood/Moon blood is drawn down the birth canal once a Moon. Furthermore, many women find the gift of prophecy comes most easily to them during their bleeding cycle. (For further information on channeling the Goddess and its uses see chapters 5, 6 and 7).

Other types of direct psychic cognition are also used by those in the Craft. They include psychic reading and the interpretation of omens and portents. The difference between these and prophecy as described above is primarily one of degree. Drawing Down the Moon (or prophecy) is most often undertaken by one individual for the benefit of the group. Psychic reading is done for the benefit of the querent and may not actually involve the summoning of the Goddess to/from the Self. And, although the reading of omens and portents can be done on behalf of a group, it is most often done by the reader for her own benefit.

To Keep Silent

Keeping silence about Witchcraft and Magick seems anathema to the overriding principal of empowerment within the women's community, but there are good reasons for its inclusion in the Witch's Pyramid. Although America is a pluralistic society and our Bill of Rights guarantees religious freedom, persecution is not unknown. Women Witches have lost their homes, their jobs and custody of their children because they were known as Witches within their families and/or their communities. Certain members of the United States Congress have tried to have Witchcraft invalidated as a religion, by attempting to repeal the right of its Temples, Groves and Congregations to receive tax exempt status as a religion. Wiccan covens have had their Circles interrupted by both the police and members of their local communities who felt threatened by the presence of Witches in their neighborhoods. Temples and Groves have been desecrated and Witches have had their lives threatened by Christians who take literally the Bible verse requiring, or at least approving, the death of Witches. (The verse which reads, "Thou shalt not suffer a witch to live" is a mistranslation of the original text, which reads, "Thou shalt not suffer a poisoner to live.")

The media, particularly daytime talk shows, fan the flames of persecution on a regular basis by linking Witchcraft to Satanism, and by trotting out a variety of "authorities" who spew forth sensationalistic and erroneous "facts" about what Witches believe in and do in the name of Satan. (Witchcraft and Satanism have no connection whatsoever. Witchcraft has its roots in the pre-Christian nature and mystery religions of Western Europe and the fertile crescent. Satanism is a perversion of Christianity. It worships the Christian devil and parodies the Catholic Mass as well as the moral and ethical canons of Christianity.) Occasionally, these same talk shows interview real Witches about their beliefs and practices. However, these Witches are usually not invited to sit on the same stage with the fundamentalist "authorities" to dispute the incorrect and incredible fabrications they deliver to the TV audience as the "gospel truth."

Although I have been a more or less public Witch and psychic for three quarters of my twenty year involvement in Witchcraft, I have very rarely encountered prejudice or persecution as a result of my beliefs. My two experiences with persecution took place while I was living and working at Circle Sanctuary — a *very* public Pagan organization. In the first instance, we were evicted from the farmhouse we had been renting. *People Magazine* ran a story on the then heads of Circle, and its involvement in Witchcraft, in the "Couples" section of their magazine. Until that time, the landlord had not been aware of our activities. After he read the article and saw the accompanying photographs, we were served with eviction papers by the County Sheriff. We then moved into much nicer housing which was more appropriate to our needs.

Later, my mother became concerned that I might be involved in a destructive cult. Although she had known about my beliefs and involvement with Witchcraft for a number of years, a neighbor boy had just been through deprogramming from a well known cult, and she began to wonder if maybe I didn't need deprogramming as well. She joined the Cult Awareness Network and began looking for a deprogrammer familiar with Witchcraft. Of course there were none, but she found someone willing to attempt it anyway.

To her credit, my mother nixed the idea of the forcible abduction and virtual imprisonment that is a hallmark of deprogramming. She knew they would get nowhere if I felt forced into anything. So, she arranged to take me on a week's vacation with her, during which time I met with a deprogrammer. She had been instructed to appeal to my intellect. My mother knew I would be interested in knowing how membership in a destructive cult was determined and what the deprogramming process was. To make a long story short, within a half hour the deprogrammer decided that I had not been brainwashed and was not involved in anything destructive to myself or to anyone else.

In the end, my mother had spent a great deal of time, effort and money to find out what I had already told her. But, it eased her mind about my involvement in the Craft, and I was returned to Circle none the worse for the experience.

Others have had experiences far worse than these. That is why it is so important to allow each woman to decide for herself if, when, how, and to whom she will break the silence regarding her involvement in Women's Witchcraft.

There are sound Magickal reasons for keeping silence about your activities as well. The operative maxim amongst Witches concerning keeping silence is, "Power shared is power lost." On the surface this may sound selfish, elitist, or like some kind of power trip, particularly to those women who are strongly committed to feminism. But that is not what is intended.

When you do Magick you must be emotionally committed to the work and must believe firmly that your Magick will indeed become manifest. If these two criteria are not met, your spell will not work. When you tell someone outside of your coven about a Magickal working you have done, you run the risk that they may not find your cause valid. Or worse, they may not believe that the spell can or will work. Their disapproval, or unbelief, may sow seeds of doubt in your own mind. When that occurs, you have seriously jeopardized the spell's effectiveness. You have shared the power you set in motion with a doubter, and thereby lost at least some of its possible effectiveness.

It is also possible that this person, not liking what you've done, will actively work against the success of your spell's Magick. This can be done through countermagick, if the person believes in and works Magick herself. Or, the other person can effectively work against its success just by thinking about it. This is often called "sending the thought," in Magickal parlance, or "broadcast negativity," in New Age circles.

It is also not a good idea to tell others where and when your coven will be meeting and what Magickal workings will be undertaken, unless you are inviting them to attend. The reasoning for this is twofold. First, you do not want interruptions while you are working. Someone, wishing to be included yet uninvited, may decide to drop by just as you are about to start. Another, knowing where you are, may decide to call you on a totally unrelated matter that she just has to discuss with you right away. And, in the worst case, someone could inform the "authorities" of your meeting and you could be interrupted by a most unwelcome official visit. Second, should the person you told disagree with your Magickal goal, she could work Magick against it at the same time that you are working Magick for it. This is not conducive to its success. (For related information on keeping the silence, see the discussion of taking a Witch name in chapter 4.)

CHAPTER FOUR

The Cauldron and the Tools

A symbol is an open-ended representation of a concept, belief or mystery. It does not define it entirely and, indeed, cannot. It merely points the way. The real value of a symbol is not found within the symbol itself, but is found through the effect of that symbol upon our awareness. It works by moving the awareness of the individual into new and previously unexperienced directions or modes of thought. A great symbol may manifest meaning in several modes at the same time. The difference in meaning lies in the perception or level of consciousness of the recipient.[1] Repeated exposure to this great symbol within similar circumstances offers the recipient a greater chance for further understanding of the symbol and what it means for herself and/or the group.

The great symbol of Dianic Wicca is the cauldron. Its use and symbology runs throughout the rituals presented in this book, offering the woman Witch a variety of opportunities to explore the value of this symbol in a variety of meaningful ways.

"In nearly all mythologies there is a miraculous vessel. Sometimes it dispenses youth and life, at others it possesses the power of healing, and occasionally . . . inspiring strength and wisdom are found in it. Often it effects . . . transformations."[2] Usually, this vessel is a cauldron, but sometimes it is a lake. Later, in the Grail traditions, it became variously a cup or chalice, a stone or a serving platter. Nearly always it is the property of a woman — usually a Goddess. In its Christian devolution it is in the hands of a Grail Maiden. Sometimes there is one cauldron, often there are three.

In Egypt the hieroglyph for the threefold Creatress — the Mother of the Sun, the universe and all Gods — was three cauldrons.[3] The Egyptians sometimes called the otherworld regenerative cauldron the Lake of Fire.[4] The cauldron represents the pot of blood in the hand of Kali and represents cyclic recurrence. The cauldron is also the property of the Triple Goddess of Fate, who is echoed in the three Witches of *Macbeth*. The Babylonian Goddess of fate, Siris —

the Mother of the Stars — has a lapis lazuli cauldron representing the blue sky itself.

Often the powers of male deities come through their interaction with the cauldron. Odin stole his power from three cauldrons of wise blood (read: menstrual blood) located in a cave (womb) in the Earth. Indra drank the magic soma (moon-blood) from three cauldrons. The Celtic God Cernunnos was dismembered and boiled in a cauldron in order to rise again from the dead. Boiling cauldrons also rebirthed Minos, Aeson, Pelops, the emperor Elagabalus and even St. John the Evangelist. Visions of being dismembered and boiled in a cauldron are a necessary part of Siberian shamanistic initiation.

The largest body of literature concerning cauldrons comes from Celtic mythology. The cauldron was the fourth treasure of the Tuatha de Dannan, the children of the Goddess Dana (Irish) or Don (Welsh). The Tuatha de Dannan were the mythical conquerors/ inhabitants and Gods/Goddesses of Ireland. The cauldron's appearance on the Witch's altar as the cup or chalice derives in part from this myth. (See the discussion later in this chapter for further information.) It is also found in the suit of cups in the tarot deck. To the Celts, the cauldron was a symbol of regeneration/reincarnation within the womb of the Goddess. This was a central religious mystery to them.[5]

The Welsh Branwen had such a cauldron. In it the dead were revivified overnight. She is the origin of the Lady of the Lake of the Basin. From this lake Her brother, Bran, raised the cauldron which became the Holy Grail of the Christian romance. He became Bron, the Fisher King of the same legends. Even in Christian tradition the Grail was referred to as an "escuele" — a bowl or cauldron.[6]

We can actually see three different types of cauldrons functioning within Celtic mythology, one for each aspect of the Great Goddess. The first is the Cauldron of Annwn (the Celtic underworld), often called the Cauldron of Rebirth and Transformation. This cauldron is described as having a rim of pearls and as being warmed by the breath of nine maidens (equivalent to the Muses or the Triple Goddess in triplicate form). The experience of this cauldron of rebirth could only be achieved by a journey through seven caers (or castles).[7] Remembering that references to any enclosure (caer/castle) equate with bodily form, we find that the only way to attain this cauldron is by passage through the seven stages of life. Simply stated, by going from life to death, then life again. As such, this cauldron is associated with the Crone Goddess and with the womb of every woman.

The second cauldron is the Cauldron of Cerridwen, often called the Cauldron of Inspiration — of initiation and the source of the beginnings of wisdom. This is the cauldron in which Cerridwen prepared for her child (and her initiates) a potion that contained the essence of all wisdom. This cauldron corresponds with the Maiden aspect of the Goddess — the protectress of those entering the Mysteries.[8] It is also a divinatory tool — a vessel of water in which to scry — a method of receiving inspiration. Badb, meaning "boiling," is Her Irish equivalent. Here is the water of the womb and the vastness of the ocean/lake.

The third cauldron is the source of plenty, the cauldron seen as a vessel for food. Its spiritual nourishment is endless and bottomless. This is the Mother Goddess, the provider of eternal plenty and fecundity, both physically and spiritually.[9] Here also is the womb of the Goddess and the womb of every woman.

These three cauldrons can be seen in the Grail legends, in which these cauldrons are transformed into the objects of the Grail quest. Depending on which Grail legend you read, the Grail is either a chalice/cup — a vessel of blood and/or water; a stone, the words written upon which bring spiritual enlightenment; or a platter — a source of spiritual and physical nourishment. The Grail as cup/container of blood and/or water (seen as the blood of Christ/death, but really the menstrual blood of Goddess symbolizing life and death) is the Crone's Cauldron of Rebirth. The Grail as stone/spiritual enlightenment is the Maiden's Cauldron of Inspiration — the beginnings of insight and wisdom as well as creativity, physical or otherwise. The Grail as platter of nourishment is the Mother's Cauldron of Plenty — the womb of the Goddess, the Earth and every woman.

The Grail romances can also be interpreted as an esoteric initiation into the feminine side of the Christian mystery — not revealed directly, but woven into a series of legends and put into the hands of the poets and troubadours who brought them to the common people. These people recognized in the stories thinly veiled allusions to Pagan/Goddess elements and became dimly aware of an inner, feminine, element not found in Christianity as taught by the established church.

If we continue with the symbol of the Grail as the womb, the central Christian Mystery of communion could be interpreted as an allegory for what happens during pregnancy. The womb as ritual cup, or grail, transforms the food and drink of the eucharist (bread and wine) into flesh/body (the bread) and blood (wine) as does the food a pregnant woman eats. And thus is the spark of divinity (represented in the Christian context by Jesus and in Pagan symbolism by all of us) reborn into the world. The body and blood of Christ are of Mary as his mother/creatress, yet they also represent the inspiriting divinity within humanity (the messiah motif of the Christians).

The heart of the Grail legends poses three riddles that must be answered correctly in order to heal the Fisher King and in so doing return his kingdom (the world) to the paradise it once was. These riddles become easier to answer when we understand the Grail/ Cauldron as a symbol of the womb. The first riddle is: Whom does the Grail serve? Answer: Humanity. This seems obvious only if you know the Grail is a symbol of the womb. Without the womb, humanity would not exist. The second riddle says: The world is in the Grail and the Grail is in the world. What is the Grail? Answer: The womb of the immanent Goddess and the womb of each woman. The third riddle asks: Where is the Grail Castle, that is surrounded with water, that is everywhere at once, and which is invisible? Again the answer is the womb of every woman. More specifically, the cervix, which is surrounded by watery secretions.[10]

The Magick of the cauldron is the Magick of the female. The symbol of the cauldron allows us to approach the Mystery of the Goddess and our connection to it and Her in a variety of ways. From the cauldron we are born. Unto it we return. Throughout our lives we dance on its rim.

The Tools

The tools found on a Dianic Witch's altar symbolize the four Elements, the Goddess Herself, our connection to Her and the power of women through that connection. And, in the case of the coven altar, symbols of the group energy are found as well. Several of the tools date from the practice of Ceremonial Magick in the Middle Ages. Two are far older and a couple are more recent. Their position on the altar is significant also. They all reflect my personal preferences and my own Magickal training and understanding. You are free to add, substitute, or subtract from this setup you see fit, based on your own internal guidance and your own system of symbology. I use the more or less traditional tools and placements here because I feel that tying into a particular symbology and placement that has been used by many people over many years significantly increases the power — or pool of energy — from which I draw performing my rituals. You may not feel the same.

A Dianic altar

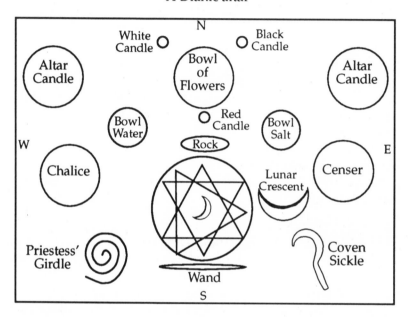

Candlesticks. You will find five candlesticks and holders on this altar. There are two altar candles on the upper corners of the altar for illumination, and three around a bowl of flowers in the center. The two altar candles are usually white, but can change color with the season or with the intent of the ritual. The three candles around the bowl of flowers represent the three aspects of the Goddess: a white candle represents the Maiden; a red candle fills the Mother's position; a black candle symbolizes the Crone.

Bowl of Flowers. Flowers represent the Goddess. Their type and color can change with the seasons or with the intent of the ritual. Roses are the traditional choice. Red roses are ruled by Venus. White roses and Wild roses are ruled by the Moon. You might try Ox-Eye Daisies for Artemis, jasmine for Diana, lavender for Hecate; iris for Isis, Juno and Hera; marigolds, peonies or sunflowers for Aradia. I place them in a bowl because it is lower than the candles and because it carries the symbolism of the cauldron. A silver or earthenware/china bowl is appropriate: silver is the metal of the Moon, the other is of the Earth.

Rock. A rock is placed between the flowers and the center of the altar. This represents the North (its position on the altar), and the Element of Earth. It can be any kind and shape. I have seen crystals, granite, geodes and fossilized stone used. You may prefer to use a "holy stone." This is a stone with a natural hole in it. It symbolizes the entrance to the womb (or cervix) and the womb itself, and as such it is an apt women's symbol. In some indigenous cultures women used to crawl through large "holy stones" in hopes of increasing their fertility. They also used to pass babies through them as a form of blessing a baby following a birth. "Holy stones" are still considered a good luck amulet amongst Witches, and many of them carry a "holy stone" in their amulet bag (see below) or wear them as necklaces.

Bowl of Salt, Wheat or Corn. One of these three is placed in the right hand bowl on the altar. Each represents the element of Earth and will be used in consecrating the Circle after it has been cast. It is up to you and your coven to decide which of these three you use.

Natural salt (sea salt or kosher salt) is a natural purifier, and is thought to repel negativity. It is included in the consecration of the Circle to act as a barrier to things unwanted in the Circle. If you are not concerned with, or do not believe that the Circle does or should act as a barrier to anything, and think of the Circle only as a container of something, then you may decide against the use of salt. You may prefer instead to use wheat or corn as your symbol of Earth.

Wheat and its methods of cultivation were a gift to humanity from the Goddess Demeter/Ceres. Corn was a gift to the natives of the Americas from the deities of those regions. It is therefore thought by some to be the most appropriate item for the American Witch to use in consecrating Circles. Please note, however, that neither corn or wheat is considered a natural purifier, as is salt.

Censer and Incense. Sitting in the Eastern quarter of the altar and representing the element of Air, both by its position and its use, is the censer of incense. It can be thought of as representing Fire as well, because the incense burns on a glowing coal within the censer. The type of incense used is a matter of personal taste, and is usually associated with the season or with the intent of the ritual. For example, pine incense is appropriate for Winter. Any of the flower scents could be burned during the Summer. If I were going to be doing some trance work during a ritual, I would burn sandalwood because it aids the inner/spiritual vision.

Wand. The wand is placed beneath the Sigil of the Moon, near the Southern edge of the altar. It represents the element of Fire by its position and its use. It is an instrument of your Magickal will, and is associated with the element of Fire. It can be used to direct your Magickal energy and to amplify the power you send with it. As such, it can be used to cast the Circle, though I prefer another tool for this purpose. The wand upon the coven altar is usually the personal tool of the woman responsible for the ritual (the Facilitating Priestess). For this reason I will describe making a wand later in this chapter.

Chalice. The chalice traditionally sits in the West on the altar, and represents the element of Water by its position and its use. Here is the remnant of the Witch's cauldron, the quintessential symbol of the Goddess, of women Witches and of women's Magick. What was central to the Goddess, Magick and Celtic mythology became the Holy Grail of Christendom, and the chalice of elemental Water upon the Magician's altar. It remains in its western position upon my altar to remind me of the history of its Magickal meaning. You may wish to move it to the central position on your altar, switching it with the Sigil of the Moon and the Moon Crown (Lunar Crescent) as given here.

Bowl of Water. A bowl of water is also present in the West for use in consecrations. Salt, wheat or corn will be added to the bowl just prior to consecrating the Circle by Earth and Water. (See chapter 6 for further information on consecration.)

Sigil of the Moon. A sigil is a seal or sign having Magickal power. The idea comes from Ceremonial Magick. However, this is not a Ceremonial Magickal sigil and was not constructed according to their methods. This sigil is the number and lineal figure appropriate to the Moon. It measures nine inches in diameter and contains three interlaced triangles with a crescent moon in its center and, as such, represents Lunar energies. It can be inscribed on silver (the metal of the Moon) or carved in wood, thereby combining it with the energies of the Earth. Because the Lunar (and Earth) energies are a direct link to the Goddess, the sigil channels the presence of the Goddess to my altar — hence its central position there.

The Lunar Crescent. This piece is also known as the Moon Crown, the Horned Crescent or the Horned Moon Crown. It sits on the Sigil of the Moon on the coven altar because it, too, represents the presence of the Goddess. This crown is worn by the Facilitating Priestess when she speaks as (channels or aspects) the Goddess. The donning of the crown acts as a psychic trigger activating the deep mind/ inner Self of the Facilitating Priestess which, in turn, subdues the usual personality and rational mind, which allows the Goddess Herself to come through.

The crown is made of silver. The headband is usually a solid strip measured to fit the head of the Facilitating Priestess and represents the Circle and the cyclical nature of life and death. However, in Dianic practice, this crown will be worn by a number of women, each fulfilling the role of Facilitating Priestess from time to time. I would, therefore, recommend leaving a small gap in the back of the headband and boring a hole in the band on either side of the gap. Then, run a leather thong (or some other strong thong-like material) through the holes. The crown can then be fitted to the head of whichever woman will be serving as facilitator for the ritual. In any case, the crescent itself should, ideally, rest over or just above the facilitator's third eye (a chakra point just below the center of the forehead and associated with clairvoyance) to aid in triggering the Goddess within her. If the Facilitating Priestess will not be channeling the Goddess, the lunar crescent remains on the Sigil of the Moon throughout the ritual.

Coven Sickle or Athame. The sickle or athame sits to the right of the Sigil of the Moon. The choice of sickle or athame is up to the coven. Traditionally, this is a sword, but a sword is not a woman's tool. A sickle or a knife is. The symbolism of the two are slightly different. The sickle is a symbol of the Crone — of harvesting and death. In hunter-gatherer societies women were responsible for gathering and harvesting plant material. When cultivation began as a result of Demeter's gift of wheat, women were instrumental in the harvest. Hence, the sickle is an appropriate (and ancient) women's tool. Its crescent shape further identifies it with the Moon and so, with the Goddess. It is both Diana's bow and Hecate's sickle (waxing and waning crescents of the Moon respectively). The sharp edge represents the gift of discernment — the ability to know what needs to be cut away — either to promote growth/provide food, or to remove disease/the unwanted.

The athame, or Witch's double-edged, black-handled knife, is the traditional tool of a Witch, male or female. In ceremonial use it is used to direct power like the wand, and is not sharp. As a woman's tool, it may be more appropriate for it to be sharp. A knife in the hands of a woman cuts food and umbilical cords, and can be used as a planting, cultivating and harvesting tool. Its edges represent the gift of discernment, as does the sickle's edge.

Since the Athame is a personal tool and traditionally the hand-made property of every Witch, you may wish the coven athame to be something especially nice. You may wish to make the blade yourselves, or to commission its making. You may each want to put energy into the making of a collectively designed handle. Or, if your coven is able to pool a fair amount of financial resources, you may wish to consider purchasing an obsidian knife.

Catal Huyuk, one of the first Goddess centered cities to be researched by archaeologists, was located near an obsidian mine. The contents of this mine were a major source of trade and income for the residents of Catal Huyuk, and were directly responsible for its growth into a major metropolitan area. I like to think (though there is no hard evidence of this) that this is the origin of the "blackness" of the Witch's knife. That the first athames had black (obsidian) blades and that later, as obsidian became more scarce, and copper, iron and steel became more available, that the "blackness" was transferred from the blade to the handle of the athame. I can also surmise that obsidian knives were used by Priestesses within the temple precincts in worship of the fiery mountain mother who provided the obsidian.

Of course, if need be, the athame upon the coven altar can be the personal tool of the Facilitating Priestess. Although this is a perfectly acceptable alternative, it is an alternative. For the sake of continuity, not to mention collective energy or group power, it would be better to have a coven athame upon the coven altar.

The Priestess's Girdle and the Witch's Girdle. As a personal tool, this is known as the Witch's girdle. It is also more simply known as the red cord. This is a red cord, six feet in length, worn in, or brought to, the Circle workings by each Witch. The ends of the cord are whipped, not tied, and a loop is whipped into one end.

There is an old belief that the wearing of knots in clothing or the hair during the performance of Magick will stop, or put kinks in, the Magick, and keep it from flowing to its intended goal. This does not apply to knotwork designs painted, drawn or stitched on ritual garb, because they do not actually tie up anything or hold anything closed.

The Priestess's girdle sits to the lower left of the Sigil of the Moon on the altar, and is the cord worn by the Facilitating Priestess during Magickal workings that call for its use. When it is not in use by the Facilitating Priestess it rests coiled upon the altar. Its use and symbolism is described below, and in some of the rituals that follow.

You have several options in creating the Priestess's girdle. It can simply be another red cord like everyone's personal Witch's girdle. Or, you may want something more symbolic of the group energy. In this case, buy a metal ring about two inches in diameter. Silver (for the Moon) is best. Attach to it a piece of heavy gauge yarn or light gauge macrame cord six feet in length for each member of your coven. They can all be red, or each person can choose her own color to contribute to the Priestess's girdle. Twist or braid these cords together to symbolize the combined energies of the group. Whip the ends together to hold the braiding in place. Then, every time a new woman joins, or is initiated into, the coven, another cord representing her energies can be added to the Priestess's girdle.

Yes, this means you will have to take it apart, add her cord, rebraid and finish off the cord again. But there is also a reweaving of energies in the group consciousness and group Magick that occurs when a new person joins the coven. This merely demonstrates that on the physical plane. In fact, you could develop a ritual around the rebraiding of the Priestess's girdle as part of the newcomer's initiation or group bonding ceremony.

The third possibility would be to begin with either of the two cords mentioned above. Then place a drop or two of blood, or a little saliva, from each member of the group onto the cord. This could be done at each individual's initiation, or during a group bonding ceremony. Blood and saliva (as well as urine, menstrual blood and hair) contain the essence of the individual and, as such, add to the combined Magickal energies represented by the Priestess's girdle. A very real part of each individual has thereby been given to the coven, to be used by the coven. If you do not like this last idea, don't use it. The taking of bodily fluid or hair is, however, a time tested, traditional, multicultural Magickal method of binding the individual to a group (or to another individual).

As an individual tool, the Witch's girdle or red cord is usually worn around the waist by slipping the tether end through the loop and wrapping it several times around the resulting waist band to hold the cord in place. The remainder of the tether end is left hanging. The cord can then act as a belt upon which to hang your athame scabbard or an amulet/mojo bag.

The cord is red because it symbolizes the umbilical cord and its blood of life, which connects us to our foremothers and to the Goddess. The color is also symbolic of menstrual blood and our connection to every woman born as a result of the cycles of our bodies. The red cord is our lifeline to the Goddess and to each other.

Personal Magickal Items

In addition to the Witch's girdle and athame, each woman may wish to bring a few other personal Magickal items to the Circle. Below is a short list of such items, and a discussion of their significance.

Personal Wand. Witches usually make their own wands out of wood. There are also a variety of crystal and metal wands available on the occult and New Age market. Although I am sure these are lovely and can work very well, it makes more Magickal sense to make your own out of wood. When you put a lot of time, thought and energy into making a wand on your own, you are putting a lot more of your personal energy/Magick into it than you could ever put into something purchased readymade from someone else. (This is the reasoning behind making your own athame handle, as well. You can even make your own blade if you have the knowhow and the access to the tools and materials with which to do it!)

Traditionally, the Witch's wand is made of hazelwood, oak or willow. Which wood you choose depends on which qualities you want your wand to bring to you. Choose hazelwood to garner wisdom. Pick oak to accrue Magickal power, strength and protection. Willow is sacred to Circe/Hecate and will bring you the shaman-istic qualities and powers of these Goddesses.

In Magickal tradition the wand is cut from a living tree branch of one year's growth on the day of Mercury (the first magician). In other words, on Wednesday. The length to cut depends on the number of inches between the crook of your elbow and the tip of your middle finger. Its thickness really depends on personal preference. I have seen wands of a variety of widths.

After you cut it, tradition further instructs that you take it home, peel the bark from it and sand it as smooth as you like, all the while concentrating on its intended use, which is to intensify and direct the Magickal energies you release through it. Once this is done, you are to imbue it with your energy by pricking your finger and letting a drop or two of blood fall on the wand, or in a small hole you have drilled in the larger end of it specifically for that purpose.

You do not have to follow the above procedure to the letter in order to create a wand for yourself. If you do not want to cut a living branch from a tree, simply locate the tree from which you would like to get a wand, wait until after a severe storm, then go out and pick up any downed branch that feels right to you. Take it home, cut it to the length specified above, peel the bark and sand it while thinking about its intended use. If you are squeamish about pricking your finger, rub your saliva on it instead. Or, you may want to wait until your Moon Time to dab a little menstrual blood on the larger end of the wand. (This might be more appropriate, because there are those who feel that the origins of the Magick wand lay in the lunar counting stick used by prehistoric women to determine the rhythms of their menstrual cycles, the conception and duration of a pregnancy, and the cycles of the Moon through the months and the seasons.)

However you decide to make your wand, consecrate it by passing it through the four elements of Earth (rub salt on it); Air (pass it through incense smoke); Fire (run it over a candle flame); and Water (sprinkle it with water from your chalice). Say something about its purpose as you do this. Name it if you wish. Finally, hold it against your solar plexus and channel your will into it to activate it. The wand is an instrument of your will, and your solar plexus is the chakra center associated with will.

Chalice or Goblet. You will want to bring a chalice or goblet to each Circle in order to share in the ritual feasting. Place it under the altar before the ritual starts to keep it out of the way. Here again, Wiccan Magickal tradition calls for a silver chalice. It can, however, be made of any material you like. The only admonishment is that you not haggle over its price if you purchase one. Consecrate it by passing it through the four elements as described above.

Amulet Bag or Mojo Bag. An amulet bag is a pouch full of natural objects to which you have attached Magickal or sacred significance. The bag itself is ideally made of a natural material. Suede, leather, silk or cotton cloth are most often used. To make one, simply cut a good sized circle out of your material. Next, punch or snip small holes about 1/2 inch from the outer edge of the material. Then simply run a thong or piece of yarn/cording through the holes. Fill it with what you like, pull it shut and tie it closed however you wish. In order to further personalize the bag you could draw your astrological chart on the inner surface of the bag, or mark it with a personal symbol you have chosen to represent yourself.

A mojo bag differs from an amulet bag in that its contents are not limited to natural objects, but are specific to a spell you are working for a specific purpose. Once the spell is complete/has worked, the bag and its contents are scattered and/or destroyed. You can do this by tossing the contents into a stream or lake, and then burying or burning the bag. Or, you can bury or burn the whole thing. Construct it as you would an amulet bag.

The amulet bag is more permanent, although you may change its contents as you are moved to do so. You can also create specific amulet bags for specific purposes like protection, safe travel, and clear insight. These bags are usually tied shut and then sealed by dripping hot candle wax onto the closure. They are worn or carried when you wish to draw on their aid. When not in use they are stored with your other Magickal things.

Jewelry. Most Witches have pieces of jewelry they consider Magickal or symbolic representations of themselves and their path to the Goddess. These are either pieces that they wear in every ritual, or are pieces that they wear at differing times, depending on their mood or the purpose of the ritual. Here again silver seems to predominate, but you will find a variety of precious and semiprecious gems and stones, as well. Most Witches like to wear a pentacle (a star with a circle around it) or a crescent Moon as a symbol of their Craft and their connection to the Goddess. Many Dianics wear a labyris — a double bladed or butterfly axe representing the waxing and waning crescents of the Moon and hence, Goddess. It is thought to symbolize life and death and the power of transformation. Historically, it was most commonly found as a symbol in ancient Crete, which is thought to have once been a seat of matriarchal culture and power. What you choose to wear is up to you. Some covens also give an identical piece of jewelry to each member as a way of connecting them to the group.

Book of Shadows. This is your own personal book of rituals. Traditionally it is kept in your own handwriting. But, Witchcraft being the practical religion that it is, you will find many Witches with a "disk of shadows" or a book kept by the Magickal hand of Xerox!

I do believe, however, that the more energy you put into a ritual, the more you get out of it. You will gain a greater understanding of a ritual, and get a good start on internalizing it and making it live within you, if you hand copy it into your own Book of Shadows. In so doing you will repeat the words in your head and mentally do the actions as you write. You also will think more about their meaning when you focus on them in the detail necessary to copy them word-for-word. One practical word of advice: Be sure to write or print largely and legibly if you plan to read your rituals within a candlelit Circle. Little chicken scratches that you can read by light of day/ceiling light don't cut it in candlelit darkness.

Originally Witches kept two books. The Book of Shadows contained only the eight Sabbats and the lunar observances (Esbats). The book that contained individual spells, notes on the development of Magickal skills, records of dreams, notes on Goddess messages received/channelled and feelings about a ritual's success or emotional content, was called a Grimoire. The first (the Book of Shadows) was a ritual book. The other (the Grimoire) was a work book. Today, however, most Witches keep everything in one or more three-ring binders with section dividers for Sabbats, Esbats, spells, dreams, Magickal skills, chants, invocations, and the like. Traditionally, the book is black, in keeping with the idea of shadows and darkness — the time of lunar/Witches' Mysteries.

Attire. Wiccan tradition runs in a number of directions when it comes to determining how one dresses for Circle work. In the "Charge of the Goddess" given in Leland's, *Aradia: Gospel of the Witches the Goddess,* Herself directs us to "be naked in [our] rites" as a sign that [we] are "truly free." For this reason some Craft traditions, including some Dianics, do their workings "skyclad." Skyclad is a euphemism for naked and means clothed with only the sky (the air around you).

Other Craft traditions, some Dianics among them, believe that out of necessity, during "the burning times" (the days of Witch persecutions) Witches wore black, hooded cloaks or robes to their rituals. The black cloak or robe leaves you less detectable when walking abroad at night. The hood hides the face. Both were believed to be desireable to protect your identity from Witches and non-Witches alike. Non-Witches would turn you in to the persecutors. Other Witches, under torture, might divulge your identity if they could clearly see your face during the rituals. Self protection is also believed to be the origin of the Witch name as well. (See below.)

Other Witches, particularly those that draw most heavily from Ceremonial Magick, have robes in several colors. Some change the color of their robes when the season changes. Some change them with the intent of the ritual. Still others create robes that they adorn with special signs and symbols that hold special meaning, that connect them with a particular culture or mythology, or that make them feel especially Magickal, powerful and capable of accomplishing their Magickal goals.

Still another school, and many Dianics fall into this category, believe it doesn't matter what you wear. Your everyday clothes are fine. They believe that the ability to do Magick or the desire to worship the Goddess has nothing to do with outward appearance. It is what's inside that counts.

In the final analysis, it is a matter of individual or group choice. If the group wants to have special, identical robes, fine. If the group feels skyclad practice is important, do it. If the group decides to leave it up to each individual to decide for herself, that is alright too. If street clothes are the uniform of choice, just make sure they are clean and fresh. They should not be what you've just spent the day in. Donning clothes for ritual is one way of helping you to set daily cares aside, to turn your mind to the ritual at hand, and to help your most Magickal Self come out. (See chapter 6 for additional information.)

The Witch Name. Many Witches choose a special name for themselves to use in Circle or whenever being identified as a Witch. There are two reasons for this. During the burning times it was important that people not identify you as a Witch. For this reason people used different names when gathering to perform the rites of Paganism and Witchcraft. Then, should someone be caught and tortured until s/he named those who participated in the ritual, s/he could give the Witch name and be assured that s/he had not incriminated others. By not using, and often not even knowing, the real names of the persons involved in Witchcraft and Paganism, the individual's safety was more or less assured.

The other reason is that the Witch name is the name most closely identified with the Magickal Self. It is the Magickal Self we want fully operational when we are in a Circle. Some Witches have further decided that, ideally, their Magickal Self should be fully operational all the time — not just in the Circle. They feel there should be no split between the way they behave and believe in the Circle or out of it. These Witches choose to use their Witch/Magickal name all the time. Some even go so far as to get their name legally changed to the Witch/Magickal name.

Those who are more or less publicly known as Witches usually choose to use their Witch names when acting publicly as a Witch, in order to protect their family members. They feel their family members should not have to suffer the consequences of their decision to be publicly recognized as a Witch.

There is also an ancient Magickal belief which says that if you know the true name of something or someone, you then have power over it/them. For this reason, some Witches take an additional name for themselves that they keep to themselves or share only with a highly trusted few. They believe this to be there true name, and keep silent about it so no one will be able to control them.

How you choose your Witch name is up to you. There are those who choose the name of a Goddess they feel especially close to, or Whose qualities they would like to emulate or develop within themselves. Others feel it is somehow sacrilegious to take on the name of a deity. Some take names of heroines from the mythology of a culture to which they feel connected, either by birth or by predilection. Others take common names from their preferred culture. Some take the name of a plant, tree, rock, or a body of water with which they feel an affinity, or that they feel symbolizes qualities they would like to take on or develop. Still others search their dreams for an appropriate name. A few use numerology to decide on the best one. The important thing is that the name feels right to you. Never mind how you arrived at it.

To Consecrate the Tools

Every tool that sits upon your altar should be consecrated, or Magickally blessed in order to imbue it with your energies. I have already described the procedure used for the wand. Here are basic instructions for the other tools, any Magickal garb you choose to wear, and your Magickal jewelry.

The rule of thumb is if you have purchased the tool or it has been given to you by someone, you need to purify it before you bless/ consecrate it. You do not want someone else's vibrations in your tool. If you have made the tool yourself out of natural materials, you need not purify it first. In the case of the athame, where you have probably made the handle but purchased the blade, purify the blade to remove all vibrations but your own before you attach the handle.

To purify a tool, put three pinches of sea salt or kosher salt in a bowl of water and stir it three times, for the three aspects of the

Goddess. (Do this with your athame if it has been purified and consecrated. If not, use your finger.) As you stir, think to yourself or speak aloud a brief exorcism and charm over the salted water. Use words of your own choosing, or say:

> Pure salt and sweet water,
> Combine now your power
> to cleanse, remove and make pure.
> All touched by your blending
> has power unending
> for Magick —
> receiving or sending.

Rub the salt water all over the tool. In the case of a robe, a liberal sprinkling will do. For your red cord, get your hand wet and then run the cord through your wet hand. As you purify your tool think about and visualize the energies of its creators and/or previous owners being washed away. You may wish to repeat the exorcism and charm as you do this.

Now dry the tool off. Salt has a corrosive effect on metal and wood. The act of drying can also be seen as removing the unwanted from the tool. Don't worry about any salt residue on robes or the red cord, just let them air dry.

To charge the tool with your own energy, I recommend holding the tool to the part of the body to which it corresponds. Then send your energy through that spot to the tool. The chalice, the bowls and the Sigil of the Moon correspond to water/bodily fluids. Hold each to your womb. The womb is your body's cauldron, and the chalice and bowls represent the cauldron upon the altar. The Sigil of the Moon represents the energies of the Moon and contact with the Goddess. The tides of your womb are effected by the Moon, and the womb of the Goddess is the great cauldron of the universe as well as the seat of the divine feminine within each one of us. For the Witch's girdle/red cord, tie it around your waist and hold the tether end to your womb. Here is the umbilical cord pulsing with the blood of life — the blood of the Mother — your lifeline to the Goddess and to all women.

There has been a debate for years in occult circles as to whether the athame corresponds to the element of Air or Fire. As a tool used to direct your Magickal will, it is associated with Fire and should be held to your solar plexus. As a tool associated with Air, it brings discernment and the ability to know what to cut away and what to keep. In this case, it should be held to the lips and blown on. You can make your own decision depending on which feels right to you. Since the wand is also a director of your Magickal will and is associated with Fire, you may wish to assign the athame to Air. Or, you can do as I do, and hold it to both your lips and your solar plexus!

Your rock, symbolizing Earth, can be placed on the ground under your foot. In this case you will draw the energy of the Earth up into the rock, with your foot acting as a magnet of sorts. Candlesticks and holders represent Fire, and are held against the solar plexus. You may wish to do handfuls of candles at one time to keep from having to stop and do this every time you need to replace an altar candle. Or, you can dress the candles (purify/consecrate them) with olive oil. To do this, place a small amount of olive oil in the palm of your hand. Close that hand around the middle of the candle. Draw your oiled hand down to the base of the candle. Remove your hand and grasp the candle in the middle again. Now draw your oiled hand up to the top of the candle. Repeat this process three times. The candle is now dressed.

The censer is obviously associated with the element of Air, so blow on it. The vase or bowl you will use for flowers should partake of your energy, as well. As a container of water, a cauldron of sorts, it is best held to your womb.

In the case of ritual garb, just put it on or hold it to your chest. Send energy to it from wherever it contacts your body. To charge jewelry, hold it between your hands and direct your energy to it through your palms.

If the altar object is a group tool like the Moon Crown, the sickle or group athame, or the Priestess's girdle, it should be charged with the energies of the entire group. (In fact, the rituals in this book assume that all objects upon the coven altar are the property of the group, and are not the personal property of any individual member.) To do this, first have whoever is serving as Facilitating Priestess purify the tool. There are then a couple of ways of charging it with everyone's energy. First, if you have a coven cauldron, place the tool in the cauldron and then have everyone direct their own energy into the cauldron using their athame, their wand, or their hands as a channel for their personal energy. If you do not have a coven cauldron, then simply hand the tool around the

Circle and let each woman add her energy to the tool in whatever way she deems fit. In either case, when all are done the Facilitating Priestess takes it in her hands, holds it out for the group to see, and seals the working with words of her own choosing, or by saying:

> Here it is,
> Charged this way,
> In it will our power stay.
> All may add a:
> So mote it be!

This phrase is used to bind a spell. It means, "so must it be" or "so be it." It is comparable to an emotionally charged "Amen."

The next step, whether it be a personal tool or a coven tool, is to consecrate it by the four elements. To do this, pass it through the smoke from a censer, pass it through or over a candle flame, sprinkle it with water, then with salt. Call upon the blessings of each element — either out loud or silently — as you use that element. Here is an example of what could be said, beginning with Air/East.

Pass the tool through the censer smoke and say:

> "Used at the beginning of the spell,
> May I speak it wise and well."

Pass it through a candle flame and say:

> "I send it now with will's full force
> to hit the spot, to stay the course."

Sprinkle it with water and say:

> "On its intended the spell rains down,
> in emotions and psychic centers it's found."

Sprinkle it with salt, saying:

> "The spell's complete, it's done its best,
> It now begins to manifest."

(If the Facilitating Priestess recites these words to consecrate group tools, she should replace the word "I" with the word "we".)

Where Power Resides

A relevant question here would be, is the power in the tool itself, or is it in the practitioner? The answer is, yes. You have charged up your tools with your own Magickal/Goddess energy, so they do hold power. Through constant use in Magickal practice they will take on more power as you direct it through them. For these reasons, it is considered improper etiquette to handle or to touch someone else's ritual tools without the permission of the owner.

However, the original power within the tools came from you. They do not have Magickal power on their own. They merely hold, channel, amplify and direct your Goddess power. It is perfectly acceptable to participate in a ritual without tools, using just your fingers or palms to direct your energy. But, like everything else in the ritual setting, the tools are meant to act as triggers to your deep mind/Goddess Self — to get its attention and to let it know it is time to focus and to perform Magickal work. So, if you cannot yet easily access this Magickal Self and bring it to the fore, it may be best to use all the tools and trappings of ritual to help you achieve this altered state of consciousness.

CHAPTER FIVE

Forming a Group

Most women, after having discovered Dianic Wicca, want to share Goddess worship, Magick and the turning of the Wheel (the cycle of the Sabbats) within the context of a coven. Usually they do not know where to find one. Sometimes, they do not feel comfortable in a particular group when they do find one. More often than I would like to think, no such group exists in their area.

There are several ways to go about finding Dianic Witches and covens. You can contact national Dianic publications and networking centers like "Of A Like Mind" and The Reformed Congregation of the Goddess (RCG). Write to them at RCG, P.O. Box 6021, Madison, WI 53716. You can take out an ad in, and subscribe to, women's spirituality and feminist publications like, *SageWoman*, P.O. Box 641, Point Arena, CA 95468, or *Woman of Power Magazine*, P.O. Box 827, Cambridge, MA 02238-0827.

You can contact the Covenant of the Goddess at COG, Box 1226, Berkeley, CA 94704. This is a loose confederation of covens and Pagan groups from around the United States, Canada and elsewhere. Although not specifically a Dianic alliance, there are Dianic covens within the organization to which they can direct you.

If you are on the west coast, try contacting the Reclaiming Collective at, Reclaiming, P.O. Box 14404, San Francisco, CA 94414. This is a group of Witches with a feminist perspective. Although not for women only, they are likely to know of Dianic covens in the region. If you are on the east coast, you might try Womanswork/Spirituality at Womanswork Connection, P.O. Box 2282, Darien, CT 06820 to see what contacts they might have for you. For contacts in the midwest, try RCG.

Another option is to attend one or more of the national, regional and local women's events held each year. They will be listed in the publications mentioned above. Some of them are oriented toward women's spirituality and some, like the Michigan Womyn's Music Festival (a lesbian/feminist event), have a different focus, but have a large number of Dianic Witches in attendance. For information on this music festival send a self-addressed, stamped envelope to WWTMC, Box 22, Walhalla, MI 49458.

At these events you may have an opportunity to attend workshops on the Craft and Craft-related subjects, as well as to attend Dianic rituals. Some events even have networking sessions or areas to enable women to connect with others living in their region of the country, state or city.

If you live in or near a metropolitan area, you can frequent the local feminist or New Age bookstore. They often sponsor classes on Craft-related topics such divination, alternative methods of healing, and the Magick of gems and stones. Feminist bookstores usually carry a selection of books about women's spirituality and the Goddess and, from time to time, have book signings by the authors. If so, attend. You are bound to be in a room full of women with interests similar to your own. Strike up a conversation with some of them. Both of these types of stores usually have a bulletin board or message board for use by customers. You can often get word of Craft-related workshops or teachers there. You can also put up an ad yourself, saying what you are looking for and how you can be contacted.

Since a wide variety of people will be reading your ad (whether it be on a bulletin board or in a Craft-oriented publication), I would suggest you be succinct and specific when writing it. If you are looking for women interested in Dianic Craft, say so. If you just say Witchcraft, men or mixed covens may contact you. If you say you are interested in women's spirituality, feminist Christian women, and others, may contact you.

If you are worried about harassment, prejudice or simply feel uneasy about having unknown individuals contact you, get a post office box and have them write to you there. If you want them to call you (your chances of success might be better if you do) give your phone number but use an assumed name. That way, no one can get your address from the phone book, or find out where you work.

I even know one person who left a message written in Theban script (a Witches' runic alphabet of sorts) on a bulletin board in the local laundromat. All it said was something to the effect of, "If you can read this, contact me at . . ." and gave a phone number. He knew that anyone who called him had to have a serious interest in the Craft because they could read the script. He got a call, too!

Another option is to place a fairly cryptic ad in your local newspaper. In this case you do not want to use words like Witch, Witchcraft, Pagan or Paganism. Words like feminist spirituality or women's religion are good choices. Or you could simply say, "Have you read books by . . . " and list Dianic Craft and/or Goddess-oriented authors. Then go on to say, "If you liked what you read and want to explore further call . . . " You get the idea.

Think, too, about what happens next. Where will you meet the people who contact you? In your home? In a coffee shop? In the park? I would recommend a public place, just in case they turn out to be on an entirely different wavelength than you are. If they seem alright, you can invite them to your house another time, exchange phone numbers, whatever.

When you meet with someone, you need to be clear with her and with yourself about what you are seeking. For example, do you want to be in a study group, a ritual group, or both? Is it important to you that everyone in the group identify as Witches, or not? Are women of all sexual persuasions welcome in the group, or would you prefer it be limited to lesbian only, bisexual only, or heterosexual only? Since Dianic Craft incorporates political, social and ecological activism within its framework, look at those issues as well in deciding with whom you can and cannot work, and what you do and do not want.

Often there is a perception that since we are all identifying ourselves as Dianic Witches, we all must naturally think, believe and act alike. No such luck. Just because we all honor the Goddess in some form, and practice Magick and apply our beliefs and practices to "real world" issues, does not mean we all do these things in the same way or understand them in the same way. For instance, those who believe it is a misuse of power to bind or blast someone or something will not work well with those who feel it is alright to do so. Most animal rights activists would find it hard to share a Circle with a woman who hunts. Neo-Luddites and technophiles probably will not do well together either.

An equally shared level of trust and respect must exist between members of a Magickal religion who worship and practice together. Without it the group will not gel and work together as one. The psychic attunement of each to the other which leads to the establishment of a group energy and, later, a group mind, will not occur. In the end, the Mysteries will only be experienced at a superficial level at best. Therefore, whether you are seeking to form a group or have been asked to join one that already exists, ask the questions to which you need answers. If those answers are not forthcoming, are vague, or are treated in an off-hand manner, or if you find the answers unsuitable, this is not the group for you. Keep looking. Or, if after joining a group you feel something is amiss and little or no effort is made to address your feeling, leave the group. There is nothing more frustrating than being in a group that does not meet your needs. It is far better to form another or to work alone than to remain unhappy just for the sake of being in a group.

One of the primary building blocks for establishing trust, particularly for someone new to Dianic Wicca, is the availability of some kind of coherent method of training. If you are establishing a group, please develop one. If you are joining an existing group, ask about their training program and how they go about integrating new people into the group. Methods may vary, but something should be available. There also should be some kind of on-going training/discussion once the fundamentals are well in hand. It is also important to spend time just having fun, sharing work, food, friendship and community service. All these activities build trust and confidence in each other, the by product of which is a richer and deeper shared experience of ritual, the Goddess, Magick and the Mysteries.

In fact, one of the best ways to improve your rituals is to meet again at the mid-point between the ritual just completed and the next one to be done. You can each share what worked and what did not work for you in the preceding ritual. You also can spend some time developing your ritual, psychic and Magickal skills at this meeting, and deepening your understanding of the rituals themselves.

You also can spend some time going over the ritual you will be doing next to make sure everyone understands the elements of the ritual as well as what to prepare in advance and/or what to bring along. This would be a good time for the Facilitating Priestess for that ritual to explain how her ritual will differ from the ritual given in this book (if at all) and to seek input and volunteers from the group to help her with various parts of the ritual, should she want or need that.

The coven meeting could also be helpful in organizing other coven activities of a more social/political nature. Perhaps you would all like to dress up in costumes at Hallows and trick or treat for UNICEF. (Contact them or your local United Way for information about how to get the appropriate donation boxes.) Maybe you would like to cook and serve a meal at the local soup kitchen or homeless shelter at Lammas or the Fall Equinox. You could prepare a ritual drama for the next "Take Back the Night" march or ecology rally/action. You could organize a food and/or clothing drive amongst the Pagan population in your area and donate it all to the agency of your choice. The possibilities are endless.

It is also a good idea to have one meeting a year, perhaps immediately before or soon after Samhain (pronounced sow-en) — October 31, the traditional Witch's New Year — to plan your liturgical year, so to speak. Everyone will want to bring their Lunar calendars and a note pad. The dates for each Esbat and Sabbat celebration should be marked on everyone's calendar, and the Facilitating Priestess for each ritual should be chosen and written down, so that everyone will remember the information.

Ideally, all Esbats and Sabbats will take place on the actual day of the Full Moon or the Sabbat. However, we don't live in an ideal world and it is far more likely that these rituals will need to take place on a weekend night in order to accommodate work schedules, child care needs, family obligations and, occasionally, national holidays. It is always best to schedule them as near to the actual event as possible. And, in the case of Sabbats, the weekend prior to the actual turning of the Wheel is better than the weekend after, even if the weekend prior to it is not as close to the actual date as the weekend after it may be. Magickally speaking, there is no point in observing the Sabbat after it has already occurred. One of the major points of celebrating a Sabbat is to lend your power to and actually participate in the turning of the Wheel. To what are you lending your power once the event has already occurred?

The Esbats are seen in a different light, and it is therefore not as important to observe them prior to the actual Full Moon. In this case, proximity to it — either before or after — is more important. It is seen as the most effective time to perform a brief spell or to complete a spell begun at the New Moon. It is a time for personal/coven work, for communing with the Goddess and/or for preparing for the Sabbat to come. It is not seen as effecting the actual cycle of the Moon in the way that Sabbat work is seen as effecting the actual turning of the Wheel.

If an Esbat and a Sabbat fall in close proximity to each other, it is perfectly alright to combine the two observances should you wish to do so, or should it be appropriate to do so. If the Esbat work is preparatory work for the Sabbat, simply move that work back one month and skip the Esbat it replaces. Or, do the potentially skipped Esbat working at the New Moon, if you find it appropriate and you all are able to meet then.

Issues of power need to be addressed within the coven. These include how the coven will be run, who is responsible for training others, who will act as Facilitating Priestess for a given ritual, what financial commitment (if any) is required of individual members, what criteria will be established for accepting new members and for bidding adieu to those who choose to leave.

Take an honest look at the skills and levels of skills possessed by the women in your group. Acknowledge the strengths of each woman and begin calling upon her to serve in the capacity best suited to her. Part of that service should include bringing other interested women in the group up to her own level of skill so that her responsibilities may be shared with equally competent women.

It may help you to work from the basic premise that everyone has power — the power to decide what is best for them and what is best for the group. Through discussion a consensus will emerge as to what is best for the group. It will usually revolve around developing and deepening the understanding of the Mysteries of the Goddess within and without, honing Magickal/psychic skills, and increasing knowledge about the ways of wise women and the Goddess throughout history and around the world. The best way to do this is to let those who know guide those who do not until everyone knows.

The choice of Facilitating Priestess for each ritual is extremely important, because it is she who guides women in the experience of the Mysteries implied and hinted at in the rituals. The process of selecting her will depend in large part on the makeup of the group, the needs of the group, the levels of skill of those involved, and the group's chosen governance procedures. The following suggestions are drawn from my experiences in a variety of Craft groups and covens, and are based on the level of skill required within the context of a ritual. That level of skill can range from the beginner to the adept. I urge you to consider these options carefully and to implement them if you find them worthy. You are, of course, free to do whatever you like. I make no claim to knowing the one, true, and only way of doing this. I do claim to know a *good* way, however, and I offer it to you here.

The Facilitating Priestess can conduct the entire ritual herself, or she can delegate parts of the ritual to others. The position of Facilitating Priestess can rotate among all members of the coven, can be shared among the experienced members of the coven, or can be the responsibility of one woman — either permanently or throughout one entire Wheel of the Year.

Those who wish to serve effectively as Facilitating Priestess need to develop some skills. A knowledge of group dynamics, an understanding of the ebb and flow of the power used in working Magick and the techniques used to raise it, channel it and when to release it are essential. All of this involves a well developed psychic or intuitive sense. Although psychic skills are innate in everyone, it is rare to find someone in whom they are completely functional without a fair amount of training. Psychic training is an important part of the training of a Witch. One who would serve as Facilitating Priestess for a group should get additional training in learning to sense the psychic energies of the group, and the individuals within the group, in order to combine it/them into a cohesive Magickal whole that can be used for the benefit of the coveners and the Magickal goals they choose.

You will notice that several of the rituals in this book require that the Facilitating Priestess channel the Goddess. In other words, the she must be able to bring the Goddess through herself to such an extent that the Goddess speaks and acts through her for the benefit of the group. This is variously referred to as "channeling the Goddess"; "mediating" — serving as an interpreter of messages from the Goddess; or "aspecting the Goddess" — bringing a particular aspect/manifestation of the Great Goddess through. This is most often referred to as "Drawing Down the Moon." As such it refers specifically to bringing down lunar deities, or the lunar deities most commonly associated with Witchcraft.

This is not play acting or ritual drama. It is a technique akin to seership or prophecy that enables the Facilitating Priestess to set aside her own ego/personality to such an extent that she can then draw the essence of the Goddess into her consciousness, and can allow the Goddess to fill her to such an extent that the Goddess moves her and speaks through her vocal mechanisms. This requires individualized training and, in my opinion, should not be attempted without training and support from someone already skilled at it. If no one in your group knows how to bring the Goddess through in this manner, then skip that part of the ritual until after the skills have been developed. Use the alternates or scripted parts given. If you do have someone in your coven who can do this, the rituals in which this is called for will fall to her. It also becomes her responsibility to teach others the skills necessary to channeling the Goddess.

Other skills helpful for a Facilitating Priestess include basic knowledge of ritual procedure, the ability to overcome, or at least control, stage fright, and the ability to project the voice so that all may hear her. These skills are developed by doing them often enough that the ritual procedure becomes internalized and the stage fright and vocal level manageable. Start by having different people do different parts of the ritual. For example, four different women can call the Quarters and another can consecrate participants. As psychic and Magickal skills develop, give and get experience at leading the spell work and guiding meditations and/or visualizations. And finally, as the ability to bring the Goddess through develops, get experience doing it within the context of the rituals. When all can do all things, then the responsibilities of serving as Facilitating Priestess can be rotated on some kind of regular schedule.

If you have gathered together a group of totally inexperienced women, including yourself, who have only a love for the Goddess and good intentions, the rituals in this book do not leave you high and dry. Each is scripted and can be performed by the beginner as well as the adept. Beginners (or anyone wishing to stick strictly to the scripts) will benefit by memorizing the various components. Time spent in memorization will help internalize the information and images presented in the scripts. This process will allow you to feel more comfortable with the ritual(s) and will allow your mind and emotions to open themselves to the experience of the ritual's inner meanings, instead of worrying about reading the words correctly and taking the right actions in the right way. As you become more and more comfortable with ritual, and as you repeat this ritual cycle over the years, you will find it becomes easier and easier, and deeper and more varied layers of meaning will make themselves known to you.

These rituals are meant to point you in the right direction and to give you a few landmarks along the way, not to set you down at the destination or at the heart of the Mysteries. How you get there is just as important as the goal. Each woman's and each coven's experience of the journey will differ slightly and significantly. Just when you think you have arrived at the heart of the matter, you will find yourselves drawn further on and deeper within Her core of being.

CHAPTER SIX

Ritual Construction

To simplify things, this chapter is an outline you can use in creating your own rituals, or as a teaching aid to help others understand the whys and wherefores of the ritual format. The ritual format arises out of the western Magickal tradition. The format is a method for preparing us to become acquainted with and to seek the aid of Otherworld beings, the Watchers (rulers of the four elements), and the Goddess.

Although we do not need to take the seemingly adversarial position toward these beings that some Magickans seem to embrace, we do need to be respectful of them and we need to recognize that they are very powerful and very different from ourselves. These beings are not abstract theories or psychological constructs. They are self-aware, self-actualized beings of another order/other orders. The ritual format employed here prepares us physically, mentally and psychically to interact with them, as well as to establish parameters or boundaries within which the interaction will take place, and beyond which it will not go.

The Goddess invoked is much more than that part of Goddess which dwells within each one of us, and with whom we personally interact on a day-to-day basis. She is the matrix from which ideas and constructs of the Divine Female and the power of the Divine Female arise — the source of creation and destruction, and the engine that drives the cycles. Her existence both permeates and stretches far beyond this world into Otherworlds, and into other ways of being. It is a part of Her we invoke into our Circle, and a part of Her that is channeled by the Facilitating Priestess who has the skills. It is She who aids us in our Magick. It is She who is our own spark of Goddess within. It is She whom we worship and celebrate in our rituals and in our lives.

Ritual Outline

Ritual Bath: Participants bathe to symbolically cleanse the body and free the mind from daily care and bring its power to bear on the purpose of the ritual at hand.

Silent Sharing of Tea: Individual time for focused meditation, and the first steps in opening the Self psychically and emotionally to the ritual work about to be done.

Lighting of the Altar Candles: A silent but visible signal to the group to assemble in the Circle for the ritual. This is the beginning of the ritual itself.

Cast the Circle: Creation of the sacred space. The Circle forms a boundary between the everyday world and the Magickal world now being entered.

Consecration of the Circle by the Four Elements: The elements are used to bless the Circle and to name it as holy/sacred, a place specially prepared for the indwelling of Goddess.

Consecration of all Participants: Each woman is anointed with oil and thus named sacred/holy/vehicle of the Goddess within. It is also a mechanism for opening the psychic and Goddess Self more fully in preparation for experiencing the presence of the Goddess and the rulers of the four elements, and for participating in Magick.

Invocation of the Quarters: Calling on the elemental rulers to come guard the Circle and to lend their aid to the rite and the women participating in it.

Invocation of Goddess: Calling on Her to join the Circle, to aid the Magick and to guide Her women.

Channeling the Goddess: The Goddess is brought through a Facilitating Priestess possessing the necessary skills and abilities. This is to be skipped if the Facilitating Priestess does not have the necessary abilities. The effectiveness of the ritual *will not* be altered if this is skipped.

Magick is Done: Each ritual calls for Magick to be performed, or it is performed according to the needs of the group.

Ceremony of Milk, Honey and Grain: A ceremony done within the context of every ritual to thank Her for Her gifts to us.

Feasting: Shared food and drink. Feasting serves to ground out any excess energy and to return participants to "normal" consciousness. It also aids in bonding and building community within the group.

Thank the Goddess: One doesn't actually dismiss the Goddess, but one does thank Her for attending the Circle and lending Her aid and support.

Dismissal of the Quarters: This is done to thank the Quarters and to send them back. Do not omit this step.

Words of Parting (Declare the Circle Open): Lets people know the ritual is over and sacred space has been dissolved.

Interestingly enough, there are 13 steps in the actual Circle procedure!

Here, now, is detailed information about these various steps.

Ritual Bath

Every ritual begins with a ritual bath. It is not meant to be a thorough cleansing of the body; that should be done ahead of time. A ritual bath is a signal to your Magickal Self/your deep mind to begin opening itself to the Circle work about to be performed. It is a symbolic washing away of daily cares and anxieties. The warm water of the bath is meant to relax the body and the rational mind in order to further open the inner/Magickal Self to the ritual at hand. Just as warm water opens the pores of your skin so, too, can it be seen as symbolically opening the psychic centers within.

Traditionally, the ritual bath is taken at the covenstead (meeting place for the ritual). It is prepared by the Facilitating Priestess, and is shared by all participants in rotation. If this is not possible for some reason, such as you will be meeting in a park, each woman should take her ritual bath at home before leaving for the Circle. Here is the method:

The bathroom should be lit by candlelight. Incense should be burning. In the rituals that follow, specific incenses are suggested. They are meant to harmonize with the overall intent of the ritual.

If nothing is specifically mentioned, use one of the incenses traditionally associated with purification such as frankincense, myrrh
or sandalwood. If you do not have any of these, burn any incense
that appeals to you. It should be one which you feel will enhance
your spiritual/mental cleansing and your relaxation process.

Draw a warm bath. It need not be very deep, unless otherwise
specified in the rituals given here. While the water is still running,
add three good pinches of natural salt (sea salt or kosher salt) to
represent the three aspects of the Goddess. Three is also the number
representing the crystallization of form out of chaos — in other
words, manifestation — and you are trying to manifest a change in
your consciousness as well as symbolically purifying the body in
taking the ritual bath.

You should also add a small amount of hyssop and/or angelica
to the bath water. These herbs are associated with purification. In
order to avoid having bits of herb sticking to my body, and to avoid
clogging the drain, I put my herbs in a cheesecloth bag. I tie it to the
faucet with a long string, which enables the bag to lie in the water.

To make a cheesecloth bag, simply cut a couple of circles about
six inches across. I use circles to follow through on the symbolism
of the ritual (i.e., working in a Circle). This is not absolutely
necessary. Feel free to use squares if you want to. Lay one circle on
top of the other to make a good filter. Place a small amount of
hyssop and/or angelica in the center of the top circle. I would use
three pinches here also, but what you do is up to you. Gather up the
edges around the herb(s) and tie the bag shut with the appropriate
length of string. Then tie it to your faucet and drop it in your
running water.

Disrobe in your room if at home, or in the ritual bath area if at the
covenstead. Take any ritual garb you wish to wear after your ritual
bath to the bathroom with you. Light the incense and candles if that
has not already been done. They should be white for purity, unless
otherwise specified by the ritual. If you are experiencing your
monthly Moon Time, and if you are at home or preparing for a
private ritual, by all means use red candles to honor the blood.

Sit or stand in the bath. Sitting is more relaxing. Standing is often
chosen in the interest of speed when the ritual bath is being shared
sequentially by a number of people. Close your eyes. Take several
deep breaths and let them out slowly. (These are also known as

cleansing breaths.) Now repeat this more or less traditional self-blessing ritual and take the actions it suggests:

Self Blessing Ritual

> "Joyous Maiden, Mother Wise, Ancient One who guides our lives,
> Bless me, for I am Your child.
> Bless my feet that I may lightly walk in your ways upon the Earth."

Make a pentagram on each foot with a wet finger.

> "Bless my knees which shall kneel at Your sacred altars."

Place a pentagram on each knee.

> "Bless my womb, without which we would not be."

Trace an outward spiral over your womb.

> "Bless my breasts and the heart within. May I nurture life and love in your image."

Make a pentagram on your breasts.

> "Bless my lips which shall utter Your sacred names."

Touch water to your lips.

> "Bless my nose that I might breathe Your essence upon the wind."

Touch your nose with water.

> "Bless my eyes that I may clearly see the choices You present me."

Touch your eye lids with water.

> "Bless my mind with visions of Your changing and eternal Self."

Make a pentagram of water on your third eye.

"Bless my hands that I may do Your work in the world."

Make a liquid pentagram on the palm of each hand.

As you perform this ritual, feel the worries of daily life being washed away. Feel your Magickal/Goddess Self come to the fore in your consciousness as the ego and the rational mind are lulled into complacency and restfulness. Spend a few moments meditating on the purpose of the ritual ahead, and do what you need to do internally to prepare for that. Instructions for what to meditate on are usually given in the rituals that follow. If not, follow your own intuition. What you are doing here is putting yourself in the first stages of a light, waking trance.

When you feel that you are done, get out of the tub and dry yourself off. I prefer not to dry off the self-blessing points. I let them dry naturally. That way, some of the water on those points is absorbed by my skin and becomes an integral part of my being, as does the blessing.

Now robe or dress yourself (unless you and/or your coven have decided upon working skyclad). Do so with intent. Robing and donning your special jewelry after the ritual bath is another step in bringing the Magickal/Goddess Self to consciousness. Think of it as putting on your Magickal persona. In a very real way that is exactly what you are doing. You have chosen your ritual clothing and/or jewelry because it makes you feel special in a Witchy way. It is an outward symbol of your inner Goddess.

Whether you are robing or working skyclad, you will need to put your red cord (Witch's girdle) about your waist. As you do, think about its symbolism: it is the umbilical cord linking you to the Goddess and to all the women who perform these rituals. It is the color of life-giving blood, whether it be the blood of birth or of menstruation. As such, it links you to Women's Mysteries and all women everywhere, and can serve as a link with those who have gone before. It encircles your body like the Circle of life. Its tether end leads you on.

The Silent Sharing of Tea

As you leave the ritual bath and go to join the others, the Facilitating Priestess or someone appointed by her will hand you something to drink. It may be an herbal tea, spring water or fruit juice. This beverage is meant to help further your relaxation. It may also be meant to aid you in opening your psychic centers. It is usually connected to the upcoming ritual in some way.

This is *not* a time to talk or joke around. It is a time to further prepare yourself mentally for the ritual while you wait for others to complete their ritual baths. I know there is a tendency to become bored while waiting for everyone to finish, especially if the group is large or some of the baths are lengthy. If your group finds it difficult to maintain silence during this waiting period, in spite of the tea, perhaps you will need to do the baths slightly differently. If this is the case, or if the group does not like the idea of sharing the same bath water, or if no tub exists at the location for the ritual, simply use a large bowl of water in the sink or on a tripod instead. Use the salt and herbs as described above. Follow the same self-blessing and robing procedure. Although this is barely different from the full bath, it does seem to be faster.

You can, of course, ask that everyone do their ritual bath at home before coming to the covenstead. Ritual garb can be put on once everyone arrives. This is not the optimum choice, however, because you will need the ego and rational mind you have just quelled to drive to the covenstead! It is far better not to break or stop the flow of the Magickal Self once it has begun, especially in the early stages of training and developing these psychic/Magickal skills. When they become second nature you may be better able to turn them on and off quickly, or to hold both kinds of consciousness at the same time. Until then it is better not to separate the ritual bath from the robing procedure.

You need not bother with the ritual bath and robing procedure if you do not want to. I am not trying to lay down the law here. However, your Magick and your Goddess connection in Circle will be much better and more complete if you take some time before the Circle to do some kind of ritualized shift in consciousness. What that will entail is up to you.

Keep in mind as well that lots of Witches have been preparing for ritual through the use of the bath for a lot of years, which adds a great deal to the power of the bath as an effective preparation for ritual work. It can also add to your feelings about being a part of a larger, world community of Witches acting in the same way at the same time.

The Use of a Circle

Witches celebrate their rites and work their Magick in a Circle. Although the use of a Circle stems primarily from Ceremonial Magick, there are additional and important reasons for its continued use. One often hears that it is the form that best demonstrates the equality of those who meet within it. There is no "head of the table" or "below the salt," so to speak. All within its confines are on equal footing. It thus demonstrates the Wiccan belief in the equality of all beings.

More importantly, the Circle is a Mandala. It connects parts of experience and leads to insight. Like any mandala, it has a center, circumference and cardinal points, and implies a rhythm that can be seen in this single image. It is the "great round" in all its permutations.

The Lunar cycle, with cardinal points at Full Moon, New Moon, first and last quarters, can be superimposed upon it, as can the seasonal cycle. The cycle of the day is here as well, with its cardinal points at dawn, mid-day, twilight and midnight. The life cycle is here too, with its cardinal points of youth, maturity, old age and death.

There are further meanings of particular importance to women Witches. The menstrual cycle is incorporated in the Circle as well. Its cardinal points are at menstruation, ovulation and the start of pre-ovulation and pre-menstruation. The Witch's Circle is often referred to as the womb of the Goddess and, therefore, as a sacred space in which we meet. It is also the mandala of our own rhythms, and names us sacred as well. It is a place in which we draw away from the world and turn inward to the core of the Goddess Self rooted within the womb and experience the Magick of the Moon and of women's power.

The Setup Within the Circle

The altar is set up in the South of the Circle, facing North. There are two reasons for which it is placed in the South. First, the Moon rises in the Southeast and moves across the sky to the Southwest. By putting the altar in the South, the Moon Herself will travel horizontally across your altar from above and Her light will shine down upon it, blessing and empowering the tools that lie there.

When the Facilitating Priestess is channeling Goddess energy, she does so by standing between the altar and the cauldron, which is placed in the center of the Circle. She stands with her back to the Moon. This allows the Moon to gently support her from above and behind as She speaks to Her women through the Priestess. Some Facilitating Priestesses visualize the Goddess walking down a moonbeam and becoming part of them by enveloping them in a big hug from behind. Others feel a connection between the Moon's light and their crown chakra (which sits on top of the head and is a link between the world of spirit and the "real" world), which opens the channel for the Goddess to speak through them.

Another reason for placing the altar in the South is that South is connected to the element of Fire and, as such, is a place of energy, activity and transformation. All of these things are involved in working Magick and in directing power. The items on the altar aid in this process. So, by placing the altar in the South we are putting it in direct contact with the energies of South. The altar itself symbolizes manifestation. So, by putting it in the South we are manifesting the transformative powers associated with Magick.

The altar faces North because North is thought by many to be the prime place of power within an Earth religion. When you stand at the altar you are facing the place of power, whether you consider it to be North, or Center, as described below.

The cauldron, the primary symbol of women's Witchcraft, sits in the center of the Circle. The center of the Circle, like the center of the altar, is the place of spirit. It is where the Goddess comes through to Her women, our point of contact with Her. It is the focal point of our Magick and our invocations. Power coalesces in the center of the Circle, and is contained and amplified by the Circle itself. Through the sacred center the cone of Magickal power is released into the world or into the care of the Goddess.

Casting the Circle and Consecrating with the Elements

The Circle is cast, using the athame or sickle, beginning in the East, the place of beginnings. The Facilitating Priestess points the athame or sickle toward the ground and walks deosil (sunwise: to her right) around the Circle. As she walks, she and all coveners visualize a bluish white beam of light/power extending from the tip of the athame or sickle to the ground. This beam marks the actual boundary of the Circle. As she walks, she recites the "Circle Casting Spell:"

> "I conjure thee, great womb of the Goddess, cauldron of a Witch's power, within who's sacred precinct are we separate from the world of care and safe from harm and strife. Inspire our Magick and make it strong. Transform the wrong to right. Feed us from Thy source of plenty and aid our work this night. In the names of Diana, three-formed Goddess of the Moon and Her reborn daughter, Aradia, so mote it be!"

She returns to the altar and puts down the athame or sickle. She, or the one so chosen, using the athame, the sickle point, or her fingers places three measures of salt (wheat or corn) from the bowl on the altar into the bowl of water on the altar and stirs it three times. The Facilitating Priestess picks up the bowl of salted water and moves deosil to the East point. She then walks around the perimeter of the Circle, sprinkling the salted water as she goes. As she moves around the Circle, she speaks The Consecration by Water and Earth:

> "By the Water of the Cauldron and the Earth from which it's formed is this Circle blessed and sealed and is our Magick born."

She completes her circuit by returning to the East and raising the bowl in salute to the Goddess. She returns the bowl of salted water to the altar. The Facilitating Priestess, or the woman so chosen, adds incense to the censer, picks it up and moves deosil to the East. She walks around the Circle with the smoking censer, while speaking "The Consecration by Air and Fire:"

> "By the Air which feeds the Fire beneath Her churning Cauldron is this Circle consecrated to Her service and blessed with Her protection."

She finishes in the East, and raises the censer in salute to the Goddess, returns to the altar and puts the censer down. The Circle is now cast. It has been triple-consecrated by three circumambulations.

If you prefer a more poetic Circle casting, you might like to substitute the following. The actions remain the same.

"By the power of Witch's blade is this Magick
  Circle made,
A strong enclosure, a power-full room,
Safe within the Goddess's Womb;
A sacred place, a world apart
Where energies merge and Magick starts."

"With Air and Fire this Circle I tread
To know our will is Magick 'tis said."

"With Water and Earth this Circle's complete
  To dare and keep silent long after we meet."

As you can see, the two are slightly different in thealogical/Magickal content. The first version uses the theme of the cauldron. The second concentrates on the powers of a Witch (to Know, to Will, to Dare, to Keep Silent).

Consecration of Participants

All participants are now consecrated. This consecration identifies each woman with the Goddess, emphasizing the sacredness of who and what she is. It establishes a link between each woman and the Goddess, thereby preparing her to commune with the Goddess more fully and with greater clarity. By anointing the third eye the psychic processes are activated (or more fully engaged) to facilitate that communication.

In its purest and simplest form the consecration is done with olive oil. The olive tree was a gift to the people of Athens from the Goddess, Athena. As a Goddess-given gift, it makes it especially appropriate for use in Women's Witchcraft. If you like, you can heat some olive oil, add Magickally significant herbs to it, simmer it briefly, let it cool, strain it and decant it. Or, you can use any of a wide variety of essential oils that are available on the market. Both of these options (as well as instructions for preparation, when appropriate) are used in the following rituals. If no such specification is noted, use plain olive oil.

You may also wish to have a vial of red liquid on the altar, with which to anoint any woman who has her Moon Time during the ritual. Honoring women's connection to the Goddess through our blood is an important part of Women's Mysteries. In this case, anoint both the third eye and the womb.

Three methods are used for this anointing process. The traditional way is to have each woman come to the altar to be anointed (consecrated) by the Facilitating Priestess. By coming to the altar, the participant is coming to the place of transformation (the South). The purpose of the anointing is to effect a transformation within the anointee — to open her more to the Goddess — and to mark the anointee as sacred. Another, often faster, method is for the Facilitating Priestess to go to each woman in the Circle and to anoint that woman where she stands. The final method is for the Facilitating Priestess to anoint the woman to her left while speaking the words of consecration. She then hands the vial of oil to that woman, who turns and consecrates the woman to her left. The bottle and words of consecration are thus handed from woman to woman around the Circle until all have been anointed and the vial has been replaced on the altar by the Facilitating Priestess.

Using the oil, inscribe a symbol on the third eye. The symbols most often employed are the pentagram, the three phases of the Moon/aspects of the Goddess (back to back crescents with a full moon between them), or the single crescent. This single crescent may also be done in imitation of the Lunar crown, with the points of the crescent upward. Use whatever feels best to the group, the Facilitating Priestess, or what suits the occasion. The spiral with three outward evolutions is often used to symbolize/trigger the opening of the third eye if psychic work, or trance work, is to be done within the Circle. When anointing with the chosen symbol, speak the "Individual Consecration:"

> "With the touch of this oil you are anointed Her
> chosen — Her daughter, Her sister, her beloved,
> Herself."

Again, there is no hard and fast rule about the consecration. This is my preference. Other options would include consecration by the four elements, using the censer and the bowl of salted water; or consecration with incense smoke only (here symbolizing spirit).

You could change the consecration point(s) as well. Instead of anointing/consecrating the third eye, you could use the heart. Or, you could do the third eye, the heart, and the womb. The choice is yours.

Another purpose for the consecration is to raise the individual's vibrational rate in preparation for the invocation of the four Quarters. This is the next step in the ritual process.

Invocation of the Quarters

This process is known as "calling the Quarters"; "invoking the Four Elements"; "setting up the Watchtowers"; or "calling the Watchers." This involves a great deal more than simply acknowledging the compass points or the four elements. Calling on Earth, Air, Fire and Water is a brief shorthand for an entire set of beliefs and concepts rooted in the western Magickal tradition, of which Wicca and Dianic Craft are a part.

The Quarters are marked on your Circle by placing a candle at each of the four true compass points. There is some debate over whether these candles should be placed on the actual perimeter of the cast Circle or just outside of it. Each group can decide for itself which is right for them.

Traditionally, the colors of these candles are yellow for East, red for South, blue for West, and green or brown for North. I feel it best to stick with these colors. You can, of course, use other colors from other symbol systems if the group is amenable. Just be aware of the Magickal baggage that comes with the decision to use those systems.

The Invocation of the Quarters is much more than paying homage to the compass points. Each of the compass points is equated with one of the four elements that compose life on Earth. They are: East — Air, South — Fire, West — Water, and North — Earth. When you invoke a Quarter you are invoking the pure essence of that element in all its implications, and you are invoking the elemental ruler of that element, as well.

The elemental rulers are powerful, self-aware and self-actualized beings that exist in the world of their pure elements. In occult literature they are referred to as the Watchers and/or the kings of the elements. They are referred to as the Watchers in the Biblical book of Genesis and in at least one Protestant hymn that I know, which begins, "Ye Watchers and ye holy ones . . . " You will also find that the elements were assigned to, or ruled by, the archangels — Raphael (Air/East), Michael (Fire/South), Gabriel (Water/West), and Auriel (Earth/North) — by about the Middle Ages. On a more Pagan/animistic level, we have the elementals associated with each of the four elements: Air — sylphs or, more commonly, faeries; Fire — salamanders; Water — undines, often thought of as similar to mermaids; and Earth — gnomes or dwarves. Other associations that you might use include: Air — eagle; Fire — lion; Water — snake, sea serpent or large fish; Earth — bull or cow (crescent horns and all). Here again, these images are a visual shorthand — Magickal compilations of the meaning, appearance, function and matrix from which these beings devolved — for what they represent. They are not the diminutive winged creatures of fairy tales, nor are they actual salamanders or lions.

Please remember that these are powerful beings and potentially dangerous essences that you are calling upon to guard your Circle, to bear witness to what you are doing, and to lend aid to your Magick. They should be treated with respect and a fair amount of caution. Not only are the elemental rulers worthy of respect and caution, but the essence of the elements should be, as well. Air is not just gentle breezes and the stuff of breath. It is also tornados and gale force winds. Fire is not just the comforting hearth fire and solar warmth. It is the searing sun of the desert and a raging inferno. Water is more than a still pond or a babbling brook. It is a tidal wave and the undertow, too. Earth is not just the womb-cave of the Mother. It is the cave-in as well.

For these reasons, the Quarters are traditionally invoked using the athame or the wand. These tools act as reservoirs and directors of the personal power of the Witch, as well as the Magickal powers summoned by her. As such, these tools are used to limit, or harness the essences the Watchers bring to the Circle, to prevent the Watchers from causing inadvertent (or possibly intended) harm.

Considering this, it is of utmost importance that you dismiss the Quarters at the close of the ritual. I have attended many rituals where the dismissal was either skipped, or done in such a way as to show a total lack of understanding of the powers involved. Here's an example of what I mean. Although I wasn't personally in attendance at this ritual, a friend of mine was and she told me the following story. At the close of a large group ritual, the same young man who had invoked Fire turned to the South to dismiss it. His dismissal ran something to the effect of, "Go if you must, but stay if you will and party with us." The Fire elementals took him up on it. The young man returned to his tent soon after the ritual ended. A few minutes later, his tent was in flames. Had he been burning candles in his tent, or was some other kind of open or contained flame in there? No. By his own account of it, the tent started burning for no apparent reason. The salamanders had a party at his expense.

In another instance, a couple had been doing some pretty intense psychic work and had invoked the undines to aid them at some point during their ritual. They got so wrapped up in the success of the work that they forgot to dismiss the undines after completing their work. The next morning they awoke to an odd smell permeating the house. They followed the smell to the basement, where the work had taken place. They found sludge and standing water covering the floor. Their sewer had backed up during a torrential downpour following their ritual. They were smart enough to realize what had happened, performed the dismissal on the spot, and the water and sludge receded within half an hour. They were left with quite a mess to clean up, though. Upon checking with their neighbors, they found that no one else had had sewer troubles as a result of the rain. They just grinned and nodded.

Once you understand the power being invoked, you can invoke the Quarters with a better awareness of your actions. Here is a set of basic invocations of the Quarters, including the ritual actions to be performed. What your coven actually visualizes at each Quarter is up to the group to decide — perhaps arbitrarily at first, but later based upon information received by the group in group meditation/trance work. Once you have decided, use the same visualizations each time, and write invocations appropriate to those visualizations. If you would like to start by using the ones I have used here, feel free to do so. Perhaps you will stick with them, perhaps not.

The Facilitating Priestess, or person chosen to invoke East/Air steps to the Eastern candle. She lights the East candle, using a taper lit from a Goddess candle on the altar. Using her athame or wand, she inscribes an East-invoking pentacle in the air while reciting the Invocation of Air:

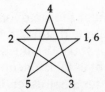

"Golden eagle of the East,
All penetrating eye,
Spread Thy wings which beat like thunder
and bring discernment nigh."

The Facilitating Priestess, or the woman chosen to do so, moves to the South, lights the red candle and, drawing a South-invoking pentagram with her athame, and recites the Invocation of Fire:

"Fiery lion of the South,
of women's blood and passion,
Transformed women with transformed lives
in our cauldron fashion."

At the West the Facilitating Priestess, or her chosen, lights the blue candle. While drawing a West-invoking pentacle with her athame, she recites the Invocation of Water:

"Coiled serpent of the West,
Leviathan of the deep,
From your womb world come to us
with pearls of wisdom we may keep."

Upon arriving at the North the Facilitating Priestess, or the chosen woman, lights the green (or brown) candle and draws a North-invoking pentacle with her athame, while reciting the Invocation of Earth:

"Spotted bull come from the North,
Horned with a crescent crown,
Wed our insight to the Earth,
Therein is Mystery found."

The Facilitating Priestess, or the woman who last spoke, completes the Circle just made by returning to the East, drawing another East-invoking pentacle before returning to the altar, or her place in the Circle.

Usually, those not performing the invocations lend their Magickal support to the speaker(s) by turning and facing the Quarter being addressed, and by raising their own athame in salute and to help hold the chaotic portions of the element at bay. Your group may or may not choose to do this. The action is not important; the mental/ Magickal lending of support and intent is.

Visualizing your own coven's images while each Quarter is being invoked aids in strengthening the reality of those images, especially if you are using images of your own creation rather than those used by others over an extended period of time. Each time you visualize them, you increase their strength and make them better able to help you with their special gifts and abilities.

The casting of the Circle is now complete, and the proper environment for the Mysteries and Magick of the ritual has been created. In many mixed covens (covens consisting of men and women) a symbolic reminder of death, rebirth and willing sacrifice takes place at this point in the ritual. In women's Circles this is skipped, because women are physically reminded of this each month by shedding blood at our Moon Time. Each woman is encouraged to meditate on this and to develop her own rituals around this and other aspects of the physio/Magickal meaning of her blood. Women in the coven may, of course, share in these specific rituals should their menses coincide. During the regular coven meetings for Esbats and Sabbats, those bleeding may be specially consecrated (as mentioned above).

Invocation of the Goddess

The shared Mysteries now begin with the invocation of the Goddess. The invocation may be spoken or sung by the Facilitating Priestess extemporaneously, or she can use the invocation provided in the rituals that follow. In some of the rituals no invocation is provided, and the Facilitating Priestess is asked to compose her own or to use the following basic call to the Goddess.

Picking up the sigil of the Moon, the Facilitating Priestess moves to stand between the altar and the cauldron. Standing with legs spread and holding the sigil out over the cauldron she recites the Invocation of the Goddess:

> "Diana of the open sky,
> Jewel of the darkest night
> reflected in the lives of women,
> Wrap us in Thy lustrous light.

Come to us here in Your cauldron,
Dance with us upon its rim.
Mistress of all Magick making,
of all spells we now begin,
Guide us in our rite's becoming,
Lead us as we go within.
Our hands have now Your Magick fingers,
Our hearts now beat with Yours as one,
Our souls are now entwined together
As the Magick now is done.
Speak with us and bless our working,
Help us as we come to see
The brightly shining light of wisdom
Here, within Your Mysteries."

Time is allotted in each ritual for the Goddess to speak (and act) through the Facilitating Priestess as She will. If the Facilitating Priestess guiding the ritual has the necessary training and skills/experience to channel the Goddess, the invocation may be changed slightly to serve as an invocation for drawing down the moon. Either one woman, or the entire group in unison, may draw down the Goddess on the Facilitating Priestess by reciting the invocation with the following changes. The Facilitating Priestess, holding the coven sickle or athame in her right hand and the altar chalice in her left, straddles the cauldron with her eyes closed and her arms raised to form the horned crescent. The woman who is reciting the invocation, or the woman chosen to crown the Goddess if all are reciting the invocation, picks up the lunar crescent from the altar and stands facing the Facilitating Priestess. She holds the lunar crescent above the head of the Facilitating Priestess (thereby encircling and hence empowering her crown chakra) as she (or all) recite(s) the invocation. When she reaches the changes in the wording of the invocation, she places the lunar crescent upon the head of the Facilitating Priestess, thereby triggering the manifestation of the Goddess within her. Change the third paragraph of the invocation to read:

"Her hands have now Your Magick fingers,
Her heart now beats with Yours as one,
Your souls are now entwined together
As the Magick now is done."

Finish as in the original.

The Facilitating Priestess/Goddess now speaks to Her women. She says what She wants, although it usually runs along the lines of explaining things related to Her Mysteries, and/or Her functions/ ways of being within both the historical and Otherworld contexts. Occasionally prophetic information is given.

A meaningful and often moving alternative to this method is to allow each woman in the Circle to approach the Goddess and to speak with her briefly, usually asking a question. The Goddess will answer/respond. Sometimes the answers are clear and simple. (Sometimes they are clearer than we'd like!) Occasionally, the answers will be challenging and perplexing, requiring further meditation on the answer given. Sometimes the answer will be another question. But always they will reveal, or point the way toward, truth.

Whichever method is chosen, when the channeling has ended, the Priestess/Goddess will close Her eyes and the personality of the Priestess will emerge again via the internal processes the uses. When she is fully herself again, she will remove the lunar crescent, open her eyes and return the crown to the altar. Although no longer fully at one with the Her Priestess, the Goddess is still present within the Circle and will inspire each woman during any Magickal workings that take place at this point in the ritual's format.

Magick is Performed

See specific rituals for the information on the Magick to be performed during the course of any given ritual. Once the Magick has been performed, move on to the Ceremony of Milk, Honey and Grain — also known as the Thanksgiving and Return.

Ceremony of Milk, Honey and Grain

This ceremony is not just the beginning of the shared feasting included in each ritual. Shared feasting is an excellent method of "grounding" ourselves, or coming back to normal consciousness, after the expanding experience of channeling deity and/or power through ourselves, and is an important part of community building — or group bonding — within a coven. However, the Ceremony of Milk, Honey and Grain (Thanksgiving and Return) is a ceremony unto itself, in which we invite the Goddess more fully into our lives through the food that we eat. We thank Her for providing it and all the other good things that have come into our lives since last the ceremony was enacted, and it is a way of giving back to Her a portion of the bounty She has shared with us. The foods used in the ceremony are highly symbolic, and the words are expressive of the ceremony's intent.

To perform the ceremony you will need the chalice, or goblet, from the altar, filled with milk. Under the altar should be a small dish of honey and a honey drizzler, a loaf of whole grain bread (preferably round), and an earthenware or silver platter on which to set these things. You will also need a bowl in which to offer portions of the ceremonial and feasting foods which are called libations.

There are two reasons for using milk. On a practical level, it allows those recovering from alcoholism, or those not wishing to indulge in alcohol, to participate fully in the ceremony. Milk is also symbolic of the all-nurturing Primal Mother who feeds us willingly, unendingly and without depletion from Herself.

Honey is used for several reasons. First, it is a product of a matriarchal society — a beehive. Second, it is a preservative and as such symbolizes the preservation of the ways of women Witches. Third, it is a healthful restorative and, thus, symbolizes our hope for a healthful and respectful restoration of the sacred ways of the Goddess and of women to the world at large.

Grain, or bread, is chosen because it was the gift of Demeter/Ceres to the world. It was once considered a prime representative of the sacred cycle of birth, growth, maturity, death, decay and rebirth in the Mysteries at Eleusis. It is a reminder of the same in this Ceremony. The loaf is round, to represent both the shape of the Full Moon (at which time the ceremony is shared) and the cycle itself, often called the great round of life and death. The platter is earthenware, in honor of the Earth Mother from whom these gifts spring, or silver for the Moon Goddess, who's rites we are celebrating when the ceremony is enacted.

To celebrate the ceremony the Facilitating Priestess assembles the "ingredients" on the platter and holds them out for all to see. As she presents them, she says:

"Sweet Melissa of the bees,Ceres of the grain,
Rhea, Primal Mother whose milk flows down like
 rain,
Quench our thirst for knowledge of Thee" (*points at
 the milk*),
"Fill us with Thy essence" (*points at the bread*).
"And may our sweet and honeyed tongues give
 voice unto Your Wisdom" (*points at the honey*).

She then places the tray on the altar and puts the offering bowl next to it. She places a portion of each item into the bowl, offering the following words of thanksgiving as she speaks:

Great living and Bountiful Mother of us all who gives willingly of Herself and all She possesses unto Her children here assembled, we thank You for all we have received and for the spirit in which it was given; and return unto You this small portion of Your goodness in token of our wish to honor You and appreciate Your gifts. May our giving to others be as willingly and as lovingly offered as that which we have received from You.

She then places the offering bowl in the cauldron. She takes a sip from the chalice and passes it to the woman on her left, who sips and passes it on. When the chalice returns to the Facilitating Priestess, she drains it and returns it to the altar. The bread and honey are likewise passed around the Circle. When the bread and honey return to the Facilitating Priestess, she places them on the floor before her. She then invites all to sit, if they have not done so already, and pulls out from under the altar all food and drink to be consumed during the feasting, which now begins.

Feasting

Each person begins by placing (or pouring) a portion of what she will be eating or drinking into the offering bowl before she eats/ drinks it. This is her own private offering of thanks to the Goddess. Although shared feasting is a time for grounding out and community building, it still occurs within the context of a ritual and within sacred space. It is not a time for inappropriate joking, gossiping or the discussion of daily drudgery. It is a time for sharing any visions, words or feelings received during the ritual and for discussing ritual, if it has not already been made clear, or for adding additional insights into that symbolism. Conversations about Magick, how it works and why, psychic development, and ritual techniques are also appropriate at this time. Discussion of the next ritual to be undertaken and what will be necessary to bring and/or prepare for it would also be good at this time. This is especially true if the group won't be meeting again until the next ritual.

Closing the Circle

After everyone has finished eating and conversations have wound down, it's time to close the Circle for the evening. Any leftover food and all eating paraphernalia is placed under the altar, as is the offering bowl. After the ritual, the offering bowl will be emptied at the base of a tree to feed the spirits and the animals.

The Facilitating Priestess asks all to stand and join her in thanking Goddess for Her presence at the ritual and within the lives of all the women present. She can say what she wants in closing, or she may recite the Words of Thanksgiving:

> "Diana's daughters — wise Witches and women —
> let us thank the Great Goddess for blessing our
> lives and our Circle with Her luminous presence."

Observe a few moments of silence so that each woman may thank the Goddess in her own way, within her own heart. The Priestess now recites The Affirmation:

> "We came to share what we all know,
> We've worked our Magick will,
> We've dared to bring the Goddess forth,
> but keep our silence still."

Dismissing the Quarters

The Facilitating Priestess, or someone previously chosen, now picks up the coven athame or sickle from the altar (and all participants pick up their own athames, if your group has decided to participate in the ritual actions of invoking and dismissing the Quarters). She now moves to the East to begin dismissing the

Quarters. While making the East-banishing pentacle she recites the "Dismissal of Air," or one of her own choosing, in keeping with her coven's chosen symbols:

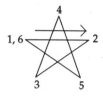

"Great eagle of the Eastern gate,
return from whence you came.
We thank you for your gifts and aid
in service to our aims.
Within your sacred realm remain
until we call you forth again."

Moving to the South the, Priestess, or the chosen woman, draws a South-banishing pentacle in the air with her athame while reciting the dismissal of Fire:

"Great lion at the Southern gate,
return from whence you came.
We thank you for your gifts and aid
in service to our aims.
Within your sacred realm remain
until we call you forth again."

She, or the woman so chosen, moves now to the West and, drawing a West-banishing pentacle recites the dismissal of Water:

"Great serpent at the Western gate,
return from whence you came.
We thank you for your gifts and aid
in service to our aims.
Within your sacred realm remain
until we call you forth again."

The Priestess, or chosen woman, now goes to the North and, drawing a North-banishing pentacle recites the dismissal of Earth:

"Great horned bull at the Northern gate,
return from whence you came.
We thank you for your gifts and aid
in service to our aims.
Within your sacred realm remain
until we call you forth again."

141

The Facilitating Priestess, or the last woman to speak, moves to the East and finishes the circuit by drawing another East-banishing pentacle and saluting the Goddess with her athame. If the dismissal of the Quarters was done by the Facilitating Priestess, she replaces the coven athame or sickle upon the altar. She then gives the traditional Words of Parting:

> "The Circle is open but never broken,
> Merry meet, and merry part, and merry meet again.
> The rite is ended."

Hugs and kisses are usually exchanged around the circle, if the group is comfortable doing so.

CHAPTER SEVEN

The Rituals

The instructions I have given in the following rituals are what I consider important for the optimal experience of the Mysteries. By doing these rituals as they are written, you will be shown one approach to the Mysteries of Dianic Wicca. It is not the only approach. Perhaps, after you have tried these rituals for one or more ritual cycles (one or more years), you will want to experiment with changing all or part of them. You are welcome to. However, my preference would be that you not attempt to change them much until you feel you understand their meanings, both intuitively/ internally and intellectually. *These rituals are meant to take you to — or point you in the direction of — deeper and deeper levels of experience in the Mysteries with each repetition of the entire ritual cycle.* Each time you experience and interact with the shared symbols, deities and beings found in each ritual and throughout the cycle of rituals, they will reveal a little bit more to you about themselves, the cycle, and/ or its/their meaning(s) for both your inner and outer life.

Each item in the rituals is chosen for a specific purpose. From the color of the candles to the items you are asked to bring to each ritual, there is a Magickal significance connected with the season, and/or with the intent of the ritual. Nothing present in the Circle space, and nothing that is said or done within the context of the ritual, is there (or is done) without a reason. Everything has a purpose.

If you know those purposes, but believe other items would represent the intent better (or, at least would not change the intent), or if you feel you no longer need these items in order to fully experience the rituals, then you can, of course, make substitutions within the rituals or you can do away with various items altogether. Not everyone is triggered to experience the Mysteries in the same way, and some people need few, if any, triggers to begin or to enhance that experience. All I am asking here is that you grasp the underlying principles of why I've chosen what I've chosen, so that you can make appropriate substitutions and/or deletions for your-self and your group and can still have an optimal experience of the Mysteries.

This is not to say that these rituals cannot be adjusted to fit the needs of the differently abled or the physically challenged. The physical comfort of the participants is most important to a good ritual experience. You cannot meditate well if your back hurts, or if you are cold. You cannot do a Breath of Fire if the smoke from the censer has triggered an asthma attack. You cannot raise a lot of power through dance if it makes your knees hurt, or if you are a paraplegic. The physical needs and comfort of your coveners will have to be considered in planning your rituals. I have not included contingency plans to cover every possibility. I trust that your own intuition and good judgement will provide you with the inspira-tion necessary to adjust these rituals to fit the needs of your particular coven, and yet to remain in keeping with the intent of the ritual/Magickal action in the ritual.

Each ritual attempts to produce a specific effect, or to trigger a particular experience of the Mysteries. If a particular speech, or series of speeches, does not work for you and your group — either because it fails to produce the desired effect, or because you have thealogical arguments with the intent — you are welcome to change it. In fact, I invite the speaker to use her own words fairly frequently throughout the rituals. Of course, should the Facilitat-ing Priestess be channeling the Goddess, the Goddess will speak as She will, and no scripted parts will be necessary.

You will also notice that I do not give step-by-step instructions for every facet of every ritual. Where scripts are not given, you are encouraged to come up with those portions of the rituals yourselves. If you like, however, you can fall back on the scripted parts in the chapter on ritual construction.

Again, in the interest of brevity and clarity, I assigned most of the ritual actions and speaking parts to the Facilitating Priestess. They need not remain so. For example, once the Circle is cast, any two other women can consecrate it by Water and Earth, and Air and Fire respectively. Four different women can invoke and dismiss the Quarters. Another may invoke the Goddess and then thank Her for Her presence and aid at the end of the ritual. The job of the Facilitating Priestess (sometimes referred to as Priestess) is to draw the Circle, to oversee the continuity, content and pacing of the entire ritual and its energy, from the beginning of the ritual baths to the closing of the Circle, to channel Goddess if the ritual calls for it, and to guide any Magickal workings or meditations/visualizations involved in the ritual. It is she who declares the Circle open at the end of the ritual.

Regarding the chants specified in these rituals: Sometimes you are asked to sing a free-form chant on aum, or any other open vowel sound. This means you are to sing/chant any notes you like. No attempt is to be made to harmonize with each other, or to sing the same notes. Let the chant happen (and end) as it will. At other times you are asked to chant something, although music is not provided. In these cases, you can either speak the words rhythmically, or you can create your own melodies. Feel free to add harmonies to the melodies you create.

The cauldron is the great symbol of Dianic Wicca. Its presence within the Circle and its use is specified in each ritual. In these rituals it has four different names to represent four different functions, each of which can be assigned to one of the four elements. When identified as the Cauldron of Rebirth (East), the cauldron in the Circle is to contain water, indicative of the amniotic fluid of the womb. When it becomes the Cauldron of Transformation (South), it is to contain fire. When it is called the Cauldron of Inspiration (West), it again contains water. When it is named the Cauldron of Plenty (North), it sometimes contains food, it sometimes contains gifts. Whether it is referred to specifically by one of these names, or whether it is referred to generically as "the cauldron," it has the greatest potential for revealing the Mysteries to the women participating in these rituals. Constant exposure to the cauldron and its meanings will help lead all who interact with it to deeper and richer meanings of the cycle and the totality of the Goddess within the individual, and within all of Nature and the universe.

All spells used in this book were written with the Rede in mind, and each spell is assumed to be worked for the good of all and in accordance with free will. If you decide to interpret and apply the spells herein in a different manner, then the responsibility for that decision will be on *your* shoulders.

I have started the ritual section with the October Full Moon. It is preparatory work for the Samhain Ritual. Since Samhain is the

Witch's New Year, it seemed appropriate to begin the ritual section with the new year. The celebration of the Witch's New Year comes to us from Celtic traditions of Paganism. They believed that all beginnings occurred in darkness, and that each new day began at sundown on the previous night. Samhain signifies the beginning of the dark half of the year, hence the New Year. Aradia's return to the Goddess at Samhain — the removal of the light and activity to the Otherworld — clears the way for the new beginnings that the Witch's New Year brings. It begins in dreams, where new ideas and new beginnings first take root and begin to grow. They germinate within and are born into the world with Aradia each Spring. And now, the rituals . . .

October Full Moon

The leaves are falling from the trees, returning to the Earth in colorful death. The salmon are running upstream to their spawning grounds where they will lay their eggs before dying. Squirrels are gathering nuts, and building nests in the tree tops to protect them from the deep snows of the oncoming Winter. The crisp, chill winds begin blowing from the North and Ursa, the great Shebear, prepares Her Winter den for hibernation.

So, too, Aradia prepares to leave us for a time. She pulls Her cloak of many colours around Her to keep Her from the cold. Her Summer's work is done. The herds have increased, the gardens have been brought to fruition, and Her women have grown in strength, power and peace. We, too, reflect on the past season and prepare ourselves to accompany Her, at Samhain, on Her journey through the darkness to the gates of the Summerland behind the north wind. How will *you* prepare?

For this ritual you will need a rust and gold (or rust and gray) cloth upon the altar, gold or orange altar candles, your usual altar accoutrements and the Cauldron of Inspiration filled with water in the center of the Circle. Since the work of this ritual will be a guided meditation/visualization, it is important that everyone be as comfortable as possible. Wear loose and comfortable clothing, if any at all. Be sure you cast a big Circle. Some may need to sit in a chair or lay down in order to be comfortable during the meditation/

visualization. If you are one of those, be sure you have a chair, pillow, and/or blanket in the Circle with you.

Burn sandalwood incense in the ritual bath area. Light gold or orange candles as well. During the ritual bath, concentrate on opening the psychic centers. Meditate on preparing for a Magickal journey in your mind. The Priestess will hand you a psychic tea after your bath. Sit down quietly and continue your relaxation, psychic opening and trance induction process.

When the Facilitating Priestess is ready, she lights the altar candles and all join the circle. The Circle is cast and the Facilitating Priestess anoints each with oil to deepen their trance and open their psychic centers. To do this, she wets her finger with oil and places it on the third eye of the anointee. She then makes a spiral beginning at that point and circling outward three times. This symbolically opens the third eye and triggers (or furthers) its opening within the anointee. As the Priestess does this, she deepens the anointee's trance by saying something like:

> "The spiral unwinds,
> down, deeper down,
> into the recesses of your deep mind.
> Here deep within,
> when you are told,
> will your life-giving symbols
> before you unfold."

After all have been so entranced, the Quarters are called and the Goddess is invoked using the material in the basic ritual outline, or in words chosen by the Facilitating Priestess.

She then leads a guided visualization around preparing for a spiritual/physical journey to the realms of the Goddess of Death, Rebirth and Transformation, which will take place during the Samhain ritual. Within the visualization the participants will find two objects that are especially symbolic to them. They will take these objects with them on their Samhain journey. One they will leave at the gates of Summerland, one will return to the land of the living with them. The Facilitating Priestess should not suggest what those objects might be. She should allow about five minutes of silence for them to find their objects. She then brings them back to consciousness and tells them to find, or to make, those objects and bring them to the Samhain ritual.

To induce the meditation/visualization, she invites all to get comfortable. She then passes the Cauldron of Inspiration around the Circle and asks each person to look deeply into it for a brief time as a way of still further deepening her trance. When each has finished with the cauldron, she hands it to the woman on her left and settles herself in her meditative posture. She closes her eyes and takes herself to her deepest regions of trance as she waits for the guided meditation/visualization to begin.

When the Cauldron of Inspiration has completed its circuit and has reached the Facilitating Priestess, she uses it to calm herself and to help her become psychically aware of the trance state of each woman in the Circle, as well as her own. She settles herself and begins the guided meditation/visualization, using words of her own choosing. If she prefers, she may draw from the following, entering the experience herself as she speaks:

"Listen now to the sound of my voice. You hear it clearly and easily. All other sounds around you fall away and are of no consequence. We are going to take a journey through a Magickal forest to a large, natural spring deep within it. You will see everything you are asked to see in your mind's eye, and you will succeed in doing everything you are asked to do.

"We begin now at your home on a beautiful, comfortably cool, Fall day. You look out your living room window, and the site of the clear blue sky and the colorful leaves on the trees draws you out of doors. You pick up your car keys and step outside, locking your door behind you.

"The air is crisp and clean, and the familiar smell of burning leaves reaches your nostrils. Your neighbors are tending their yards, but you have other things to do. Samhain approaches, and the Magick and Mystery of the season internally prompts you to seek out the wild places. You get in your car and drive to a forested area with which you are familiar. (*Pause.*)

"When you arrive, you get out of your car and approach the trail you usually follow through the woods. You are about to set foot on that trail when suddenly you hear a crow cawing nearby and to your left. You turn and look. As you look, the crow lands on a narrow, yet well-worn path just to the left of your usual trail. How strange. You've never noticed that path before. The crow caws again and flies off down the path. You follow her. (*Pause.*)

"The woods are lovely — silent and deep. The light filters beautifully through the multicolored canopy of leaves above your head. (*Pause five heartbeats.*) The only sound you hear is the crunching of fallen leaves beneath your feet as you walk. (*Pause five heartbeats.*) The dank smell of rotting undergrowth meets your nostrils. (*Pause five heartbeats.*) The crow is nowhere to be seen.

"You pause now, suddenly feeling very alone. You psychically open yourself to impression. You look for an omen to guide you on. The path ahead seems more difficult. It's narrower and more overgrown with brush.

"Just now, a short distance up ahead of you, you hear the sound of downed twigs and branches snapping. You look up just in time to see a large doe leap from the woods onto the path in front of you. Seeing you, she flicks her tail and bounds off down the path. You follow at once, but your pace is slowed by the underbrush. (*Pause.*)

"The path smooths out a little now and widens just a bit. It is much easier to walk. So you hurry along, hoping to catch another glimpse of the doe. But she's gone. You realize now it's pointless to hurry, and that you are missing a great deal of beauty around you in your rush to keep up. You slow your pace and notice the Fall flowers on the forest floor at your feet. (*Pause five heartbeats.*) You notice as well a growing number of ferns along the path. (*Pause five heartbeats.*)

"Now, as you keep walking, you begin to hear the babbling of a brook. The sound grows louder as you approach it. (*Pause five heartbeats.*) You see now, directly ahead of you, a small, wooden bridge over the brook. Before stepping on to it, you bend down and pick up a few fallen leaves. (*Pause five heartbeats.*)

"You step onto the bridge now. It sounds hollow beneath your step. You stop in the middle, and lean on the bridge railing to watch the water run its course below. (*Pause five heartbeats.*) The sound and the movement of the water relax you and put you in a mild trance state. The leaves become any worries you've brought with you to the woods, and any worries you have about your present journey. One by one, you drop these worries into the water with the leaves and watch them flow away. (*Pause.*)

"You notice now that the path follows the stream bank, and you follow it now to the stream's source. The walking is easy, and the sunlight warms your body and soul. You are relaxed, happy and in tune with the water and these words.

"Up ahead you see a horseshoe-shaped grove where the path terminates at a round pool of water surrounded by a low, grassy bank. As you arrive you are quite taken with the loveliness of the spot, and sit down on the bank to gaze into the water. (*Pause five heartbeats.*) As you look in the water, you see tiny bubbles of air rising up through the water from the pool's shallow bottom. You realize this is a natural spring — the source of the stream.

"Continue gazing at the water now. Soon you will see two objects or symbols appear on the surface of the water, or bubbling up from its shallow depths. When you see them, you will immediately know what they are and what they represent. It is important that you remember them, for you will need them in our Samhain ritual. One will be left in Summerland. The other will be your passport back to the land of the living. Look for them now. (*Pause about five minutes.*)

"It's now time to make your journey home. Remember your symbols. Plant them firmly in your mind. Arise now and follow the path back through the woods. The path seems familiar now, as you follow the stream back to the bridge. (*Pause five heartbeats.*) As you cross the bridge, you see the doe drinking from the stream. She bounds off down the path when she sees you, and you follow at a lighthearted pace. (*Pause five heartbeats.*)

"Though the path is still overgrown in places, you have no trouble making your way along. The ferns and the Fall flowers are behind you now. You move deep within the woods again, but make rapid progress toward the wood's edge. (*Pause five heartbeats.*) The crow caws a short distance down the path, and you know you will soon reach your car. (*Pause five heartbeats.*)

"As you step out of the woods and into your car, you notice that the sun soon will be setting. You have just enough time to return home before dark.

"As you drive home you become more and more aware of the goings on around you. The Magick, the Mystery, and the trance-like quality of your walk in the woods are fading into memory as your waking consciousness begins to assert itself. (*Pause five heartbeats.*)

"As you arrive home and get out of the car, the street lights are just coming up, and your consciousness comes up with them. You know that when you step in your door and turn on the lights, you will be fully awake and conscious. Open the door. Turn on the lights. You're home! Eyes open. Wide awake."

Clap sharply twice to fully bring back any laggards.

The Ceremony of Milk, Honey and Grain follows. Appropriate foods for the feast might include salmon and apple juice, or cider. During the feasting remind the participants to find, or to make, their two objects/symbols and to bring them to the Samhain ritual. Ask them not to discuss their visions of objects with others. When all are ready, thank the Goddess, dismiss the Quarters and declare the Circle open.

The rite is ended.

Samhain Ritual

Wear black clothing for this ritual. The red cords will be necessary, as well. The participants will also need to bring their two objects for the journey. A cauldron of water is in the center of the Circle. Alongside it are an unlit taper, matches and a ladle. An unlit candle lantern should also be present. Carved pumpkins are at the Quarters, and there are vines on the altar. Frankincense and myrrh should be on hand for burning in the censer. A chalice, or goblet, of red fluid (e.g., cranberry or raspberry juice, cherry Kool-Aid) is placed at the North point of the Circle.

The Facilitating Priestess can dress as Aradia in a cloak/robe of many colors, or Aradia can be envisioned as leading the way to the Summerland, followed by the Facilitating Priestess and all the coveners. If the Facilitating Priestess dresses as/becomes Aradia, she should be wearing black clothing under the cloak, or robe, of many colors. Under the altar should be two black veils made of a sheer material, the Lunar Crescent, and a bell.

Someone assembles the women in a room other than the ritual room. Lights are extinguished. She asks them to sit or stand quietly and to prepare for their journey through darkness to the Summerland, where they will meet with those who have gone before, where they will see into their future, and where they will meet the Dark Goddess. All wait in silent meditation for the Facilitating Priestess/Aradia to lead them "home." Each holds the two objects made for this ritual.

The Facilitating Priestess/Aradia casts the Circle, leaves a gate in the northwest and calls the Quarters. She then lights the candle lantern and leaves the Circle through the gate she has created in the northwest by cutting a doorway in the Circle with her athame. All lights in the house are extinguished except the altar candles and the Quarter candles within the carved pumpkins.

The Facilitating Priestess/Aradia goes to the room where all the women are gathered, and beckons them to follow her, saying nothing. If all have their eyes closed and do not see her, she says only "Come" and beckons to them. Should Aradia wish to speak through the Facilitating Priestess at this point, She will. If not, silence remains.

The women, still holding their objects, follow the Facilitating Priestess/Aradia, who leads them on a widdershins (counterclockwise) journey — the way of death — through the darkened house to the edge of the Circle before the northwest gate. She stops, picks up the chalice of red liquid and addresses the group:

Before you enter the realm of death you must be marked in the sign of life so that ye may return to the land of the living this night.

She marks each on the forehead with a deosil spiral beginning at the center and spiraling outward. As each woman is marked, she passes through the gate and into Summerland/the Circle.

When all are within the Circle, the Facilitating Priestess/Aradia closes the northwest gate by tracing the arc of the Circle that she had previously cut open with her athame. This reseals the Circle. Still standing in the northwest, She turns to face the group and says:

> "Spirits of the Mighty Ones, blessed immortals,
> women and Witches who have gone before and
> who rest here still, we come in peace and friendship
> to honor you and to commune with you. We ask of
> you a greeting."

She waits for a sign. This may be the flicker of a candle, a noise in the room, or something that indicates to Her that the group's petition has been accepted. If no sign is forthcoming, skip to the Divination Section. If a sign has presented itself, proceed as follows:

All are seated within the Circle. The Facilitating Priestess/Aradia lights the taper beside the cauldron and says,

> "Let us speak with the blessed and the dead."

The candle is passed around the Circle. As each woman receives the candle she speaks aloud (or within herself) a greeting, a blessing or expresses her inner feelings to a dead ancestor, friend or the blessed immortals—Goddesses or Witches who have passed over permanently. When she is finished, she passes the candle to the next woman. When the candle returns to the Facilitating Priestess/ Aradia, she addresses the Dark Goddess, saying:

> "Darksome Shining One, whose name is the mystery of mysteries, and through whom we experience both death and life; oh ineffable three-in-one who sits at the hub of the universe and keeps the stars in their courses, bless these words spoken to our beloved departed. Rest them well in Your considerable care. And when we ourselves one day come to stand upon Thy mist shrouded Isle of Apples, grant us visions of our future lives so that we may wisely choose the next, just as we ask you now to bring us visions of the year ahead."

Divination Section

If the "conversations with the departed" was skipped because of the lack of an omen, the Facilitating Priestess/Aradia asks the Dark Goddess for guidance and visions, saying:

> "Dark Shining Mystery, Hidden One, behind Who's veil our future lies; allow us a glimpse of what is to come as we stir Thy Cauldron of Inspiration, and look into its shadowed depths."

The Facilitating Priestess/Aradia sets the cauldron in front of Her, dips the ladle in and begins to slowly stirr the water. She says:

> "Herein lies your future. It eddies and swirls and spirals outward to meet you as you stir the Cauldron of Inspiration at this, the turning of the year. Stir briefly, and peer within to see dimly what lies ahead for the coming year."

She passes it to the woman on the left, and so it continues around the Circle until each has taken a turn. Each remains in meditation on her future after she has passed the cauldron on. When the cauldron returns to the Facilitating Priestess/Aradia, She stirs it, glimpses Her future, and speaks of Her need to withdraw deeper into Summerland to rest and to be refreshed among the blessed immortals before Her return to Earth and Her women in the Spring.

If the Facilitating Priestess has been Aradia to this point, She rises and removes Her cloak/robe of many colors revealing the black clothing/robe beneath it as She speaks of Her need to rest. She places the cloak under the altar, removes all altar tools from the altar, puts a black veil on the altar, snuffs all altar candles except for the candle lantern with which She guided participants, and dons the other black veil and the Lunar crescent. As She does all of this, She speaks of leaving Her women in the care of the Dark One; the Queen of Mystery and the guide of all dreams and waking, the Mistress of Winter's slumber and death.

The Facilitating Priestess, now embodying the Dark Goddess, rings the bell three times, holds up the lit candle lantern, and says:

> "Behold the Mistress of Magick: the Whispering Guide through the dark night of this season and your soul.
>
> You stand in darkness at the hub of the year, the center of the spiral of life and death, the axis of the universe revolving in stillness, and await your return to the land of the living. The price of your passage you hold in your hand. Leave one on My altar as you begin your spiral of return."

All rise and pass before the altar, placing the object chosen to be left in the Summerland upon the altar. The women, still holding their other object, now link themselves to each other by their red cords. The Facilitating Priestess/Goddess, using the candle lantern to cut a gate in the Circle, leads the women deosil (clockwise) — the way of life — through the darkened house to the room from which they began. Leaving them there to contemplate their experience, she returns to the Circle, reseals it, takes off her veil and crown, dismisses the Quarters and opens the Circle, using only the candle lantern as a tool. She gathers the gifts from the altar, puts them in a basket, and places them under the altar to be buried at the foot of an evergreen tree later that night. She then returns to the room full of waiting women, turns on the light, and says:

"The Goddess lives, as do we. The Wheel has turned another notch and a new year begins. The rite has ended."

Alternate Ending

If the Facilitating Priestess has not embodied/channeled Aradia, she bids farewell to Aradia and welcomes the Queen of Mystery, saying:

"Rest ye well, Aradia, in the land of shimmering sunlight and warmth. Walk with our dear ones in the shade of the apple trees, and share the sweetness of honeycombs and heather wine with them. Then, at Winter's end, return to us in all your radiant glory."

The Facilitating Priestess pulls a thin black veil out from under the altar. She removes all objects from the altar, and drapes the black veil across it in a diamond shaped pattern. All lights are extinguished. She invokes the Queen of Mystery in the darkness:

"Oh jewel of the night sky by Who's light we dimly see the pattern of our lives, we stand in darkness at the hub of the year, the center of the spiral of life and death, the axis of the universe revolving in stillness, and await our return to the land of the living. The price of our passage — our gifts to the dead — we hold in our hands and would give to You, if You would but show us the way."

The candle lantern is lit, and the Facilitating Priestess holds it above the altar. She directs the women to begin to spiral clockwise out of the room. As each passes the altar, she leaves the object to be left behind on it, and grabs the tether end of the red cord of the woman behind her. They file out of the Circle and return to the room where they started. The lights are turned on and all say,

"We live."

The Facilitating Priestess, who has remained in the Circle, using only the lantern from the altar, dismisses the Quarters and opens

156

the Circle. All altar tools are left under the altar. She removes the gifts from the altar, and buries them outside at the foot of an evergreen. She goes to the room (now lit) where all are waiting, and says,

> "The Goddess lives, as do we. The Wheel has turned another notch and a new year begins. The rite is ended."

The women are asked not to speak to each other of their visions. A meal is shared of pork, apples, cider, pumpkin dishes and nuts. The meal is to include a Dumb Supper, in which a place is set for the dead at the head of the table. A plate of food and a goblet of drink are filled for them and they are invited to join the feasting. Soul cakes are shared at the end of the meal .

The Ritual of Thanksgiving and Return is not done in this ritual because the ritual takes place in the Summerland. It is believed that one may not return to the land of the living if food has been eaten in the Summerland.

The other symbolic object that went on this journey to the Summerland and has returned from it now becomes a power object for its owner. It has gone beyond death and has returned, like its owner. It will now serve as a constant reminder of the ability to survive death and return to life again. It also represents the owner's ability to go in and out of Otherworld realities successfully . She may wish to keep it with her any time such a journey is attempted.

November Full Moon

The altar is set with only the black veil and a single dark candle wreathed with the crescent crown. The veil reminds us that we are in the presence of the Dark Goddess of Mystery. The candle reminds us that She dimly shows us only a part of Herself. The rest is veiled in Mystery and Magick. The cauldron sits in the center of the Circle. Alongside it are slips of paper and pens. Each woman brings her dream diary with her.

When all who are participating in the ritual have arrived, prepare the self-blessing/ritual bath. As they come out of the bath, give each a cup of psychic tea to help relax her and to help her open her psychic centers. Ask each to sit down with her tea and dream diary, and to find a dream symbol she is having trouble interpreting while she is drinking her tea.

When all have finished their tea and found their symbol, the Facilitating Priestess lights the Dark Goddess Candle on the altar, thereby calling the women to the Circle. Since all altar tools are unavailable, an alternate Circle casting must be used. (The tools were harvested — removed from the altar — by the Dark at Samhain. They rest in the Otherworld, and will return to the Circle at Yule.) Either join hands or link to each other via the red cord. Walk around the Circle three times while reciting the Circle Casting Spell in unison. Walk a little faster and speak a little more emphatically with each revolution. Finish with a "So mote it be".

If someone in your group is unable to move in this fashion, or is uncomfortable with movement, simply have everyone sit, join hands or link to each other with the red cord, and visualize a blue light forming around the Circle while reciting the Circle Casting Spell in unison. Or, instead of reciting the Circle Casting Spell, chant it into being while visualizing the same blue light getting stronger, brighter and thicker as the chant continues.

Have the woman closest to each of the Quarters invoke it. If your group is not yet comfortable with spontaneous/channeled ritual (or parts of ritual), choose four women to invoke the Quarters ahead of time, so that each may prepare something to say. Or, if even that seems too difficult, simply use the invocations provided in the basic ritual in chapter 6.

It is sometimes helpful if each of the women chosen to invoke a Quarter has an affinity with the element she will be invoking. For example, the most scholarly/intellectual woman would be well suited to invoke Air. The most passionate political activist would do well invoking Fire. The woman who is the most intuitive or psychic could handle the invocation of Water. And, the most avid gardener or plant person could invoke Earth.

Once the Quarters are called, the Facilitating Priestess for the ritual will invoke the Goddess, calling upon the Dark Goddess to guide the work they are about to do on their dreaming. The Priestess invokes as she will, or she can say:

> "Darksome Queen whose name is spoken only in
> whispers, Wise One in whose presence the secrets
> of our souls become revealed, be with us this night

as we plumb the depths of our subconscious un-
knowing. Make clear our dreaming and bring us
through insight to action."

The Facilitating Priestess then asks each woman to take a slip of
paper and a pen and to draw her dream symbol, or write a brief
phrase describing it, on the paper and then drop it in the cauldron.
When all have finished, she passes the cauldron and the Goddess
Candle from the altar to the woman sitting at the West Quarter.

This process starts in the West because it is the direction associated with dreaming, the subconscious/unconscious, and the psychic realm in general. The Goddess Candle is used not only to
provide light, but to remind each woman that the Goddess is
guiding her interpretation, and is illuminating her mind as well as
the slip of paper.

The woman in the West draws a slip of paper and holds it up in
the candlelight. The woman whose symbol it is identifies it, and
gives a synopsis of the dream in which the symbol occurred.
Although the woman holding the symbol and the candle has
primary responsibility for interpreting the symbol, that does not
necessarily mean that she works alone. She is free to ask for input
from the rest of the group and can facilitate any ensuing discussion,
as well as offering her own insights. Getting further clarification
from the dreamer and checking her reactions to possible interpretations will help, as will a final summation before the primary
interpreter passes the candle and cauldron on to the person on her
left.

Continue around the Circle until each symbol has been addressed and each woman has served as interpreter. The cauldron
is then returned to the center of the Circle and the Goddess Candle
is replaced within the crescent crown on the altar. If anyone has any
Magick to do, now is the time. If not, proceed with the Ritual of
Milk, Honey and Grain as given in the basic ritual, or by using
words of your own choosing. All participants settle to feasting, and
share any discussion appropriate to the Circle.

When everyone is ready, the Facilitating Priestess thanks the
Dark Goddess for Her presence and aid with words she feels
appropriate. The women who invoked the Quarters now dismiss
them, and the Priestess declares the Circle open.

The rite is ended.

December Full Moon

If the Full Moon is prior to the Winter Solstice, there are several activities that are appropriate at this time. If the coven meets at the same place for each ritual, the group could go and select a Yule tree for the covenstead. Or, if no covenstead exists, each woman could — with the help of her coven sisters — choose her own Yule tree.

Whichever it is, be sure to encircle the tree, explain why you wish to take it and get its permission. Once the tree has been cut down, be sure to leave an offering to the tree's spirit and to the Goddess as a "thank you" gift. A gift from the plant kingdom would be most appropriate — a flower perhaps, or herbs.

Should you wish not to sacrifice a tree in this manner (or even if you do), the day could also be spent in making religio/magickal decorations for a living tree nearby (or for the cut tree). Since this Full Moon anticipates the Goddess's announced pregnancy at the Winter Solstice, and its subsequent assurance of the return of light and Aradia to the world, the decorations should symbolize the Goddess, pregnancy and birthing, and light. Do not hang them on the tree(s), however. Save that for the Solstice itself. Instead, have each woman bring her decorations to the Circle for blessing during the Full Moon ritual.

You will also need to make a wreath that will encircle the Cauldron of Rebirth. Work four candle holders into the wreath to represent the four Quarters, and have on hand a taper for each in the appropriate color: yellow/East; red/South; blue/West; green/North. A white votive candle will sit in the center of the Cauldron of Rebirth.

Remember, you still do not have altar tools (they were removed at Samhain), and the altar is still draped in black. The only ornament on the altar remains the Dark Goddess candle surrounded by the lunar crescent crown. Mark the Quarters with your Quarter candles, but do not light them.

Again, because you do not have your altar tools, an alternate method of Circle casting must be employed. Use one of those previously mentioned, or create one of your own. For this ritual, the Quarters will be called and the Goddess will be invoked simultaneously.

All sit on the floor (or on chairs) around the Cauldron of Rebirth. The Facilitating Priestess, addressing the Goddess, says:

"Dark Shining One, Magna Mater, within Whose
womb lies our hope and all possibility, deliver us
from darkness into light. Grow great with child
and bring to us the child of promise. Re-birth the
world."

The Facilitating Priestess, or she who will light the North candle on
the wreath, says:

"From the mountains craggy peaks take rocks to
form Her frame. From the subsoil of the plain take
clay to flesh it full. *"(Lights North candle.)*

The Facilitating Priestess, or she who will light the Eastern candle,
says:

"From the four winds gather the wisps of a perfect
mind. *"(Lights East candle.)*

The Facilitating Priestess, or the lighter of the South candle, says:

"From the volcano's fiery depths pump blood into
Her veins." *(Lights West candle.)*

The Facilitating Priestess, or she who will illumine the West, says:

"From the ocean's vast expanse draw the waters
for Your womb and rock Her gently, safe within
You. *"(Lights West candle.)*

The Facilitating Priestess says:

"Impart to Her a spark from Thy Spirit and, at Her
birthing, breathe life into Her lungs. *"(Lights Spirit
candle within the Cauldron of Rebirth.)*

All say in unison:

"Return to us Thy darling daughter;
Return to us the light.
Return to us the green and growing
and end this lifeless night."

Repeat this three times, getting faster and louder each time. End
with the Breath of Fire. (Symbolic, in this case, of breathing life into
Aradia — an act of sympathetic Magick.)

161

Once this is completed, proceed with the blessing of the ornaments. Have each woman hold the ornaments she has made against her womb and speak a blessing upon them using words of her own choosing. When she is done, she should put them in or near the Cauldron of Rebirth.

After each woman has spoken her blessing, the Facilitating Priestess shall speak a spell over them while stirring the contents of the Cauldron of Rebirth (and any surrounding it) with her hands. As she stirs she says:

> "The spark of spirit here within
> will make the Magick now begin.
> By Your hands which stir this brew,
> bring to us the babe anew.
> Each ornament hung on the tree
> unlocks the spell we send to Thee."

The ceremony of Milk, Honey and Grain is enacted. All settle in for feasting. At some point during the feasting whoever will be Facilitating Priestess for the Yule Sabbat instructs the coven about what to prepare before coming to the ritual, as well as what to bring to the ritual. The following information is included:

Before the Yule Sabbat the coveners will gather in the afternoon to decorate the Yule tree with the Magickally charged ornaments. The cauldron, filled with ornaments, will be placed under the tree for all to draw from. Also under the tree will be all the coven tools, each in a nicely wrapped box. (The Samhain Priestess will need to see to this.)

A coven gift exchange is also customary at the Yule Sabbat. If your coven decides to have one, I would recommend doing it in the following way: Each woman is asked to bring a festively wrapped gift from the heart. This would be something particularly significant or Magickal to the giver, small enough to fit in the palm of the hand, and something any among you would enjoy/appreciate. These are to be gifts from the Goddess, so the giver's name should not be included in the gift. A gift to the Goddess should be present as well. Therefore, the Facilitating Priestess for that ritual should prepare an extra gift to be included in the exchange.

The Priestess for the Yule ritual also tells everyone that a meal will be shared before the Circle, so everyone should bring a dish to pass as well as a special Yule goodie to be added to the communal plate of treats during the ritual. She invites all to come dressed in the colors of the season.

Once all of this information has been communicated, the Facilitating Priestess for the present ritual thanks the Goddess for Her presence, douses the wreath candles with a word of farewell to the Quarters and declares the Circle open.

The rite is ended.

YULE
(Winter Solstice)

Gather in the afternoon to decorate the tree and to make merry. Put on the lights on the tree, but do not light them. As you put the handmade Magickal ornaments on the tree, remember the spell spoken over them at the December Full Moon — see it and feel it being activated.

The festively wrapped boxes containing the tools are under the tree. Decorate the rest of the house with pine boughs, wreaths, holly and ivy, and red, green and white candles.

Enjoy your meal together using the candle wreathe from the December Full Moon as a centerpiece. Light the candles when sitting down to the meal, and remember what they represent. Set a place for the Goddess at your table, and serve Her a portion of everything served. At the end of the meal, the hostess will take the plate outside and offer the food to the Earth by burying it, or leaving it for the wild ones to eat. This plate then should be washed and used to hold the special Yule goodies everyone has brought to be shared during the ritual.

If the house has a fireplace, this is the time to light the Yule log. (This is usually a very large Oak log.) Build the fire and add the Yule log when the fire is blazing well. The lighting of the Yule log (or the alternate described below) is an unspoken sign that it is time to begin preparing the Self (and the Circle space) for the ritual.

If there is no fireplace, take a log about 12 inches long and 5 inches in diameter, and drill three holes in it, each large enough to hold the butt end of a 10-inch taper. These candles represent the three aspects of the Goddess and are traditionally white (Maiden), red (Mother), and black (Crone) (although pine green can be substituted for black if you prefer using the colors of the season). Place this log on a table around which all can gather. Light the candles.

One by one participants should leave the fire to take their ritual bath and then return to the fire, placing the gift they brought into the Cauldron of Plenty under the tree. Conversation at the fire, if any, should be subdued and should center around individual feelings about the season or, perhaps, a sharing of poetry and song about the meanings of Yule.

The ritual bath, in this case, should be a complete submergence in water. In this way, each person symbolically becomes the babe in the Goddess's womb. The bathroom should be dimly lit with red, white and pine green candles. Pine incense should be burning. Your thoughts while in the womb/tub are of course your own, but might center on the renewal of your spirit, your own growth in the Goddess and the cyclical nature of life, or the comfort of being surrounded by and nurtured by the Goddess.

When the last bath has been completed, the Facilitating Priestess invites all to gather comfortably and quietly around the tree. Each brings a new, unlit taper. The Facilitating Priestess stands ready to turn on the lights on the tree. The room is dark, except for the Yule fire. She says:

> "The fire that has burned within our hearts now burns within the womb of Summerland's Dark Queen. Our spells have been received and our prayers answered as She begins Her metamorphosis from Elder Crone to Great Mother. The Mother of Us All is again with child. She announces Her joyous gifts to us and light returns to the world!"

The Facilitating Priestess turns on the tree lights and pauses for a moment so all may admire the tree. She then lights her taper from the Yule fire and turns to the group, saying:

> "A point of light within Her night
> grows to a Child with future bright.
> Her body's formed 'til Imbolc night
> when first it stirs by candlelight.
> The spell's complete,

the womb unlocks
upon the night of Equinox.
Pass it on."

The Facilitating Priestess lights the candle of the woman to her immediate left, and asks the woman to speak of what she would like to nurture within herself until it flowers at the Spring Equinox. Or, she may speak of what it is like to be pregnant with a child (if she has had that experience), or of what it is like to wait expectantly for something, or of the importance of inward growth/development before its outward manifestation occurs. When this woman is through speaking, she lights the candle of the woman to her left, and says,

"Pass it on."

Continue around the group in this manner until all candles are lit and all wisdom has been shared. All now join in the following chant:

"We're each a link within Her chain,
from life to death to life again."

Begin with a whisper and build to a shout as you repeat the chant. (This symbolizes the growth process from inner-whisper — to outward manifestation — shout.) On the last repetition, raise your candles in the air on the last "life" as a way of affirming the truth of this statement and as a way of releasing its power into the world.

The candles are now put aside, and the Facilitating Priestess distributes the wrapped altar tools in whatever manner seems best. Each woman opens her gift. The Facilitating Priestess asks each to take home with her the tool she has received, to place it on her altar and to consider herself pregnant with it. This means that each woman should meditate on the tool's meaning and use, and should charge it daily to lend it power and life. She should care for it and feed it in whatever way seems best. Since the cauldron was not wrapped, the Yule Priestess will assume the responsibility for nurturing it. The coveners are asked to bring their charge with them to the January Full Moon.

Next, the women are told to prepare to receive their gift from the Goddess. All close their eyes and, in a meditative state, open themselves to the Goddess. The Yule Priestess takes the Cauldron of Plenty to each woman in turn who, with eyes closed, picks a gift out of the cauldron. The Priestess is the last to choose. Before opening the gifts, she reminds the coveners that these are gifts from the Goddess, and that the giver of the gift is not to identify herself to the recipient. Should anyone receive her own gift, it simply means that the Goddess meant for her to keep it.

The communal plate of Yule goodies is passed, with a thanks to the Goddess for Her bounty and Her presence in the lives of those present. Feasting and merriment continue into the night. The Facilitating Priestess buries the last gift in the Cauldron of Plenty — the gift for the Goddess — in the ground at the close of the evening's festivities.

The rite is ended.

January Full Moon

At some point prior to the ritual the Facilitating Priestess for this ritual calls each woman to remind her to bring her tool/child to the ritual. Each is asked to bring a crystal as well.

The altar is draped in white to symbolize the snows of Winter and the purity of new beginnings. Upon it are only the candle of the Dark Goddess, here representing the darkness of gestation as well as the Crone Goddess of Winter. It is wreathed by the crescent crown. An unlit white candle in a holder and matches are placed next to the cauldron. Ritual baths/self-blessings are taken as usual. After the bath each sits in quiet meditation upon her child/tool while awaiting the beginning of the ritual.

As the Dark Goddess candle is lit, all gather in a circle around the altar. Each has her tool and her crystal. Since the time of quickening does not come until Imbolc, the altar tools presented by the women are not yet used. Instead each tool is presented in the order of its use during the Circle casting and opening of the Circle. The tool is placed before the cauldron, and its use and purpose is described, as well as any insights about it the mother received during her time of gestation with it.

All then close their eyes and visualize the tool's role in setting up the Circle as its mother recites an appropriate portion of the Circle casting/opening for that tool. After the recitation, she picks up the tool and puts it in its accustomed place on the altar. The cauldron is done last. The white taper is lit and replaces the cauldron at the center of the Circle.

The tools will remain upon the altar as a group from now until the quickening (at Imbolc). They now represent the combined energies of the women in the group, thereby increasing the group's power and effectiveness. Thoughts of this nature should be on the minds of all present as the tools are placed upon the altar.

The women settle themselves comfortably in a sitting position with their crystals over their wombs. The Facilitating Priestess asks them to focus their attention on the candle's flame and to put themselves in an open and receptive state. She leads a guided meditation on fire and ice using her own words, or using what follows:

"We are in the depths of Winter and it seems the entire world is hushed and still — slumbering under a blanket of crystalline ice and snow. The songbirds are silent and nowhere to be found; the fox buries her nose in her tail for warmth and snuggles deeper in her den; the great shebear sleeps the long sleep of hibernation, nurturing her unborn young within her body; and the Snow Queen walks the Earth, leaving radiant crystals that reflect the light of the great solar fire where e'er She sets Her ice blue feet clad only in snowflakes. You hold just such a footprint in your hands now.

"Within this ice-like structure, formed in fire, you can see your future and its past reflected in its many facets. When you hold it up to the candle's flame, you see within it the molten fire that formed it, and are reminded of the flaming furnace that stirs at the Earth's core — a spark of which burns within you and warms you at this time of bone-chilling cold. You'll remember it when you see your warm breath crystalize in the air before you as you exhale in the cold of this Moonlit Winter's night. And it is this same internal fire that nurtures the yet unborn through this long, dark, night of Winter.

"It nurtures the cub in the belly of the bear and warms the seed in the ground. The mantle of snow you crunch under foot protects the seed and insulates it against the

167

icy fingers of the Snow Queen's wrath — the same fingers which etch lovely crystalline pictures on the windows of your bedrooms and dens.

"The light trapped within your crystal's facets foretells the light and warmth that are even now returning to the Earth, and which hold the promise of the brilliant colors of the living Earth as She clothes Herself in the coming Spring, Summer and Fall. But for now, we dwell in the land of ice and snow and slumber 'neath blankets of eider down and are pregnant with all possibility.

"Take a few moments now to meditate on the possibility of you — and the rest of Winter — and the fire and ice which leads to the coming quickening.

(Pause for at least five minutes to allow each time to meditate. Then continue:)

"When you are finished, please place your crystal near the candle — pointing toward yourself — thus helping to encourage the Sun's heat to return to the land and your life. When all have finished, we'll share the fruits of the past Fall's harvest and close the Circle."

As women complete their meditations, they place their crystals on the floor around the candle as directed, thereby creating a sunburst pattern on the floor.

Pass apples, cheese and cider. Pass the Goddess's plate so that each may return thanks to the Goddess for Her bounty. Appropriate discussions follow. The time, place and Facilitating Priestess are chosen for the Imbolc ritual. What to bring is reviewed. (Shoes comfortable for dancing and a candle.) The Goddess is thanked for Her presence in the Circle and in the lives of the women present. The Quarters are dismissed and the Circle is declared open.

The rite is ended.

IMBOLC

(The Quickening)

The promised one moves in the womb of the Goddess. The seed germinates in the ground. The back of Winter is broken. The time of activity begins unseen, as we move toward rebirth. Another name for this festival is Candlemas. Many Witches take a clue from this name and gather early in the day to make all the candles the coven will need for the next year. This will require candle molds, wicks, and wax in a variety of colors. None of this equipment is costly and will certainly save you money in the long run.

The ritual itself celebrates the quickening: the defeat of Winter, the growing light. This is also the lambing season, the first births of the new year. As such, Imbolc has traditionally been considered the ideal time for initiations. However, it is my opinion that initiations are better suited to the Spring Equinox because it celebrates the birth of Aradia, Maiden Goddess and Daughter of the Great Mother in the mythic cycle employed in this book. An initiation births a Witch and ritually signifies the birth of the Goddess within the individual Witch. Therefore, I feel it best to birth the new Witch on the day the Goddess Herself is reborn on Earth.

The Imbolc ritual begins with the ritual baths to cleanse away the unwanted in the Self. It would also be good to spend some time in the bath moving the arms and legs in imitation of Aradia moving within the womb of the Goddess. Imagine your young Goddess-Self moving within you as well. Meditate on what you want to quicken within your life.

After the bath, each woman waits quietly for the others to finish. She continues to think about what she wants to quicken in her life and about her own young Goddess within. The Facilitating Priestess serves each woman a cup of red raspberry leaf tea as she comes out of her bath, with the words:

"Nourish the Goddess-child within."

Red raspberry leaf tea has long been prescribed by wise woman herbalists for pregnant women. It nourishes both mother and child by providing needed calcium and toning the system in general, and thus would be a good choice here.

After all baths have been completed, the women assemble in the Circle as the altar candles are lit. The altar cloth is white, as are the altar candles, to symbolize the snows of Winter and the new beginnings the quickening symbolizes. Any flowers you choose to have on the altar should be white. All tools are present on the altar. The cauldron is in the center of the Circle. Each woman places her

candle near it. The cauldron contains water, and a spoon for stirring
it sits nearby.

Tonight the altar tools quicken as well, and are ready for use.
That is, they are ready to begin moving and acting as channels for
power. The Facilitating Priestess casts the Circle and consecrates
participants as usual. She then calls the Quarters, or calls upon
various women to help with these tasks. All participants direct
power to these tasks, even if they are not those chosen to speak and
perform the ritual movements/gestures. The Facilitating Priestess
invokes the Goddess with words of her own choosing. She then
goes on to say words to the effect of:

Tonight we celebrate the beginning of the end. Every ending is
a beginning and every beginning, life. The Snow Queen, at the
height of Her power, begins to give way as Spring takes root in the
ground. The lambs are born in the snow and root in their mother's
soft fleece in search of her warm, white milk. A girl child stirs
within the womb of She Who Waits and the light grows stronger.
May we quicken as well.

She then asks each woman to tell what her candle represents:
what the woman wishes to have quicken in her life. As each is
finished speaking, she lights her candle from one of the Goddess
candles, to symbolize her wish that the Goddess help her in this
quickening, and sets her candle near the cauldron. She then uses the
ladle to stir the waters of life in the cauldron, which represent the
amniotic fluid within the womb of the Goddess. This movement
within the waters is the release of her spell, the quickening she
desires.

When all have finished the Priestess says, "So mote it be!" Or, all
may finish with this chant, or a similar one of their own devising:

> "Fire burn and Cauldron churn
> to make the Wheel of Magick turn.
> By North and South,
> by East and West,
> grant us each what we request."

The Facilitating Priestess says:

> "From the personal and individual we turn our
> attention outward to our Mother, the Earth, and

ask Her to awaken from Her Winter's rest. We ask those who dwell upon the Earth to wake up as well."

All begin to move in a deosil direction by spinning on their own axis: two steps per revolution, followed by a stomp on the ground. The spinning body thus represents the ladle within the cauldron, stirring it to life and transformation, as well as the young Goddess stirring in the womb of the Great Mother. The stomp on the ground is to get the Earth's attention, thereby waking Her up from Her Winter's rest. As the women spin, they call out what they would like to see wake up. For example:

First half of spin: "The Great Bear,"
Second half of spin: "Within Her den,"
As you stomp: "Wake up!"

Continuing now with the same pattern:

"The sap within the trunk of the tree, wake up!" or,
"The corporate polluters who need to stop, wake up!"

If possible, speed up little by little as the dance continues. When all are going as fast as is reasonable and prudent (considering the lit candles on the floor), stop spinning but continue stomping, to a chorus of,

"Wake up!"

Once the power peaks, all drop to the floor and blow out the candles to release the power of the spell. Any excess energy within each woman is channeled into the Earth to aid in Her awakening. A final "So mote it be" from the Facilitating Priestess finishes it and indicates to the women it is time to move on to the sharing of Milk, Honey and Grain.

After the ceremonial sharing, all settle to feasting and sharing appropriate conversation. When this seems done, all arise. The Facilitating Priestess thanks the Goddess for attending in the usual way or through words of her own choosing. The Quarters are dismissed and the Circle is opened.

The rite is ended.

FEBRUARY FULL MOON
(A Blessing Way for Goddess)

A Blessing Way honors the pregnant Goddess and presents Her with gifts appropriate for Herself or the baby. In this case, they are gifts that can be consumed by fire, such as herbs or incenses, symbolizing a variety of wishes for Mother and/or baby. Each woman is asked to bring such a gift to the Circle. Such offerings might include dried rose petals for love/bonding; sage for blessings of spirit; hops for plentiful milk; lavender for an easy and relaxed birth; wormwood to bring the aid of Artemis (divine midwife) to the impending birth; hazelnuts for mom to eat to give the child wisdom, or acorns for strength and endurance; or whatever else occurs to you.

Begin with the ritual bath, but this time add some parsley root water to the bath. Parsley root water is a Green Witch brew meant to protect and care for the pregnant mother and the baby. To make parsley root water bring pieces of the root to boil in a stainless steel or enamel pot of covered water. Reduce the heat and simmer for 20 minutes to one hour. Allow to cool completely. Strain through cheesecloth and add the resulting brew to the bath water.

You can also use any of the following protective herbs in the bath by making a tea of it/them and adding it to the bath water, or by tying it/them in a piece of cheesecloth and adding the bag to the bath water as the tub fills. You can use basil, Sacred Basil, angelica, Star Anise, ash leaf, bittersweet, chamomile, coriander, cumin, dill, garlic, hyssop, juniper, any of the mints, motherwort, mugwort, mullein, parsley, purslane, rowan berries, St. John's Wort, sesame seeds, Solomon's Seal, or others. You may wish to add herbs for happiness, luck and/or love as well.

This ritual bath is also different in that it should be done in pairs. One woman takes the role of the pregnant Goddess/Self, and one woman takes the role of the well-wisher who ritually and lovingly bathes Her. The woman as Goddess should relax and enjoy, opening herself to the comfort and good wishes offered by she who washes. They then switch places and begin again. A flowery incense indicative of joy, happiness and Goddess blessings (such as jasmine) should be burning in the candlelit bathroom. When the bath is finishe, each woman proceeds to the living room/waiting area and is given a cup of mint tea by the Facilitating Priestess, who says:

"Share the joy."

All sit quietly thinking about the upcoming birth and the coming of Spring. When all have finished their tea, they proceed to the ritual area as the altar candles are lit.

If anyone is uncomfortable with the notion of being bathed by another, she need not feel pressured to participate in this way. She can take her bath by herself, imagining her hands are the hands of the Goddess (which in a very real sense they are) bathing her, and that she is the pregnant Goddess being bathed by her own hands.)

The altar cloth and candles are white. The incense should either be the same scent as in the bath area, or it should be frankincense. It is important for this ritual that there be a charcoal block burning in the cauldron. Be sure to fill the cauldron with earth or sand to set the charcoal block on. Put a fireproof pad underneath the cauldron if need be.

The Circle is cast, the participants are blessed, the Quarters are called and the presence of the Goddess is invoked in the usual manner, or through words of your own choosing. Each has with her a gift for the Goddess and the Child. The Facilitating Priestess lights the charcoal block in the cauldron, saying:

> "The Goddess is great with child. Aradia will soon return to the Earth. The waters of life will burst forth from the Great Mother in the form of Spring rains to ease Her daughter's passage into life among us again. But for now we want to honor the two who are one and wish them continued strength, health, joy and an easy birth as they move toward separation. In honoring the Mother with Child in this fashion we are continuing a women's tradition known in different forms among native peoples the world over. Some dance it. Some sing it. Some anoint with unguents and oils. Some offer good wishes and gifts, as we do here. May the Cauldron of Transformation change our wishes to realities. May the smoke of our offerings waft its way to the nostrils of She Who Waits."

One by one the women come forward and make their offerings, saying what they wish or keeping silent. When all have finished, each woman reaches out to the woman on either side of her and places one hand over the womb of each of these women. Those who are comfortable with it may begin to undulate their belly in imitation of labor and delivery. All chant rhythmically:

"Pregnant Mother, Goddess Wise,
Birth your Child between Your thighs.
Make Her healthy, make Her strong,
Bring Her to us 'fore 'ere long."

Repeat three times, getting louder each time. Release with a yell.

Move on to the Thanksgiving and Return, the sharing of food and discussion — including what to bring to the March Full Moon, if it precedes the Spring Equinox. If not, details on what will be necessary for the Spring Equinox are given. When all are ready, the Goddess is thanked, the Quarters are dismissed and the Circle is opened.

The rite is ended.

MARCH FULL MOON

(If prior to the Spring Equinox)

As the equinox approaches, we know life is about to burst forth on the Earth. Manifestation begins anew, and our thoughts begin to turn outward to the world. Each woman brings a hard-boiled egg to the Circle. The Facilitating Priestess provides a variety of crayons and grasses — either real grass, or green "Easter" grass.

The altar is draped in the green of the coming Spring and the white of the passing Winter. The altar candles are snowy white. Any flowers on the altar should be Spring flowers (daffodils, daisies, crocuses or others). A flowery scent should be available for the censer. Other appropriate decorations might include rabbits, chicks, four-leaf clovers and other symbols of the coming Spring, fertility and luck. Women wear green and white, or nothing at all if they prefer. The cauldron is in the center of the Circle, with a bed of grass within: the Witches' Ostara basket.

The ritual begins with the ritual bath. (The room is illuminated by candlelight, incense is burning, salt is in the bath water and purifying herbs in cheesecloth are in the water as well.) Each woman should purify herself in the bath, and should purify her egg by passing the egg through the four elements. Salt and water are in the tub. After she bathes the egg, she passes it through the smoke of the censer, thereby purifying it by fire and air.

When each woman is finished, she returns to the main area and shares a cup of mint tea, or a Spring tonic to prepare her body for the coming seasonal change. (A traditional Spring tonic is a cup of sassafras tea. Other ingredients that might be added include licorice root, ginger, dandelion root or leaf to cleanse the system and remove toxins; comfrey and red raspberry leaf to clear the lungs and add vitamins and minerals to the body.) Each woman relaxes in silence and clears her mind, putting herself in a receptive state for the ritual. Perhaps she thinks of the coming Spring, the melting snows with their rivers of cold runoff, the sap running in the trees, the tree buds about to burst forth, or the shebear awakening in her den with cubs at her side. She thinks of herself coming forth into the light after a long Winter inside. She contemplates the return of the Maiden, Aradia.

As the altar candles are lit, everyone proceeds to the ritual area, eggs in hand. The Facilitating Priestess welcomes all to the Circle. An attunement exercise is performed to open the women to each other, to the Goddess and to the work. (This could be a free-form AUM chant, a chant favored by the group, a squeeze of the hand, a kiss passed around the Circle or a brief guided visualization consisting of opening and blending imagery.) After completing this, the Facilitating Priestess says:

> "Tonight, more than any other, the Full Moon truly represents the pregnant belly of the Great Goddess, for ere She waxes full again She will give birth, and Aradia will again walk among us. The Mystery of manifestation is about to be played out before our eyes, and we are in awe of Her ways and Her wisdom.
>
> In concert with the Mother, our own Goddess within urges us to turn outward to the world and begin Her work of manifestation on the personal, political/social and ecological levels. Tonight we will Magickally begin that work and symbolically see its fruition."

175

The Circle is cast, the participants are blessed, the Quarters are called and the Goddess is invoked following the usual pattern. At the point at which Magick is to be done, the Facilitating Priestess invites the women to think about what they would like to see manifested in the world during the coming year. Once they have something in mind, they are to use the crayons to draw symbols appropriate to that goal on their egg. Each is to then hold the egg against her womb and to concentrate on that goal until all have finished drawing on and "incubating" their eggs.

The Facilitating Priestess will then ask all to birth their egg in their own fashion and then to place it in the cauldron/nest, naming its purpose as they do. (Here, women could go through actions indicative of labor and delivery, they could imitate a chicken or bird laying an egg, or they could sing a birthing chant.) Once all of the eggs are in the cauldron/nest, the Facilitating Priestess asks everyone to hold hands and to begin walking around the Circle. As they do so, she says:

> "Birdwoman, Lady, on the nest
> bring to us what we request
> for we would have it manifest!"

Everyone continues to chant:

> "Manifest, manifest, manifest . . . "

As they all chant, they drop hands and start flapping their wings in imitation of birdwoman flying to Earth with their requests. As they do so, they continue to walk around the Circle, getting faster and faster as they do. When the power peaks, all drop to a squatting position in imitation of laying the eggs. Their hands then go to the ground to drain off any excess energy at the completion of the laying.

The Facilitating Priestess now brings the cauldron of eggs to where she is sitting. As she takes them out and puts them on a plate, she explains:

> "Our eggs and wishes have been Magickally laid
> and Earthed in preparation for manifestation. Their
> birth into the world remains. As I pass the plate
> around, please take your own egg, and manifest
> your desires by cracking it open and freeing it from

176

its shell. Since we know that the will of the Goddess is best accomplished by the willing hands of Her women, please eat your egg. It will give you the strength and sustenance to manifest Her handiwork, through your desire, into the world around you."

Since most people like salt on their hard-boiled eggs, she passes the salt, with the words:

"We are the salt of the Earth and we preserve the ways of the Wise Ones in our hearts, in our minds, and in our works."

Proceed now with the sharing of Milk, Honey and Grain. Feasting and friendship follow. When appropriate, thank the Goddess, dismiss the Quarters and open the Circle. Discuss what needs to be prepared/brought to the Spring Equinox ritual.

The rite is ended.

OSTARA

(Spring Equinox)

Ostara is the birthday of the Goddess/ daughter, Aradia, as well as the birth of Spring and the renewal of the life it brings. For this ritual the Facilitating Priestess will need to be someone comfortable with channeling the Great Mother. In other words, she will manifest the Great Mother through her own body and go through the birthing process with Her. For this reason it may be helpful if the Facilitating Priestess has given birth in actuality. It is not, however, a necessity for channeling the birthing Goddess.

The birthing can take place in one of two ways. Either a doll, hand-sewn by the coven, can be birthed by the Priestess/Great Mother. Or, each member of the coven can be so birthed. Each coven should decide what feels best for itself. A doll might be chosen because sewing/handwork and the care/nurturance of babies/dolls have always been a sacred/Magickal task among women. Clothing could be made for the doll that would change with the seasons, and it could become a representation of the Goddess Aradia on your altar.

I would also suggest that the doll be stuffed with Magickal/
symbolic and fragrant herbs, instead of standard stuffing materials. Herbs associated with the Sun and/or the four elements would
be appropriate. For example, you may wish to include angelica, ash
leaves, bay leaves, camomile, eyebright, frankincense, High John
the Conqueror, marigold flowers, peony petals, rosemary or sun-
flower petals or seed, to name a few. You may also wish to enclose
crystals and/or other stones you might find worthy. Once the doll/
Daughter has been birthed, she will be blessed by the four elements, and blessed by all Her Goddess mothers in the Circle.

If you choose to birth the women in the coven instead, it would
be best to do this skyclad. If this is not comfortable for one or all,
clothing may certainly be worn. White and/or purple (for newness
and divinity) and red (for the blood that comes with birth) are most
appropriate. Be sure each woman brings her red cord to the Circle.

The altar cloth is green, as are the altar candles. Fresh flowers are
on the altar. The cauldron is wreathed with red flowers to symbolize the blood of birth. Birthing symbols of the coven's own choosing
are laid out around the Circle and/or at the four Quarters. A
birthday cake, preferably round to represent the world and the
great round of life, death and life again, waits under the altar to be
shared during the feast. Candles on the cake are arranged in the
shape of a sunburst.

The ritual bath, as usual, is used to cleanse away everyday cares
and considerations. You are privy to the most sacred of all Mysteries this night and must prepare yourself to bear it witness. The font
of the female opens for you, and you are about to see the root of
feminine power and sacredness manifested before you. It is a rare
privilege granted by the Goddess to Her chosen.

To enhance your meditation, purple and red candles should
burn in the bathroom, and sandalwood incense (a purifier and
inducer of mystic vision) should be burned in the censer. A red
rose, symbol of a cervix beginning to open, may also be present to
aid in the meditation.

Another red rose could be in the area where all gather after their
bath to drink a glass of cool spring water, representative of the
waters of life that are about to burst forth through the open cervix/
rose. Women should now be chosen to invoke the Quarters. These

women will bless Aradia by the four elements, should the doll ritual be used.

As the altar candles are lit, the women assemble in the Circle wearing their red cords (if the cord ritual has been chosen). (Whichever ritual is chosen, the Facilitating Priestess should wear a red skirt, symbolic of the blood of life. This skirt should be cut full enough to allow her to straddle the cauldron or crouch over it. If the doll ritual is being enacted, the doll should be tied around her waist and it should be hidden under the skirt.) The Circle is cast, the women are anointed and the Quarters are called. A special Quarter calling may be used in addition to, or instead of, the usual one. In this case, a Goddess associated with birthing and midwifery is called upon at each Quarter.

East — Artemis:

> "Artemis, Virgin Protectress of the pregnant feminine at the moment of her delivery, draw nigh and offer aid to All-Woman at the point of transition. Defend Her, and us, from all unwelcome intrusion at this Her moment of fruition."

South — Brigid (pronounced "Breed"):

> "Blessed Brigid, midwife to the Queen of Heaven who each year births anew the Sun, be with us here. Again assure us of the deliverance of Aradia — the fair-faced flower of the sky, the light of our lives, the gem of the ocean and fragrant daughter of the green Earth."

West — Ilithyia (fluid of generation):

> "Ilithyia, Mother of the Amniotic Fluids, within whose grasp lies the progress of labor, come to us. May the rhythms of Her belly undulate in sync with You. May the rhythms of Her belly easily push Her daughter through."

North — Meshkent:

> "Building blocks of life, Meshkent, upon who's firm foundation crouched the laboring women of

Egypt, attend us here. Guide the babe from out Her body and read the future in Her eyes."

The Doll Ritual

The Facilitating Priestess says:

"Tonight the Goddess has given us the unparalleled privilege of allowing us to witness the creation of the world anew. She assures us that the beings of the Earth will take yet another turn around the great wheel of life by manifesting Her daughter among us. Tonight we sit in awe of the great power that is woman and reaffirm its primacy in the natural world. For know ye the Mystery that without birth, there is no life. Without life there is no death. Without death there is no rebirth. And the Great Goddess, through Her women, rules them all."

The birthing Goddess is now drawn into/out of the Facilitating Priestess. In this case, the donning of the crescent crown will act as a trigger to bring the Great Mother through. An invocation is spoken, either by another woman who holds the crown above the head of the Priestess until she finishes speaking and puts the crown on the Priestess's head; or by the Facilitating Priestess herself, who holds the crown in front of her as she speaks, crowning the Goddess incarnate when she feels Her blossom in her consciousness. In either case, use this invocation, or one of your own:

"Mighty Mother of us all through whom we live, move and have our being, enter into the body of your Priestess and handmaid here. Reveal to us your Mystery of Mysteries. May Your vision be hers, and her words, Yours. Animate her body with Your essence. Inspirit her soul with the soul of nature and bring through her the renewed life we await. Hail Diana, Creatrix and Queen! Hail Aradia, divine daughter and guide!"

When the Great Mother is fully present within the Priestess, She will do as She pleases to deliver Her Daughter. She may dance rhythmically through Her contractions, in which case the coven may wish to aid Her by drumming on the ground or by swaying in time. A softly spoken rhythmic chant that builds in volume and/or speed as the birth approaches may be helpful. A simple chant of "Come Aradia, Come!" could be used. Or use another of your own choosing, so long as it compliments the rhythm of the dance. A good chant that is particularly appropriate to this ritual is the "Cauldron of Changes" chant:[1]

> "Cauldron of Changes,
> Blossom of Bone,
> Font of Eternity,
> Hole in the Stone"

The Priestess/Goddess may stand and/or squat above the cauldron the whole time, rocking with Her contractions while singing the child into manifestation. The coveners can support Her efforts by singing along, or dancing around Her. She may laugh through the entire process, or make low, guttural, animal noises that the coveners can imitate, or they can support Her with their silence.

Since it is impossible to determine beforehand what She will do, it is impossible to plan your response to it/support of it. Go with the flow. You may be too overcome with awe by the Mystery being played out before you to do anything but watch and respectfully wait for the Magickal moment of birth. Each of you may react in different ways. Each way will be appropriate and important to express. Tears are not uncommon, nor is laughter. If She speaks, listen. If She asks you to do something, act.

When the birth is imminent, She will squat over the cauldron and pull the child/doll out from beneath Her skirts. Again, react as you are internally prompted to do — laugh, cry, hug each other. Finally, quietly sing "We All Come From the Goddess"[2] as She displays the baby/doll for all to see.

At the end of the chant the Facilitating Priestess, still channeling the Goddess, will present the child to each Quarter and ask for a blessing. The same women who invoked the Quarters shall give the blessings, saying what comes to them or saying the following:

East — using the censer:

> "May Your spirit soar like an arrow loosed from
> Your Mother's bow. May Your mind be quick and

keen, and may all you speak and hear have the ring of truth."

South — using the candle:

"May a passion for life burn within You. May You have the courage of Your convictions, and may Your will be done."

West — using water:

"May Your eyes be gifted with second sight, Your heart with understanding. May You hear the unspoken as well as what is said, and thus be known as Wise."

North — using salt:

"May You be blessed with abundant health and may Your body serve You well. May all Your works come to fruition, and may You live a charmed life upon the sacred Earth."

The baby/doll is then handed around the Circle so that each Goddess Mother/covener has a chance to hold Her and give her own blessings and good wishes. Meanwhile, the Facilitating Priestess returns to normal consciousness, removes the lunar crown from her head, and replaces it on the altar. When the baby/doll is returned to the Facilitating Priestess, she gives it her own blessing and places Her in the Cauldron of Transformation, in which the Goddess/child will change from young babe to young woman via Her first bloods at Beltaine.

The Facilitating Priestess thanks the Great Mother for Her labor of love in again giving to the Earth Her daughter. Milk, Honey and Grain are shared. Then all sit down to celebrate Aradia's birthday by sharing Aradia's birthday cake. The candles on the cake are lit and the life-giving warmth of the Sun at this season is considered. Thoughts about this (and about Aradia as a solar deity) can be shared with the group, or considered privately by the individuals. When all are ready, the candles are blown out by the group, and the cake is cut and distributed. When the feasting is done, the Goddess is thanked, the Quarters are dismissed, the Goddess/midwives are thanked and the Circle is declared open.

The Cord Ritual

If the Doll Ritual seems inappropriate to your group, the Cord Ritual may be done instead. Here again, the Facilitating Priestess must be someone accustomed to having the Goddess move through her and animate her body and soul. For this ritual each woman must wear her red cord tied around her waist in such a way that a long section of it is left hanging in the front (the tether). The Facilitating Priestess wears her cord as well, but tied more loosely so that it is resting more or less on her hips. Her tether should be off to one side.

Again, considering the action and symbolism involved in the ritual, skyclad might be easier for all concerned, but it is not mandatory. As in the Doll Ritual, any clothing worn should be red, white, and/or purple. (The green of the season is on the altar.) The attire should be comfortable and should allow you to crawl or to draw yourself into a ball in a squatting position. The red skirt of the Facilitating Priestess should again be full enough for her to stand with legs fairly far apart because she, as Goddess, will birth each woman from between her legs.

Proceed with the preparation, Circle casting, anointing, and Quarter calling as in the Doll Ritual. After calling the Quarters (and the midwife Goddesses) the Facilitating Priestess says words to this effect:

> "Tonight the Aradia within us all is reborn and our hope for the world and for ourselves is renewed as we are touched by, and experience, the all encompassing love and power of the Great Goddess in Her most creative moment. The world is again recreated in all its teeming diversity, and we stand in awe of Her miraculous will and the power that is woman. And a promise made to a dying world in the Fall is fulfilled in the Spring. For know ye the Mystery that without life there is no death and without death no renewal, and the Great Goddess rules it all."

The Great Mother is now drawn into/out of the Facilitating Priestess with the crescent crown and invocation recorded in the Doll

Ritual. Here again the Goddess will labor and do as She wills, and that activity can be supported by the coven.

When She is ready to begin the actual birthings, She will adopt an open-legged stance next to the Cauldron of Rebirth. This will be a signal for the coven members to line up behind Her. The first woman in line will squat down behind the Goddess. When the Goddess is ready, She will bend down and reach one hand between Her legs. The woman to be birthed hands her tether to the Goddess, who uses it to help draw the woman through Her legs. The Goddess will now tie the end of the cord around Her own cord at Her waist in a loop, so that the woman and cord may move along Her red cord. In this way, the red cord becomes an umbilical cord, pulsing with the blood of life that comes from the Goddess to the newly born woman, and pointedly shows each individual's connection to Her and Her life-sustaining abilities.

This process is repeated for each woman until each has been reborn and is standing, attached to the Goddess, in a circle around Her. The Priestess/Goddess now raises Her arms in a crescent shape and the women sing, "We All Come From the Goddess." At some point during the singing the Priestess/Goddess will begin to remove the umbilical cords from her cord. As each woman is untied, she moves deosil (the way of life) out to the Circle's perimeter.

When all are again standing in a Circle, the Goddess may choose to speak, or She may simply choose to withdraw. When She withdraws, the Facilitating Priestess will remove the lunar crown and return it to the altar. She thanks the Goddess for being present with them and for revealing Her Mystery to them. Proceed with the ritual sharing of Milk, Honey and Grain, followed by the birthday cake/feast, the dismissal of the Quarters/midwives and the opening of the Circle.

The rite is ended.

APRIL FULL MOON
(Garden/Seed Blessing Ritual)

The April Full Moon is a good time to Magickally prepare the garden and to bless seeds that have already been planted or are ready to go into seeding flats or into the ground. It is fairly likely that the frost is out of the ground by this time.

Ideally, the garden space will be a communal garden tended by all coven members, who will share in its harvest. It could either be on land owned by one or more members of the coven, or it could be a plot rented in a community gardening space set aside by some towns and cities for that purpose. Failing this, even apartment dwellers can raise some culinary herbs, or a vegetable or two in clay pots on a balcony or in front of a well-lit window. Growing our own food and medicines organically (if we can) is a good way of empowering our lives by seeing to our own nutritional and health care needs.

Garden Plot Ritual

Here's a chance for the child within, or for the children of coven members, to have fun and to prepare a ritual at the same time. Conveniently enough, Ostara egg dyes are available at this time of year in all grocery stores! Get some, preferably the type that have a wax crayon included for writing or drawing on the eggs.

Get together to color your hard-boiled eggs on the day of the Full Moon. You are going to put at least one egg at the cardinal points at the edge of the garden, and at least one in the center of the plot. You may bury them at other places within or along the perimeter of the plot, as well. Figure out how many eggs of each Quarter color you will need. You might make the center eggs purple (for the Goddess) or orange (for the Sun), or a combination of colors that appeal to you. Use the wax crayon to draw fertility symbols; symbols of Earth, Air, Fire/Sun and Water; or to write the words to a growth charm of your own choosing.

When you have finished, you can cast a Circle and call down the blessings of the Goddess and the four Quarters, and chant over the eggs. Or, you can carry the symbols of the four elements out to the garden space with your eggs, and bless the entire plot by the four elements. Begin in the East and walk around the edge of the garden carrying the yellow/East egg and your censer with incense. As you walk, you ask for the blessings of Air on your garden: gentle breezes to bring bees and beneficial insects to pollinate the plants and to eat harmful insects; an absence of destructive winds; cool breezes on the days you need to be out thinning, weeding, harvesting and preserving, and the like. When you return to the Eastern point, "plant" your egg by digging a hole and burying it.

Next, carry the red/South egg and a candle or wand around the garden, beginning and ending at the South. As the circumambulation is made, ask for the blessing of Fire: sunshine, moderate heat, and the long hours of daylight needed for growth and maturation. When this is done, "plant" the red egg at the South.

Carry a chalice of spring water and the blue egg around, beginning and ending in the West, sprinkling the perimeter of the garden as you go. Ask for the blessing of Water: gentle rains at optimum intervals for growth, absence of hailstorms, and the like. "Plant" the blue egg when you return to the West.

The green egg and a symbolic sprinkling of salt or earth from the surface of a rock begins and ends at the North, where the egg is "planted." Blessings of Earth are called down: fertile soil, proper nutrient balance, and the ability to both retain and drain water in the appropriate amounts.

Move to the center of the garden and call down the blessings of the Goddess on the purple egg, presenting it to each Quarter as you do. (Turn in place and face the East holding out the egg. Turn to the South, West and North with egg extended as well.) Hold it up to the sky and down to the Earth as you speak. Then "plant" it in the center of the garden. Your garden is now Magickally prepared for planting.

If you are afraid of being seen doing all of this, you may abbreviate the ritual as follows: Take your colored eggs to the garden along with a hand trowel. At the East point, dig a little hole with your trowel, calling on the blessing of East in your mind as you do. Breathe on the egg three times (once for each aspect of the Goddess), and bury the egg. At the South, call on the blessing of South while you dig. Hold the egg to your solar plexus and send energy through it to the egg. At the West, spit on the egg three times and "plant" it, calling on the blessing of West. At the North, the act of burying the egg will be its consecration by Earth. Call on the blessings of North as you dig. At the center, call on the blessing of the Goddess as you dig. Display the egg to the four directions, up and down, and bury it. You can divide the tasks according to the number participating. Burying and blessing the eggs could be two separate tasks.

Or, if that still seems too risky for some reason, bless and consecrate the eggs by the elements and by the Goddess in your Full Moon Circle, and save them until you actually go out to plant the garden. Then slip them in the ground while marking the rows or planting the seeds.

Seed(ling) Blessing

If you will be planting in flats or pots, gather in the afternoon and prepare them to receive the seeds. Bring seed packets. If you have already sprouted seedlings, bring them along.

Although it is too early in the season to harvest any of the ingredients, you may wish to share a meal of Spring foods. This can be an act of sympathetic Magick in itself. While you are preparing and eating the food, do so with intent. Visualize the seeds, roots or cuttings you are about to plant as fully-grown. See yourselves harvest and prepare a Spring meal from your own garden and surrounding lands. Your Spring meal might consist of watercress soup, a salad of greens, asparagus and herbed rice with a plate of young dandelion greens on the side. For the meat eaters, Spring lamb is appropriate.

At the beginning of the meal, offer first portions from each platter or bowl to the Goddess and to the Earth by preparing a plate and place for Her at your table. Take turns speaking one-line prayers of thanks to the Goddess, to the Earth and to the plants or animals for giving of themselves for your sustenance. The great Mystery is on the table before you. The preparation and consumption of food is a sacred act and privilege.

The ritual bath area should contain at least one green and growing plant. Burn green candles and an earthy or flowery incense. Solar herbs for growth, or herbs associated with vegetation Goddesses, could be placed in cheesecloth and added to the bath water as well. Mint tea should await bathers when they have finished, as the mints are among the first herbs to grow in the Spring. They also are very relaxing and are a good aid to digestion.

The altar cloth and candles are green. The cauldron holds the seed packets everyone brought. The trays of seedlings and prepared flats and pots surround the cauldron . A watering can is present, as well. Coven members can be decked out in green, wear necklaces of seeds, and have flowers in their hair, if they wish.

The Circle is cast, participants are anointed and the Quarters are invoked. Vegetation/Earth Goddesses are called upon to bless the seeds and plants. To do this, everyone sits on the ground and begins pounding rhythmically upon it to get the attention of the Earth Mother. All chant:

> "Sun to Earth, seeds to ground,
> Gentle waters now come down."

As the chant continues, the Facilitating Priestess calls up the blessing of the Earth Mother on the seeds and plants, and lays the spell, saying (or singing):

> "Earth, Mountain Mother, fertile plain; You who
> sustains our lives with the bounty of Your body,
> bless with growth these seeds we sow. May our
> seedlings quickly grow. And when harvest time is
> near, bless the scythe that cuts them clear. By our
> hands the spell is done, when seeds and Earth shall
> rest as one."

Packets of seeds that are not to be sown outdoors are distributed. The Facilitating Priestess says:

> "As we plant and water these seeds, let us plant
> and tend to seed ideas as well. Magickally plant an
> idea in the world as you plant the seeds and as you
> speak its meaning."

Each woman speaks her seed idea as she plants. These can range from personal growth to social/political goals, or ecological and spiritual concerns. Each should speak from her heart. When all of the seeds are planted they, and any seedlings present, should be watered well. Here again, wishes may be expressed, this time through water metaphors. For example, "may change for the good rain down upon the Earth." Or, "may the fact that we are all interconnected to all-that-is soak into and percolate through the fertile ground of human consciousness." At the completion of this task, a final charging-up should be done in unison. All say:

"May all we've asked for manifest, manifest, manifest . . ."

The ritual of Milk, Honey and Grain is shared. Feasting ensues, and instructions for what to bring to the Beltaine ritual are given. The Goddess is thanked, the Quarters are dismissed and the Circle is declared open.

Seed packets to be sown outdoors are removed from the cauldron and are planted outside now, or when conditions are optimal. Seedling flats go home with their respective owners, to be tended and transplanted out at the right time.

The rite is ended.

BELTAINE

(The Red Ritual)

In the mythic cycle/seasonal cycle of the life of Aradia, Beltaine celebrates Her rite of passage into womanhood. She passes from girl-child to fertile woman and enters into the heart of Women's Mysteries, the unique power that belongs to the female alone. With it comes rights and responsibilities. She enters the house of the Moon and feels its influence within the ebb and flow of Her own body. She sees for the first time how the monthly cycle of Her body reflects the larger cycle of the seasons of the year, and of all life which passes into existence through the feminine. Her blood also connects Her to every woman born of woman, and this ritual celebrates that connection, and the connection to the Great Goddess as First Ancestress.

This ritual requires the red cords and red clothing, or white clothing with red "stains." (Or no clothes at all!) The altar cloth and candles are red. A bouquet of red carnations or roses sits upon the altar. The bouquet includes one flower for each woman present. There is a garland of flowers for Aradia, as well. Wine, pomegranate juice, cherry juice, cranberry juice, or menstrual blood is in the chalice. The cauldron contains glowing coals upon which water may be sprinkled to create steam. If this cannot be managed, burn a smokey incense (like frankincense tears) on the coals. Incense, a candle, water and salt are placed around the cauldron. The youngest woman present will enact the part of Aradia. The eldest will be the First Ancestress and will wear the lunar crescent.

The ritual bath area should be lit with red candles; red carnations and white gardenias (or carnations) should float in the bath water. Add a few drops of musk oil to the water. An earthy incense should burn in the censer — patchouli, or another of your preference. Each takes the ritual bath, beginning with the woman enacting the roll of Aradia. During the bath, thought should be given to the special significance of menarche and how nice it would have been if we each had been honored in this way. Take time to honor yourself. As each woman emerges from the bath, the Facilitating Priestess gives her an herbal tea made for the bleeding woman. This could be a pms tea, a tea for cramps, or one to encourage the flow. The choice is yours.

When all is ready and the altar candles are lit, the Facilitating Priestess casts the Circle, consecrates it and consecrates all present, and then invokes the Quarters. She then calls the woman acting the part of the First Ancestress to join her behind the altar. The Facilitating Priestess picks up the crescent crown and turns to face the women. She invokes Her saying:

> "Oh Ancient of Days, Prime Progenitress, She who lived first so that we might live and our foremothers before us, be with us now to welcome your daughter, Aradia, into the community of all women and into the Circle of Life. Grant us Your presence and wisdom, and share our joy."

The Facilitating Priestess crowns the First Ancestress and pauses a moment to allow Her to speak if She will.

The Facilitating Priestess then calls the woman enacting Aradia to the front of the altar. She places the garland of flowers on Her head and says:

> "Aradia, daughter of All Mother, today You enter the community of all women and assume the responses and responsibilities of a woman grown. The ebb and flow of Your body connects You to the cycles of the Lady Moon and the tides of Yemaya; to the Great Mother, Gaia, and the divine female in all Her manifestations. This is the time of Your

greatest power and the elements will bless you to it."

The Facilitating Priestess takes the chalice from the altar, stands beside Aradia, puts her arm around Her and gently guides Her to the Eastern Quarter. There she raises the chalice and invokes the element and Goddesses of Air, saying:

"Hear me O Mighty Ones, Great Queens of the regions of the East, we ask that you attend us here and consecrate this woman born with the power and wisdom of the spirits of the Air."

The woman standing at the East takes the chalice from the Priestess and, dipping her finger(s) in it, anoints Aradia on the forehead (third eye) with the red fluid, saying:

"I give You the gift of focused attention. Of it is born intuition and action as well as awareness of Yourself and Your needs. With it You'll know Yourself and others — their truths and their false-hoods; their intentions toward you for good or for ill. You'll see to the heart of every matter and act with wisdom, integrity and honor. Each month when You bleed, remember me and my gift with an offering of incense and smoke."

Aradia throws incense on the coals in the cauldron. The Priestess regains the chalice and guides Aradia to the South. Holding the chalice aloft, she invokes:

"Hear me oh Mighty Ones, Great Queens of the regions of the South; we ask that you attend us here and consecrate this woman born with the powers and the wisdom of the spirits of the South."

The Priestess hands the chalice to the woman at the South, who anoints Aradia's womb with the fluid therein, saying:

"I give to You the gift of passion and the responsi-bilities thereof: to give of Your body to those You feel are worthy; to take delight in the pleasures of the flesh along with the emotional honesty and

clarity it demands; to know and to respect Your
need — and the needs of others — for separation as
well as for union; for privacy as well as for intimacy;
for gentle love as well as for driving lust. Know,
too, that Your body can now create, nourish and
birth a child — a sacred task not undertaken lightly,
if at all. Be mindful of the choice. Each month when
You bleed remember me with an offering of fire."

Aradia takes a new candle from beside the cauldron, lights it from
the cauldron's coals and sets it up to the South of the cauldron.

The Facilitating Priestess takes back the chalice and escorts
Aradia to the West, where she invokes, with raised chalice:

"Hear me oh Mighty Ones, Great Queens of the
region of the West; we ask that you attend us here
and consecrate this woman born with the wisdom
and powers of the spirits of the West."

The woman in the West takes the chalice and anoints Aradia's
breasts, saying:

"Mine is the gift of intuition — to know Your body
and the cycles of its seasons. Such knowledge of
your body will increase Your psychic abilities and
will ease the transition into and out of Your greatest
time of personal power, which is centered within
Your bleeding time. Go into Your Moon Temple at
that time and divine the future, integrate the past,
decide Your course of action for the present, and
remember me with an offering of fluid."

Aradia takes the chalice and pours a small libation from it into the
cauldron. She then returns the chalice to the Priestess, who takes it
and guides Her to the North. The Priestess invokes with raised
chalice, saying:

"Hear me oh Mighty Ones, Great Queens of the
region of the North, attend us here and consecrate
this woman born with the wisdom and the powers
of the spirits of the North."

The woman standing in the North takes the chalice and anoints Aradia's feet, saying:

> "May Your feet rest firmly on the understanding I bring - the knowledge of the sacred ground upon which You walk. The Earth, Herself complete with cycles and seasons of life and of death as reflected in Your body and Hers. Your own divinity is a diminutive reflection of Her Holiness. Each month, when You bleed, remember me with an offering of salt."

Aradia throws a pinch of salt into the cauldron.

The Facilitating Priestess returns the chalice to the altar, picks up the bouquet and gives one flower to each woman in the Circle, except for Aradia. Aradia, escorted by the Priestess, is then presented to each woman in the Circle, beginning with the woman to the left of the First Ancestress. Each woman hands Aradia her flower with a wish for Her. Each woman then connects her red cord to the waist portion of the cord of the woman to her right, saying something about the monthly blood connecting us to the women who have gone before us, or about it being a red thread woven into the tapestry of all women's lives.

When Aradia comes to the First Ancestress, She receives a flower and a wish from Her. Aradia is then placed in the Circle to the right of the First Ancestress. The Facilitating Priestess ties Aradia's cord to the waist cord of the woman on Her right. The Priestess then ties the cord of the First Ancestress to Aradia's waist, saying:

> "Thus is the last connected to the first and the first to the last within the Circle of women. Your blood connects You to all who have gone before and to all who are yet to come, and binds You directly to She Who Bled First. And the red thread spins on in the hands of the Ancient of Days."

She touches the hands of the First Ancestress.

The Facilitating Priestess steps to the center of the Circle near the cauldron, replenishes the smoke, removes her own cord, lays it in a circle around the cauldron and the four elements on the floor, and says:

"And when we come to the time when our bleeding
stops and it returns to the elements form which it
came, we will gladly stand on the rim of the cauldron of transformation (she straddles it) and embrace and honor the changes it brings."

All women untie themselves from each other and remove the cord
from their waist, dropping it at their feet in a ritual foreshadowing
(or remembering) their own menopause. The Facilitating Priestess
says:

"And our connection to each other will turn from
red to gray. "(*She indicates her hair.*)

The First Ancestress is thanked, and the crown is returned to the
altar. The ritual of Milk, Honey and Grain is celebrated. All sit to
feast and to share stories of their own menarche — how they felt,
and how their mothers reacted. Any information relative to the
May Moon is passed on. The Quarters are dismissed and the Circle
is declared open.

The rite is ended.

May Full Moon

The idea for this ritual comes from the old Pagan custom of giving
or exchanging May Baskets. This was originally done on May Day,
but is just as appropriate to the May Moon. Originally May baskets
were given to potential lovers as an indication of sexual interest in
the recipient. Later, they became a flirtation device — as if to say,
"I like you, let's date." Still later, they were given as a sign of
friendship, and were often given in secret. This is how I came to
know the custom when I was a child.

In Iowa, where I was born, the little children would make May
Baskets for their friends. The baskets consisted of popcorn, nuts,
candy and a trinket or two. We would then get up early on May
morning and quietly leave them on the doorsteps of our friends'
homes. The first year we moved to Wisconsin I excitedly made my
baskets on Beltaine Eve and delivered them on May morning, and
was absolutely crushed when I didn't receive any myself. To make
matters worse, no one even knew what they were or who they came
from! I never again gave or received a May Basket. So, I would like

to revive and expand upon this beautiful, touching and enjoyable custom here.

There are lots of different ways and reasons to do this, and the contents of your baskets will vary according to their purpose. If pair bondings exist within your coven, the lovers can make baskets for each other filled with the beloved's favorite treats and/or symbols of their love. If there are single members in your coven who have lovers outside the circle, they can have the joy of preparing a basket for a totally unsuspecting recipient. Or, perhaps some in the group would like to make their feelings of love and/or friendship known to another for the first time. Maybe there are children, or elders, known to you who you would like to surprise in this way.

Another approach would be for the whole group to make a May Basket consisting of food and donate it to a food pantry. Or the group, as a group, could volunteer their services at a local soup kitchen for the day. You may prefer to make up a bunch of identical baskets and give them to the women and children at the battered women's shelter, or to the residents of a nursing home or an emergency housing shelter.

The contents of the baskets will, or course, be determined by who the intended recipient(s) is/are. Use your imagination. Bits of food, herbal tea blends, bath sachets, little toys, symbols of love or friendship, and flowers are all good bets. The basket, too, will differ with its intended use, and can range from a beautiful handwoven basket to a paper cup with a construction paper handle stapled to it. The baskets are always relatively small.

However you choose to do it, have everyone bring their basket and "ingredients" to the Circle for preparation and blessing during the ritual. Have each also bring something to give to the Goddess as well.

For the purposes of this ritual, the cauldron will be thought of as a May Basket for Goddess. Decorating it with nice satin-like ribbons tied to the handles may enhance that effect. Once the Circle is cast, the elemental symbols can be placed around the cauldron in case anyone wants to use them in blessing the contents for their basket or for blessing the basket itself.

A profusion of May flowers on the altar is appropriate. Daffodils, tulips, and flowering twigs are all appropriate. A sprig of apple blossoms would make a lovely and symbolically correct handle for the Goddess basket. The blossoming apple branch symbolizes She who rules the great round of life and death. Avalon, the realm of the Goddess of death and rebirth, is an isle of apple trees. The apple itself, when cut across, reveals the pentacle with its attendant stations of life represented by the five points. The apple blossoms symbolize the rebirth occurring at this time of year.

Keep the apple blossom branch in a vase of water until the Goddess basket is complete. Attach it as the last edition to the basket. Apple blossoms, like life, are very delicate and fragile, and must be treated with care and respect.

Begin with the ritual bath. May flowers and jasmine incense fill the senses in the bathroom. This ritual bath, in addition to its usual function of cleansing away care and relaxing mind and body in preparation for the ritual work, is also an act of love and caring for the self. Take a few moments to realize how wonderful and how worthy of love you are as you do the ritual cleansing/blessing.

As each woman comes out of the bath, she is presented with a cup of apple blend tea by the Facilitating Priestess, with the words:

"You are an appreciated and important part of my
life, and I care about you."

All sit and wait for the rest to finish their baths. While drinking the tea, think about how good it feels to be cherished and appreciated by someone, and how nice it was to hear some one express that to you. Each then spends some time thinking about how good it is going to feel to prepare and present a basket to someone.

The Facilitating Priestess summons all to the Circle by lighting the altar candles. She sees to it that the Circle is cast, that the participants are consecrated, and that the Quarters are called. Whether she does all of this herself or asks others to help her is up to her. The Goddess is invoked, and She speaks to Her women saying what She will.

The elemental symbols are placed around the cauldron and all settle to making their baskets. When each has finished, each is given a chance to bless her basket by the elements, if she hasn't already. She then tells about the basket and its contents, if she wishes, including presenting it to its recipient if it goes to a coven sister. She then blesses, and tells about her contribution to, the Goddess basket, and places it within the cauldron.

Finally, the Goddess basket is blessed by all by standing and extending right arms to the center above the cauldron and interlocking hands, thereby forming the hub and spokes of a wheel. If all are ambulatory and willing, they begin slowly turning this wheel of Magick by walking slowly around the cauldron, hands still interlocked. As they circle, the Facilitating Priestess intones the blessing:

> "Keeper of the Cauldron, Lady of the Grail before
> Whose shining countenance all Nature is hushed
> and sinks to sleep, accept this gift of loving hands
> and hearts made in Your honor and remembrance
> by these women here, whose lives You have touched
> with love and wonder. May Your bejeweled eyes of
> darkness and light rest kindly upon us and guide
> our going forth and our returning within until we
> are all with You again."

All now begin to chant:

> "Cauldron simmer and cauldron churn,
> Make the wheel of Magick turn,
> accept our gifts, accept our praise,
> give us love and guide our days."

Repeat often, gaining in speed and intensity. When the Facilitating Priestess feels the power is about to peak, she will indicate it by causing a dip at the hub of the wheel. All will then release hands and throw them up in the air, thereby releasing the power to the Goddess.

If the women do not wish to move, the hub and spokes of the wheel of Magick can still be formed over the cauldron, either from a sitting or standing position. They then bounce their arms up and down as though lightly churning butter. When the power is about to peak, the Facilitating Priestess emphasizes the downward bounce and all release hands and raise that arm in the air.

The Ceremony of Milk, Honey and Grain is shared. Feasting follows. Plans are made to distribute baskets to shelters, if the group has agreed to do this. In that case, this ritual would have been changed to suit those particular needs, although the Goddess basket and its blessing and power raising would remain the same.

The Facilitating Priestess for the June Moon reminds everyone of what they are to bring to the June Moon, as well as what the focus of that ritual will be. The Goddess is thanked, the Quarters are dismissed and the Circle is open.

The rite is ended.

The June Full Moon

By this time the night air is warm and inviting, as Summer approaches. This is a wonderful time to worship outdoors in the light of Her full face — to dance with the Moonbeams, to bathe yourselves in Her shimmering softness, and to breathe Her essence upon the wind. This ritual will entail drawing down the Moon, and each woman will have a chance to invoke the Moon Goddess of her choice and to commune with Her.

Since you will probably be meeting at a site other than someone's home, each should take her ritual bath at her own home, complete with candles and incense of her choice. While relaxing in the bath and cleansing away daily cares, spend some time selecting and reflecting on the Moon Goddess you wish to contact/have move through you. Dress for Her/as Her. Bring reminders of Her to help mark the Circle's edge (e. g., stones, statuettes, crystals, shells, flowers, herbs).

At the site you will need: a card table to use as an altar if using the ground is objectionable; a white altar cloth (symbolic of the Moon's face); your usual altar accoutrements; Quarter candles that will not go out (votive candles in paper bags, hurricane chimneys on platforms or something similar of your own devising); your coven cauldron filled with water, and a ladle beside it. If the weather has been such that you can safely have a fire in the center of your Circle, have one. Be sure to clear a spot for it first. Ring it with stones and have enough water on hand to douse it when you leave.

Drums and other rhythm instruments can be used in this ritual. Melodic instruments can be used, as well. Melodic instruments like harp, flute, recorder or guitar may be more appropriate to the invocations section. Remember that in the country sound travels a great distance, so unless you want to attract an audience, play all instruments and do any chanting softly.

When the Facilitating Priestess is ready, she signals a drummer to start playing softly at a walking pace (the heartbeat of the Goddess). This brings the women to the Circle. All join in a free-form AUM chant to attune themselves to each other as the heart/drum beat continues. When the chanting ceases of its own accord, the Facilitating Priestess will light a single taper to the accompaniment of continued drumming. As she lights the candle, she says:

> "In the beginning the divine She of all creation
> opened Her eyes and there was light. Her right eye,
> the Sun. Her left, the Moon."

The Priestess moves to the East and, lighting the East Quarter candle, says:

> "She laughed, and the four winds burst from Her
> divine lips and encircled the globe."

The Priestess moves to the South and, lighting the South candle, says:

> "She lusted and the seed of all creation took root in
> Her womb."

The Priestess moves to the West and, lighting the candle there, says:

> "She labored and the waters of Her womb cas-
> caded down and covered the Earth."

The Priestess moves to the North and lights the North candle, saying:

> "She delivered and the bounty of Her creation
> burst forth upon the land and in the sea."

The Priestess returns to the East, salutes with the taper and says:

> "Thus the world was created,
> the cycle begun —
> All life now connected,
> existing as One." (Drumming stops abruptly.)

The Facilitating Priestess returns to the altar, lights the altar candles and incense, and proceeds to cast the Circle, to consecrate participants and to call the Quarters. At this point, she moves on to the drawing down of the Moon. She may use the words often quoted in other books, or she may use this alternate, and perhaps more ancient, method: picking up the cauldron she turns and faces the Moon, lifting the cauldron to it. If the Moon is directly overhead, she lifts the cauldron above her head, speaking or chanting an invocation to Diana as she does. As she speaks the invocation, she attempts to capture the Moon's reflection on the surface of the water within the cauldron—a true drawing down of the Moon. She may need to move around the Circle in her attempt to draw the Moon into the cauldron.

If unable to gain a reflection, or if the ritual is done indoors, she may symbolically draw the Moon into the cauldron by placing the lunar crescent crown around the lip of the cauldron, or by sinking it within the cauldron if the cauldron is a large one.

As she attempts to draw down the Moon, she may speak or chant what she is moved to say, or she may say:

> "Diana Moon, midnight's Mother, twilight's lover,
> and conjurer of each day's dawning; I invoke and
> call upon Thee Great pearl of Wisdom. I invoke
> Thee by starlight and soul's flight; by heartsong, its
> singing; by life, love and laughter and joy ever after
> to descend into the waters of life here represented,
> so that each may partake of Your essence and drink
> down the Moon."

She lowers the cauldron to the ground (if she hasn't already), ladles some of the Moon-reflected water to her lips, and drinks. Each covener now comes forward, speaks her own invocation to the Moon Goddess of her choice, channels Her if she is able to, pauses for a moment when done, drinks down the Moon from the cauldron — partaking of Diana's essence in so doing — and returns to her place in the Circle.

While each recites her invocation, melodic music may be played softly and others present in the Circle should look for/be open to signs of the presence of that Goddess. If a fire is blazing in the center of your Circle, a flurry of sparks may ascend at a significant moment during an invocation. A log may crack or an image may appear in/from the smoke of the fire. An owl may hoot or screech. A whippoorwill may sing. A dog may bark in the distance, or a coyote may howl. If other Magick is to be done, now is the time, perhaps scrying in the fire and/or the cauldron may be appropriate, or an energy-raising dance around the fire for an agreed upon goal, with or without music and drumming.

Move now to the Thanksgiving and Return (Ceremony of Milk, Honey and Grain), and on to the feasting. An abundance of strawberries (chocolate dipped or not) would be appropriate to this Moon ritual because the June Moon is often referred to as the Strawberry Moon. (How about strawberry short cake, strawberry pie or tarts, or even strawberry Kool Aid!) During the feast, each covener could share what she saw, heard or felt during a particular invocation. When the feasting and conversation winds down, the Facilitating Priestess for the Summer Solstice tells everyone what they will need to bring and to prepare beforehand, and reminds them of the ritual's symbolism.

Diana and the other Goddesses are thanked for their presence by having each woman say the name of her Goddess, beginning with the Facilitating Priestess/Diana and continuing around the Circle. When the Circle is completed, the Priestess finishes the thanks. The Quarters are dismissed and the Circle is declared open. Be sure your fire is out before you leave.

The rite is ended.

THE SUMMER SOLSTICE

(The Mystery of Musk and Patchouli)

This is the time of fertility realized. The Earth is lush and green, flowers bloom everywhere, pollination occurs, warm sunlight caresses the skin and moist breezes kiss the night. Aradia becomes fully mature and the embodiment of the Magick of love — of Herself and of other(s). She participates, and we with Her, in the Mystery of Musk and Patchouli, of muscle and moisture, of hard sinews and soft curves, of fire and velvet.

Diana, Her Mother, has assured us that "all acts of love and pleasure are My rituals." In preparing for this ritual, you will need to decide how you are most comfortable participating in this Mystery. You may wish to experience it alone — learning to love yourself in totality, and learning to appreciate the wonders of your physical form, your embodiment of the divine within in this lifetime. Perhaps you will wish to share this Mystery with your permanent or current partner, or you may just wish to experience a mystic union with the Earth Herself.

Once you have decided, you (or you and your partner) will need to prepare a love bower to which you will go as a part of the ritual. Ideally, the ritual and the Mystery will both take place outside, weather and inclination permitting. The love bower can be anything you like, as simple or as elaborate as you wish. It could be a sleeping bag and an air mattress deep in the woods, out under the stars, in a cave, or in a trough dug in the ground. It could be a room rented in a fancy hotel, or it could be your own bed/room at home bedecked with flowers, incense and crystals. Whatever it is, it should stimulate the physical and mystical experience of the Mystery. On this night all become Aradia, and mark Her passage into the manifestation of love and sexual expression.

As with any Mystery, the experience of it marks a transition. Something old passes away or is no longer needed, and something new takes its place. Something is willingly sacrificed so that something new can be born/created. Think about what that sacrifice will be for you. What will pass away as a result of this experience? Find a symbol of that thing, or write it on a slip of paper, and bring it with you to the ritual. Likewise, think about what you hope will be born, or transformed, within yourself as a result of experiencing the Mystery. Find a symbol for it and place it in your love bower.

You will also need to bring fresh cut flowers to the ritual site. These flowers should be red, yellow or orange, or any combination thereof, to represent/remember the Solstice — the Sun/Aradia at Her peak of power.

If you will be meeting on open land, take your ritual bath at home, floating rose petals and lovage (symbols of love) in the water, and burning musk or patchouli incense in your censer (to arouse the passions). Use candlelight, of course. The object here is to pamper yourself and to get those love juices flowing through the body's senses by using warm water; earthy, sensual scents; the Mystery, shadows and alluring sight of candlelight. While you are bathing, bite into a peach, plum or nectarine, and meditate on its sensual nature: its smooth (or fuzzy) skin, its juicy and succulent interior and the hard pit within. You may wish to drizzle the fruit with honey, or to eat a honeycomb in honor of sweet Melissa. (You may also wish to have these foods available in your love bower to feast upon during or after the Mystery.)

If meeting at someone's home, do the ritual bath there. Dress in a sensual fashion, as you feel Aradia would dress, or wear nothing at all. You may wish to wear cowrie shells, or put flowers in your hair. There should be a fire in the cauldron. If you are meeting outside, you may wish to dig a fire pit, thereby making a cauldron of the Earth Herself. An altar cloth of orange and/or yellow would be appropriate for the Solstice. Your other altar accoutrements should be present as well, with the chalice taking the central position. The chalice becomes the Loving Cup and will be filled with damiana tea (with extra available in a thermos). The following herbs (fresh, if possible) should wreath its base: coriander (the immortality of love), catnip (for playfulness and sensuality), Red Raspberry leaves (to keep the female system in tone and functioning well), Red Clover blossoms (for truth and fidelity within a relationship — between lovers and "to thine own self be true"), and rose petals (for the ability to love and nurture, and to see beauty in all things).

For this ritual it is helpful to use anointing oils that will arouse the passions and, since different scents do it for different people, it is important to offer a choice at the point of individual consecrations. Rich earthy scents do it for some people, so offer patchouli oil as a possibility. Flower scents do it for others. Rose Geranium oil is most often Magickally associated with rituals of this type. Musk oil also is very arousing. Have a small vial of each (or others of your own choosing) on the altar, and let each person (or each couple) decide beforehand what they would like. Have each hand their choice to the Facilitating Priestess at the point of consecration.

Quarter candles, bonfire and altar candles are lit. This signals the women to gather at the entrance of the Circle with their cut flowers. The Facilitating Priestess signals the drummer(s) to begin the "Triple Cauldron Chant." (Drummers chant the continuo, all others chant the verses.) As they chant, the women walk around the Circle three times, the Facilitating Priestess in the lead. After the third revolution, she stops and places her flowers on the ground behind her. All do likewise, thus forming the Circle.

Triple Cauldron Chant

Drummers rhythmically say:

> "Transformation,
> Inspiration,
> Well-spring of Eternal life."

All others sing:

There's a cauldron deep inside me and it's made of   blood and bone

There's a cauldron called the ocean and there's heaven's starry dome

Rid-ges end - ing in the fore-st   ly - ing 'neath two rounded peaks
is the   end - ing to your quest-ing, is   the   Grail font that you seek.

The Facilitating Priestess says:

> "Tonight, as Aradia, we each feel the pull of our
> body yearning to experience the sacredness of
> itself. Whether alone, or in pairs, we are about to
> experience the transformation of our bodies into a
> divine instrument of loving expression. May each
> breath inspire Her manifestation, and may we
> drink deeply from Her well-spring of eternal sus-
> tenance."

The Circle is cast and consecrated. Participants are consecrated with the oil of their choice, and the Quarters are called:

East:

> "Heady breezes fill our nostrils with the scents of love and lust. Make us supple as wind-kissed tree-tops gently bending in a breeze. Caress our skin and lift our spirits. Guard us in our loving place."

South:

> "Smoldering embers of passion too long pent, burst forth in flames of love and lust. Ignite the sparks down deep within us and stoke the furnace where we lie."

West:

> "Elixir of Life — moist lips, moist thighs, waters of women, bless our sweet rapture with ebbing and flowing."

North:

> "Great mountains, deep clefts, caves, passages and mounds — our bodies, like yours, are now sacred ground. Be with us, enjoin us, and grant us skilled hands."

The Facilitating Priestess finishes by returning to the East and saluting with her Athame.

Restoke the cauldron fire if necessary. The Facilitating Priestess speaks of the transformative nature of experiencing a Mystery, of how some things pass away as a result of the experience, and of how new things take their place. She invites women to come forward, one at a time, and toss into the cauldron fire the symbol of what they expect to have pass from their lives as a result of experiencing the Mystery of Musk and Patchouli. She is careful to remind them that their expectation and what actually is forever transformed/gone *may* be two different things and to be open to, and aware of, this possibility. While women approach the fire, the coveners quietly chant:

Cauldron Fire

Cauldron fire, burn a - way this rel - ic from my bygone days

After the Facilitating Priestess has thrown in her own symbol, she moves back behind the altar (if she isn't already there). There she begins preparing the Loving Cup. She fills the chalice with the hot damiana tea, and places a small amount of each of the herbs from the herbal wreathe encircling the cup into a tea ball and snaps it shut (the rose petals are not included). When all have finished at the cauldron fire, the chanting stops. The Facilitating Priestess then explains what she is doing and the Magickal/symbolic meaning of the tea and each herb in it. She says something to the effect of:

> "Before leaving the Circle tonight to partake of the Mystery we will share the Loving Cup. In it I've placed hot, strong damiana tea and honey—known as an aphrodisiac by wise women for centuries. In it you'll also taste a hint of coriander for the immortal nature of this loving; Red Clover blossoms for truth within your relationship, and for being true to yourself; catnip for playfulness and sensual luxuriousness; Red Raspberry leaves to tone the female system and to keep it functioning well; and finally, I'm floating rose petals on the surface to enhance your ability to love and to nurture and to see the beauty in all things and everyone, including yourselves."

She stirs the tea ball around in circles, using its chain as a handle. As she does so, she speaks this, or a similar, spell:

> "Magick brew within this cup,
> stir our passions, heat them up.
> All our fears shall come to naught
> by this cupful's potent draught.

> The Cauldron Keeper of Cauldron Wise
> says all is sacred where our love lies."

The Facilitating Priestess drinks from the cup and passes it to the woman on her left. She, in turn, drinks and passes it on. Thus, all receive the draught. The Priestess stands ready with refills as necessary. When the cup returns to her, she places it on the altar and prepares to open a gate in the Circle to release the women to their love bowers. Before they go, she reminds them to return by dawn's new light to offer thanks in the cauldron fire for any new insights gained through experiencing the night's Mystery, and/or to bless a symbol of the same by the four elements. After they do so, the ritual is ended for them and they are to return home, keeping the night's experiences close to their hearts. She then opens a gate in the northeast quadrant of the Circle, and all depart for their bowers.

The Facilitating Priestess is the last to leave, closing the gate behind her. She either banks the fire (if her bower is within sight of the fire) or she lights a candle from the fire, puts the fire out, and takes the lit candle with her. Before dawn she returns to the Circle, opens the gate, and rekindles the cauldron fire — either by adding wood, or by lighting it anew using the flame from the previous fire, which she has carried with her in the form of the lit candle. She makes her own offering and then withdraws to a distance, leaving the gate open, and waits until all have returned and left again.

When all have departed, she returns to the Circle and seals it. She then pours any remaining tea on the ground (or on the fire) as an offering to the Earth and thanks to the Mother, dismisses the Quarters and opens the Circle. She then douses the fire, packs up the ritual equipment and goes home, probably to sleep!

The rite is ended.

July Full Moon

(Ritual for Independence)

July 4th marks Independence Day in America, yet many people in this country are far from independent. The number of homeless people is rising constantly. Many of them are women and children. The vast majority of working women in the United States do not earn enough money to support themselves, much less any dependent children they might have. Many women opt to stay in abusive situations because they could not support themselves if they left. Racism, sexism and the abuse of women and children cut across all economic lines, and the number of people living below the poverty level grows daily. True independence belongs to a privileged few.

But Aradia come to Earth to change all that! In addition to revealing to us the Mysteries of the seasonal cycles and of our own lives, She also encourages us to fight oppression and tyranny wherever it is found. Whether or not the July Full Moon falls on or near July 4th, it is a good time to work for freedom from oppression because the spirit of independence is so close at hand during this month.

I have two visions for this ritual. One is that the coven agree on an issue of oppression and jointly work Magick to transform it in a positive way. The other, perhaps more likely, scenario is for each woman in the coven to work her own particular Magick on the issue nearest and dearest to her. Each should use her own best method of creative expression, including drawing on the Aradia within. For example, those with artistic talents could draw/paint/ photograph a picture, or series of pictures, representing the transformation of her chosen issue, visualizing it actually occurring as she creates it. Someone who enjoys dancing could choreograph the changes she wants to bring about. Another could do a brief ritual drama. Someone who likes to write could pen a "declaration of independence" for her issue. A song or chant could be created and shared.

The Facilitating Priestess, in addition to working her own spell, should take notes within the Circle on the spells of others, so that all may be placed in the Cauldron of Transformation as a final and unifying Magickal act during of the ritual.

If you have one, a statue or picture of Lady Liberty/the Goddess of Freedom would enhance your altar. Goddesses of justice, freedom, strength and/or virgins (complete unto themselves) can be invoked during the ritual, or at the four Quarters, in addition to the elements.

Since this ritual could take awhile — especially if individual Magick is to be worked — it is important to be comfortable. Casting a large Circle around living room furniture, or around folding chairs is a good idea. The use of a performance area also will require a large Circle.

The altar is set up as usual. The Cauldron of Transformation has a fire laid within it. The Magick offerings should take place between the altar and the cauldron since both represent the spiritual presence of Goddess.

Each participant should feel free to ask the group for assistance in the completion of her spell. The group could help by repeating an affirmation, mantra, or chant; by providing rhythmic accompaniment for a dance, or to raise power; by adding their own positive statements regarding the transformation of the issue at hand; and in other ways appropriate to the spell.

The ritual format remains the same. The ritual bath signals the beginning of the ritual. The donning of ritual garb and/or the red cord completes this process, and links you to the Goddess and to every woman born. It especially links you to all women performing on this ritual this night. It links you to the ways of wise women and to the spirit of Aradia, who walks the Earth with us and guides our efforts on this night.

After the bath, all sit quietly drinking tea or spring water, and all meditate on the task at hand. When the Facilitating Priestess is ready, she calls everyone to the Circle by lighting the altar candles. All other lights are doused. The Circle is cast, the participants are consecrated and the Quarters are called.

The Facilitating Priestess turns and faces the Moon and invokes the blessings of Diana on the rite. She then invokes the activist spirit of Aradia to indwell within the Circle and the participants. As she does this (or when she finishes), she lights the cauldron fire to symbolize both the presence of Aradia and the transformative power of Her activist spirit. Once this is done the individual (or group) Magick is performed. The Facilitating Priestess takes notes for use in the final spell. At the end of the group's contributions, she sets the cumulative spell of transformation, and tosses the paper containing her notes into the cauldron fire while all chant/shout:

> "Change it!
> Re-arrange it!
> Engage it — now!!!"

The Magick is followed by the ritual of Milk, Honey and Grain. Feasting and appropriate discussion ensue. When all are ready,

Diana and Aradia are thanked, the Quarters are dismissed and the Circle is declared open.

The rite is ended.

LAMMAS
(The Green and the Gold)

At this point in the life cycle of Aradia, she reaches physical and emotional maturity and chooses a permanent partner. As a result, Lammas was (and is) the traditional time of handfastings/trysts (weddings). In days past, people used to gather and celebrate these unions en masse. These marriages often lasted for only a year and a day, and were dissolved the following Lammas by simply having the couple stand back-to-back and walk away from each other. Other hands joined at Lammas remained so for life.

With the rise of Christianity, this custom gradually faded away until all that remained was the Lammas Faire: a gathering of kindred and folk to share food, gossip and fun in the form of horse races, divination/fortune-telling, clowns, kissing booths (what's left of the handfasting ritual) and confectioneries. It survives today in Britain in the form of the village or church fete, and in this country as the church social or picnic, and often has the ulterior motive of raising money to pay the church heating bills for the upcoming Winter, or to bolster the village library or building fund.

If your coven is a part of a larger community of Wiccans and Pagans in your area, organizing a Lammas Faire — Pagan style — would be fun. Handfastings/trysts could be included, or a Lammas Love (representative of Aradia) could be chosen and She could be symbolically united with the person of Her choice in a ritual drama.

If your coven is not a part of a larger Pagan community, either by choice or by circumstance, a trip to the nearest Renaissance Faire could serve the same purpose. You could also engage in a brief ritual drama consisting of the symbolic handfasting of Aradia and Her partner. This drama is meant to be "in fun," yet it points to a deeper Mystery underlying it. While the child within will have fun, ask the deeper mind to be open to the Mystery.

No Circle is needed for this drama. In fact, it could begin before attending the Lammas Faire/Renaissance Faire and could be completed later, when the coven is alone again. The part of Aradia should be chosen by lots. The part of Her partner can be chosen in a number of ways. The partner can also be chosen by lots, or Aradia can choose Her partner through a game of "blindman's bluff," or the partner can be chosen in some other way. In the case of blindman's bluff, Aradia is blindfolded and counts aloud to thirteen while everyone scatters. When She reaches thirteen, all freeze in place and She searches for Her partner. Women can call to Her from their various positions, enticing Her to them and away from others, or all can remain silent. Or, some sort of contest can be arranged, in which case the winner becomes Aradia's partner. Or, Aradia can be blindfolded and a number of small personal/ Magickal items — one from each coven member — can be placed before Her on the altar (or on any table). She will handle each item and choose the one that feels best to Her. The owner of that item becomes Her partner. Or, Aradia can hide in a woods and the person who finds Her becomes Her beloved. Here, She can entice and lead all on a merry chase if She wishes.

However Her partner is chosen, Aradia makes the following statement as lots are drawn, as blindman's bluff is played, as the contest begins, as items are handled, or as She hides and leads the chase:

> "Oh ye who would wed me, you think on this song —
> Whoever will wed me will lose me 'ere long
> For courting's a pleasure and marriage is bliss
> but old age and dying soon follow all this.
> Beginnings bring endings and endings, rebirth
> in cycles unending ruled by love and by mirth."

When Her partner has been decided, the Facilitating Priestess takes the red cord from around Aradia's waist (or picks one up from the altar/table) and binds the hands of Aradia and Her partner together at the wrist (the handfasting), saying:

> "By this lifeline two lives are entwined."

Aradia and Her partner then remain bound together for the remainder of the day. This will provide some interesting insights for the couple and some good-natured fun for the rest of the coven.

As evening approaches, the coven returns to the covenstead to prepare for the night's ritual. If dinner is to be shared prior to the ritual, salmon with hazelnut stuffing or venison are traditionally associated with this holiday. If you are vegetarians, skip the meat or fish and focus on bread/wheat dishes. Lammas is also loaf-mass: the celebration of the wheat harvest and the beginning of harvest time in general.

The altar is covered with green and gold cloth(s). The usual altar accoutrements are present. The cauldron is wreathed with the fruits and vegetables ripe at this time. Items of woven wheat are especially appropriate — around the cauldron, on the altar, at the Quarters — wherever you like. They represent the wheat harvest and the intertwining of lives through handfasting/trysting, as well as the intertwining of life and death.

The green and gold theme is carried into the ritual bath area through the use of green and gold candles. A small wreath of braided grasses floats in the bath water (or two small joined wreaths). Incense reminiscent of orchards and vines is most appropriate. An herbal tea of fresh leaves, such as comfrey, awaits all after the bath.

Aradia and Her partner are still joined, so they will have to help each other through the bath process as well as in dressing for the ritual. Dress however you like, or not at all. You may wish to carry the green and gold theme into your clothing, or you may wish to wear clothing you feel is appropriate to ceremonies of union.

During the taking of tea, think back over the day. Remember the fun and seek the Mysteries hidden in the games. Think about what it means to be fully mature/ripe, and what it means to be pair bonded, and its place in the grand cycle. What did you see? What did you feel? What did you learn? What bears further meditation and thought? What does it mean for your life?

As the altar candles are lit, finish your tea and join the Circle. If you are pair bonded and your partner is present, walk hand-in-hand to the Circle and retain that link in the Circle (thus becoming representatives of Aradia and Her partner). If you are not in a bonded relationship, remember past experiences — the joy and the lessons, or why you've chosen not to be in a bonded relationship. If you are bonded but your partner is not present, establish a link to that love in your mind. Aradia and Her partner stand in the center of the Circle, one on each side of the cauldron, bound hands over the cauldron, facing the altar and the Facilitating Priestess. She welcomes everyone to the Circle, saying what she will, or saying:

Today we have celebrated the union of Aradia with Her true love. Tonight we celebrate the ripening of the harvest and share in the meaning of its first fruits.

All chant:

The Green and The Gold

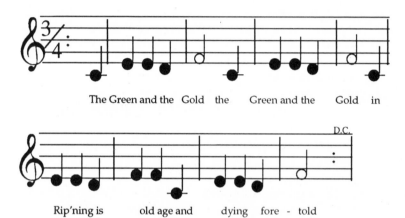

As the chant is repeated, the Facilitating Priestess casts the Circle and Aradia and Her partner place all the fruits of the harvest into the cauldron, the origin of the horn of plenty. A loaf of freshly baked bread and a wheat weaving should be on top. (Preferably this should be a weaving of two interlocked circles to signify the two lives joined. If unavailable however, a woven circle representing the wheel of the year / the life cycle will suffice.) Participants are anointed, with bonded pairs being anointed together.

For this ritual, the Quarters are called in pairs, with Aradia and Her partner acting as the axis for the pairings and the turning. The cauldron represents the axis of the world. Aradia and Her partner each hold their free hand out to the direction nearest to them. East and West are called first by the Facilitating Priestess, the couple, or anyone the group has decided will do so:

"Spirits of the East and West
bring to us your very best:
knowledge and wisdom,
youth and old age,
sunrise and sunset,
most ancient of days."

The couple turn deosil around the cauldron, arms extended to North and South:

"Spirits of the South and North,
Here, attend, we call thee forth.
Passion, its ending
maturity, death
noon day and darkness
the end of this quest."

The Great Goddess who rules all cycles is invoked. The Facilitating Priestess speaks as she will, or she can say:

"Mother of the sacred round
within whom life and death are found,
be with us here and guide our hands,
as we would weave another strand
that leads from birth to death and then,
spins around to birth again."

The Facilitating Priestess approaches the couple at the cauldron, enfolds their hands in her own, and says:

"The harvest now begins apace,
these two, their lives now interlaced,
face life as one,
then life alone,
the die is cast,
each thread is sewn.
They'll move through life
to bleached white bone
only to arise in Spring
infused with new life which it brings."

The coven again chants "The Green and the Gold." As they do, the Facilitating Priestess removes the cord from the couple's wrists and drops it into the cauldron, signifying their separation at death and the cauldron's power to transform death into life again. As the cord is dropped into the cauldron, pairs in the Circle drop hands and the chanting stops.

Allow a brief pause before moving on to the Thanksgiving and Return. This ritual is often quite moving for people. They may wish to hug each other or to speak what is in their hearts at that moment. Individuals within the Circle often will have a new and deeper understanding of just how important other people, particularly their coven siblings, are in their lives and may like to say so, or they might just appreciate them with a loving glance or, perhaps, tears.

On the other hand, it may dawn on someone that they no longer belong in the group — that others outside the group are more important — and that perhaps they need to consider withdrawing from the group or starting another. If so, the group can make plans to ritually mark the person's leave taking/rite of passage at the August or September Full Moon.

Proceed then with the Thanksgiving and Return, using the loaf of bread from the cauldron as well as the usual milk and honey. All then settle in to feast on the first fruits in the cauldron and anything else people have brought to share. When all are ready, the Priestess thanks Goddess, dismisses the Quarters and declares the Circle open.

The rite is ended.

August Full Moon

Around my neck of the woods August is the month when hunters begin to prepare for the upcoming hunting seasons. The August Full Moon is also known as the Wort Moon: Wort as in Wortcunning, which means, basically, plant knowledge (i. e., the ability to heal through the use of plants). Wort means plant. Therefore, it is appropriate to do a ritual to protect endangered species at the August Full Moon.

The use of the word "endangered" can be thought of in several ways during the ritual. Each woman is, of course, allowed to define it in the way(s) she feels best suit(s) her. Endangered can mean those plants and animals on the Endangered Species List. It can mean any animal endangered through non-respectful hunting practices. (Non-respectful hunters are those who do not, prior to the hunt, speak with the Goddess and/or the spirits of the animals to secure permission from each for the kill. It also includes those not skillful enough to mercifully drop the prey with a single shot, and those who do not feed their families with what they kill.) It can mean any plant considered to be a noxious weed and thereby targeted for destruction, even though it may have beneficial medicinal properties. Or, it may be a plant labelled as toxic by those who misunderstand its proper use and/or dosage.

For the purposes of this ritual, each woman is to choose an endangered animal or plant and to become that being for/during the ritual. Allow creativity to flow here. Make a mask representing your choice. Make a costume as well, if you wish. Research its behavior and/or life cycle. Learn where it is found and what conditions are necessary for it to flourish. Meditate on it and take its essence into yourself. Practice becoming it, and gift it with the ability to speak through you to others.

On the night of the ritual, each arrives with her mask (and costume) prepared. (Or coveners could gather in the afternoon to make their masks out of materials they've brought with them.) The ritual bath is prepared by drawing a shallow bath. Since all will be asked to take the ritual bath in the manner in which her species of choice would bathe/get wet, chances are some will need to use the shower to represent rainfall.

Brown and green candles illuminate the bath area. The incense chosen should be reminiscent of animals — musk or patchouli, for example — or plant scents like pine, cedar, or any of the floral incenses.

After the bath, costumes are donned by those who have them, the red cord being worn underneath the costume. Masks are donned during the ritual. Those without costumes can dress as they prefer or can choose to go skyclad.

Everyone is given a psychic tea consisting of eyebright, cloves, camomile, peppermint, Lemon Balm and thyme mixed to taste and steeped in stainless steel, enamel or glass for at least 15 minutes. This will aid in opening the psychic centers through which the transformation from woman to endangered species will begin. Each woman mulls over her being in her mind as she stirs and drinks her tea while waiting for the ritual to begin.

The altar tools are laid on the gold and green altar cloth(s) used at Lammas. Or, the coven may prefer to use the traditional white of the Full Moon. The cauldron contains an unlit votive candle. As the Facilitating Priestess lights the altar candles, the women assemble in a Circle. The Facilitating Priestess casts the Circle around them in the usual manner. The participants are consecrated with a special oil designed to open the third eye.

This oil is prepared by simmering equal parts of eyebright, mistletoe berries, mandrake root, cloves, mugwort, angelica, Bay Laurel and thyme in a stainless steel, enamel or glass pan in a small amount of olive oil for 10 minutes. The mixture is then removed from the heat and is allowed to cool completely. It is then strained through cheesecloth to remove the plant materials/sediment. The remaining oil is then placed in a special vial. It is labelled, "Psychic Oil - for external use only." (This oil does not keep well. Make it the day of, or the day before, the ritual. Refrigerate it if not using it the same day. It also helps to make it in the hour of the Moon or when the Moon is in a water sign.) The Facilitating Priestess puts some oil on her finger and then places her moistened finger on the third eye of the woman in front of her. Without lifting her finger from the third eye, she makes an outward spiral to encompass the entire area of the third eye, thereby opening it through sympathetic Magick. All are consecrated in this manner. The Priestess does herself last.

The Quarters are then invoked by the Priestess, or by those chosen to do so. The Goddess as Lady of the Beasts, Mistress of the Wild Things and Goddess of Vegetation is invoked by the Facilitating Priestess. As she does so, she lights the votive candle in the Cauldron of Transformation. She may invoke with words that come to her, or she can say:

Diana, in whose sacred grove the wild things run free, Lady of the beasts on land, Birdwoman of the airborne, Le Mer of sea creatures, Ruler of the rooted ones; come forth and enliven our Circle, our Magick, and the endangered of Earth. As we transform and partake of their essence, we'll shift the shape of their future as well. All beings endangered are helped by our Magick. All beings endangered are safe through this spell.

Each begins to become her chosen being through meditation, visualization, or whatever means work best for her. Feel the body begin to change. Let movement and sound come as it wishes. When each feels the transformation is almost complete, she stands astride the Cauldron of Transformation and dons her mask. That action is the trigger/key to complete the metamorphosis, though the ability to speak is retained.

All spend a few minutes acting as their being — moving as it would move, sounding as it would sound, speaking its wisdom and affirming its continued existence. When the Facilitating Priestess feels that the power is moving toward its peak, she begins the following spell:

> "Life assured and life engendered,
> in the web we all are one.
> Life protected and remembered —
> Chant the spell and be it done!"

As others hear her, they join the incantation. As it builds in power and volume, each removes her mask and raises it to the sky above her, dancing with it above her head. When the Facilitating Priestess feels the power peak, she drops to the floor placing her mask at the base of the cauldron. All simultaneously do the same. Placing the masks at the Cauldron of Transformation releases the spell to become manifest around the world. All sit and catch their breath, ground out if they need to, and return completely to their own natural state. The Ceremony of Milk, Honey and Grain is shared. Feasting and appropriate conversation follow. Any information necessary regarding the September Full Moon is discussed by the Facilitating Priestess for that Moon and all present. When ready, the Priestess thanks the Goddess, dismisses the Quarters and opens the Circle.

The rite is ended.

September Full Moon

The September Full Moon finds the harvest season in full swing and moving toward its completion. Some crops are already harvested and processed. Others are coming in daily, and a few remain to be harvested. The season of thanksgiving is here. This is a good time to show our appreciation for all the Magick that has become manifest in our lives since those early Spring workings we did to put our Magick in motion.

For this ritual, each woman is asked to bring three pieces of yarn, each eighteen inches in length. One piece should be either silvertone or white (for the Moon Goddess). One should be yellow or gold (for the Sun Goddess). One should be brown or green (for the Earth Goddess). Also present should be a crescent-shaped branch, longer than the cauldron is wide, for use in the Fruition Amulet. This branch should be of either willow (to foreshadow the coming Crone time) or of Apple wood (signifying the harvest time). A bowl of dried, shelled, corn, some slips of recycled paper and some pens; or some fresh corn husks and Magic Markers will be necessary, as well.

The Cauldron of Plenty contains fruits of the current harvest. The traditional white altar cloth, or a gold one, gold altar candles and the usual altar paraphernalia, including harvest decorations, and the Quarter candles are in place. Perhaps you will want to gather early to share a supper of the produce from your garden(s). In any case, such foods should be available for feasting within the Circle in addition to the milk, honey and grain.

Proceed with the ritual bath as usual, including incense and candlelight. Serve a tea of your own choosing as each woman comes out of the bath. Using the fresh herbs available would be appropriate, as would any of the apple blends on the market. As each woman bathes and then drinks her tea, she silently reflects on the variety of things that have become manifest in her life during this growing season. Remember the minor things as well as the major . Remember the unplanned as well as the planned; the steps completed in an as yet unfinished operation; what worked and what did not. All of the women come to the Circle as the altar candles are lit. The Facilitating Priestess asks everyone to place their three lengths of yarn near the cauldron. She picks up the bowl of dried corn and asks each woman to take a handful as she offers it to her. As she stands before each woman and offers the bowl, she says:

> "Join me in creating the mandala of our sacred space."

As each woman receives her corn, she turns around and lays it on the ground behind her, thus creating her own arc of the Magick Circle. When all have finished, the corn is returned to the altar and the Circle is cast. Participants are consecrated and the Quarters are invoked by the Facilitating Priestess or by those previously chosen to do so. The Goddess is invoked. Everyone sits down. The Priestess explains the construction and the purpose of the Fruition Amulet in words of her own choosing, or she can say:

> "A Fruition Amulet is a Magickal and visual representation of the success of our harvest and an offering of thanks for it. The branch is the fertile crescent of the Moon. The tri-colored yarns represent the Sun, the Moon and the Earth, each of which has a profound effect on the growing season. On the corn husks (or recycled paper), symbolic of this month's Corn Moon, we will write all of the things that have come to pass in our lives as a result of our efforts and of Her aid. These will then be braided into the yarn and kept in a place of honor until the next planting season. At that time the amulet will be buried to encourage another successful harvest next year. The braiding represents the interplay of Sun, Moon and Earth. The insertion of the husks (paper) in the braiding puts them in a place thought sacred for centuries — suspended between heaven and earth."

If you have chosen to use recycled paper instead of the corn husks, make the appropriate substitution and deletion in the above.

As she speaks, she hands the branch around the Circle, and all attach their group of three yarns and begin to write on the corn husks/paper. Remember to pull the yarn tight around the husks/ paper and to knot all three yarn ends together at the end of each woman's offering.

To keep everyone occupied while each woman braids her offerings, the Facilitating Priestess moves the bowl of corn to the center of the Circle, next to the cauldron. Each woman takes a small handful of corn from the bowl. Each tosses the kernels, one by one, into the Cauldron of Plenty, naming each kernel with something for which she is thankful. She can name what she is including in the Fruition Amulet as well as any number of other things for which she is thankful. Feel free to toss in kernels at random. No particular order needs to be observed, although I would recommend that everyone listen to each other as kernels are tossed, and not speak over each other or at the same time as someone else.

When all have finished with their kernels of thanks, and the Fruition Amulet is completed, bless it by the four elements and lay it on top of the Cauldron of Plenty. The elemental blessing can be words of her own choosing, or the Facilitating Priestess, as she passes the amulet through the smoke from the censer, can say:

"By the Air that brings Her essence . . . "

Passing it near the flame of the altar candles, she says:

"By the Fire that burns within . . . "

As she sprinkles it with water, she says:

"By the Waters of Her wellspring . . . "

When sprinkling it with salt, she says:

"By the Earth of which it's been . . . "

Placing it on the cauldron, she says:

"Is this charm made,
Is the spell laid,
here, upon the cauldron's rim."

All link together in whatever way seems best (tie cords together, hold hands, use eye contact, or whatever else works best for the group). The Facilitating Priestess says:

Fruitful Mother of Abundance, the harvest time has come again in our lives. The seeds we planted have quickened, grown and matured, and we have reaped their rewards. For all that You have done for us, and all that's yet to come, we thank You.

All pick up the last line as a rhythmic chant, as follows:

"For all that You have done for us and all that's yet to come, THANK YOU!"

Repeat this, getting louder and louder and then softer and softer until it dies away in a whispered, "Thank You!"

Move on to the Ceremony of Milk, Honey and Grain, followed by feasting on the bounty of the season and appropriate conversation. The Facilitating Priestess for the Fall Equinox ritual — the Croning — reminds all of the point of the ritual and what they are to bring. When ready, the Priestess thanks the Goddess, dismiss the Quarters and declares the Circle open.

The Fruition Amulet is hung in a place of honor within the Facilitating Priestess's home until the next Spring, when she will bring it to the Spring planting ritual to be buried as part of the blessing of the garden space. (Either her own or the coven's communal garden, if it has one.) Failing any garden space at all, she will bury it wherever she and the coven feel it appropriate to do so.

The rite is ended.

THE FALL EQUINOX
(The Croning)

The Fall Equinox signals the beginning of the Fall and the end of the growing season. Though a few things remain to be cut down, in the main the harvest is in and will most certainly be complete by the time the leaves have fallen from the trees and Samhain/ Hallows is again upon us. From here on in, the nights are longer than the days until the Spring Equinox, when we will again celebrate the coming forth into the light cycle of life and new beginnings.

Now, in the twilight of the year, we honor the coming of the Crone and the special gifts and lessons She brings. So, too, Aradia enters the twilight of Her years and becomes Crone. And we, along with Aradia, are reminded of endings — of what is allowed to fall away and what is saved for seed, and that which must be cut off to encourage new growth and the renewal of the cycle.

For this ritual, each woman is asked to bring a small pouch filled with seeds and/or nuts in the shell, a pair of scissors, several sheets of construction paper in Fall colors, and a black ink pen or fine line marker. The altar cloth should be rust and gold to symbolize the colors of the season, or rust (for the season) and gray (for the gray hair of the Crone). The altar candles should be gray. In addition to the regular altar accoutrements, bring a hand-held, working sickle, if your coven does not already have one. The sharpness of the sickle adds to its power as a symbol of the Crone.

As always, the Cauldron of Transformation is in the center of the Circle. An incense of frankincense and myrrh, an ancient funerary blend, should burn on the altar and in the ritual bath area. Fall flowers and other items indicative of Fall should be on the altar and in the bath area, and gray candles should be in the bath area, as well.

In addition to washing away daily care and preparing the Self for ritual and to walk with the Goddess, the individual bather should open herself to the Aradia within and to the traits of the Crone She will manifest through her. This will be encouraged further within the Circle, but beginning preparations should be made in the bath.

As participants emerge from the bath, each is given a cup of herb tea by the Facilitating Priestess, who bows slightly to each woman to acknowledge the croning Aradia surfacing within her. This tea could be anything you like or could contain herbs to relax and soothe (mint or mint blends); to open the psychic centers (the psychic tea); or a blend meant to ease the croning of the body (sage, licorice, and/or red raspberry leaves).

Each may dress as she chooses. Wearing Fall colors and/or a hooded robe (indicative of the Crone) might be appropriate. The pouch of seeds/nuts should hang from the red cord, and from its tether end should hang the scissors. Each woman places her construction paper and pen around the cauldron before she gets her tea from the Facilitating Priestess.

While drinking her tea, each woman gives some thought to what she would like to cut out of her life and/or what things she should simply let fall away. Each woman thinks, too, of those things in life which need re-planting now for rebirth in the Spring. Thought is given to these same types of actions on the social/political/ecological scale as well.

As the Facilitating Priestess lights the altar candles, the women assemble in the Circle. The Priestess says:

> "The celebrants at Eleusis knew, as did those who gathered in Diana's grove in Italy, that without death there can be no life, and that in dying, we are promised rebirth. Thus is the Earth eternally re-newed as are we ourselves in our own time. Though the Maiden kills capriciously, upon a whim for perceived hurt; and the Mother kills to protect Her

223

beloved; the Crone it is, with cool eye and deft precision, who administers the coup de grace to us all. It is She who sets in motion the change from life to death and life again. It is She who turns the wheel in Fall and She, Aradia's becoming."

The Facilitating Priestess or her chosen delegate casts the Circle and consecrates it by the elements. All participants are consecrated with oil to bring out the Croning Aradia, as follows:

"Aradia, Goddess-woman born, today You become Crone. Come forth within (Witch name) here, and guide her hand, heart and mind within this Circle. Bring her elder wisdom of seasons in the Sun spent harrowing and winnowing until her harvest's done."

The Quarters are called by the Priestess (or her delegate), using words of her own choosing, or using the invocations given in the chapter on ritual construction. The Priestess, holding her athame in one hand the sickle in the other, and forming a horned crescent with her arms, with her feet apart, invokes the Crone, saying what she will, or by saying:

"Morrigan, Cailleach Bheur, the Washer at the Ford; Midwife of all endings, Mistress of the Night Mare; the Self we fear to face, come forth! Draw nigh! and visit Thy Ancient Grace upon Aradia, Goddess-woman Croned this night, made so within this place. Give us Your wise, discerning eye, to know what goes, what stays. Give us the will to persevere when trouble comes our way. Give us Your sure internal knowing that death ends not our days. And when we come to stand before You, in barrow, mound or hill, work Your Magick, spin the thread that gives us lives to fill. (*Crone may speak if She will.*)"

The Facilitating Priestess replaces the athame and sickle upon the altar, and invites all to sit around the cauldron. She instructs them as to the methods of individual Magickal transformation to be used, by saying something to the effect of:

"Take a few minutes now to draw a variety of leaves on the construction paper you've brought. Allow the discerning eye and steady hand of the Croning Aradia to help you decide what needs to be cut out of your life. Write or draw a brief phrase, or symbol, representing these things on the leaves you've outlined. Then, use your scissors to cut out the leaves, and drop them into the Cauldron of Transformation one by one. Cutting out the shapes will signal to your deep Self to begin this culling action in your life. Dropping them one by one into the Cauldron of Transformation shows your deep Self just how effortless and easy the removal of these things can be from your life — as easy and as graceful as leaves falling from a tree. You may speak these little deaths aloud as they fall into the cauldron, or you may keep silence. Do what is best for you."

"Once you've completed this process for yourself, turn your attention to your bag of nuts and seeds. Think now about the good things in your life that you'd like to re-seed for renewed growth, those things that you'll nourish within yourself over the coming months of Winter. Name those things, either aloud or within, as you place a nut or seed for each one within the Cauldron of Transformation. Please remember to keep a few nuts or seeds in your pouch for use in the next portion of the working."

All set to work. When everyone is finished with both parts of the personal work, the Facilitating Priestess seals the various spells with a "so mote it be!" She then asks everyone to stand, and she explains the next part of the Magickal working in whatever way is best for her, or as follows:

"From the personal we move outward with the hobbling gate of the Crone into the larger world.

Here we use our sharpened shears to cut out the
outmoded, the unnecessary, the harmful, the dead."

Women begin circling deosil around the cauldron with a limping
gait. They hold their scissors in their right hands. As they walk they
begin to call out the things they feel need to be removed from the
garden which is the Earth. They walk slowly, and speak in rhythm
with the walking. As each wish for removal is completed, all hold
their scissors out toward (or over) the cauldron and snip them twice
while saying:

"Cut ... it ... out!"
(*snip*)   (*snip*)

They gradually increase their gait, though still limping, and gradually get louder. When the Facilitating Priestess feels that the power
is peaking, she says:

"And all the things we've spoken here ... "

Everyone stops in place, turns and faces the cauldron, scissors
extended toward it, and snips repeatedly while shouting:

"Cut it out! ... Cut it out! ... "

They continue until it feels done. The Facilitating Priestess says
something to the effect of:

"Now that the world has been cleared of the unwanted, it must be seeded with the desired replace-
ments. Speak now of your wishes for the world as
you drop your remaining nuts or seeds into the
Cauldron of Transformation."

When all have finished, the Priestess says:

"So it's sown,
Now be it grown."

Repeat this statement often to raise the cone of power and to release
it again. Or, if that doesn't feel right, the spell then is seen as
releasing the entire working into the cauldron to begin the transformations.

The Ceremony of Milk, Honey and Grain is celebrated and all
settle to feasting on foods of the season. It might be particularly

significant to include nuts and seeds in the feast, particularly hazelnuts because they are thought to bestow wisdom.

When all are ready, thank the Goddess, dismiss the Quarters and declare the Circle open.

The rite is ended.

NOTES

Chapter One

1. Penelope Shuttle & Peter Redgrove, *The Wise Wound , Myths, Realities and Meanings of Menstruation*, Revised Edition (New York: Bantam, 1990), p.58.
2. Ibid., pp. 60-61.
3. Joseph Campbell, *Masks of God: Occidental Mythology* (New York: Penguin, 1965), pp. 52, 60, 64, 72.
4. Shuttle and Redgrove, *The Wise Wound*, pp. 192 - 195.
5. Ibid.
6. Ibid, pp. 253-256.
7. John Matthews, ed., *At the Table of the Grail*, (New York: Arkana, 1987), pp. 122-123.
8. Robert Briffault, *The Mothers*, Vol. III, (London: George Allen and Unwin, 1969), pp. 183-184.
9. Ibid.

Chapter Three

1. Paul Huson, *Mastering Witchcraft, A Practical Guide for Witches, Warlocks & Covens* (New York: G. P. Putnam & Sons, 1970), p. 37

Chapter Four

1. John Matthews, ed., *At the Table of the Grail: The Grail as Bodily Vessel*, (New York: Arkana, 1987), p. 193.
2. Emma Jung and Maria Von Franz, *The Grail Legend*, (New York: Putnam, 1970).
3. Wallis, Budge, *The Egyptian Book of the Dead*, (London: British Museum, 1895) p. 114.
4. Ibid, pp. 205 - 206.
5. Robert Graves, *The White Goddess*, (New York: Creative Age Press, 1948), p. 409.
6. Joseph Campbell, *Masks of God: Creative Mythology*, (New York: Viking Press, 1970), p. 531 .
7. Adam McLean, "Alchemical Transmutation in History and Symbol," in Matthews, *At the Table of the Grail*," pp. 60-61.

8. Ibid.
9. Ibid.
10. Penelope Shuttle and Peter Redgrove, *The Wise Wound: Myths, Realities and Meanings of Menstruation*, (New York: Bantam, 1990), pp. 219 - 222.

Chapter Seven

1. Rick Hamouris, "Bring in the May," chant by Candace Haddad on the cassette tape, *Welcome to Annwfn* by Deborah and Rick Hamouris and friends.
2. Chant by Z Budapest, on the cassette tape *Chants: Ritual Music*, by the Reclaiming Collective.

BIBLIOGRAPHY

Bardon, Franz, *Initiation Into Hermetics* (West Germany: Dieter Ruggebera & Wuppertal, second edition, 1971).

Beyerl, Paul, *The Master Book of Herbalism* (Custer Washington: Phoenix Publishing Co., 1984).

Briffault, Robert, *The Mothers*, 3 vols. (London: George Allen and Unwin 1969).

Budge, E. A. Wallis, *The Egyptian Book of the Dead* (London: British Museum, 1895).

Campbell, Joseph, *Masks of God: Creative Mythology* (New York: Viking Press, 1970).

Gimbutas, Marija, *The Language of the Goddess* (San Francisco: Harper & Row, 1989).

Goodwich, Nora, *Priestesses* (New York: Harper Perennial, 1990).

Graves, Robert, *The White Goddess* (New York: Creative Age Press, 1948).

Huson, Paul, *Mastering Witchcraft* (New York: G. P. Putnam & Sons, 1970).

Jung, Emma & Von Franz, Maria, *Grail Legend* (New York: Putnam, 1970).

Leland, Charles G., Aradia: *Gospel of the Witches* (Custer, Washington: Phoenix Publishing Inc., 1990).

MacGregor Mathers, S. Liddell, *The Greater Key of Solomon* (Chicago: deLaurence Scott & Co., 1914).

Matthews, John, ed., *At the Table of the Grail* (New York: Arkana, 1987).

Regardie, Israel, *The Golden Dawn* (St. Paul: Llewellyn Publications, 1971).

Shuttle, Penelope and Peter, Redgrove, *The Wise Wound: Myths, Realities & Meanings of Menstruation* (New York: Bantam edition, 1990).

Starhawk, *The Spiral Dance* (San Francisco: Harper & Row, 1979).

Walker, Barbara G., *Women's Encyclopedia of Myths and Secrets* (San Francisco: Harper & Row, 1983).

Walton, Evangeline, *The Mabinogian* (New York: Ballantine Books, 1974).